Gel

A Novel

LEE A. KOLESNIKOFF

Order this book online at www.trafford.com
or email orders@trafford.com

Most Trafford titles are also available at major online book retailers.

Cover Design by Jill Murphy

Print information available on the last page.

ISBN: 978-1-4907-8855-5 (sc)
ISBN: 978-1-4907-8856-2 (hc)
ISBN: 978-1-4907-8854-8 (e)

Library of Congress Control Number: 2018942771

This is a work of fiction. All of the characters, names, incidents, organizations, and dialogue
in this novel are either the products of the author's imagination or are used fictitiously.

Trafford rev. 05/22/2018

www.trafford.com

North America & international
toll-free: 1 888 232 4444 (USA & Canada)
fax: 812 355 4082

Thanks to my beloved Eugenia; companion, wife, and precious love.
She encouraged me, waiting patiently as I wrote.

Thanks to Nick Kling for his advice and review of my manuscript.
His frequent encouragement has been an irreplaceable
asset to my endeavors. I am grateful for his efforts.

Contents

Returning

Claudia Morgan raced through the Gilbert Building lobby's revolving door determined to get to her desk on time. It was impossible. Had she not left her watch on the nightstand, she might have known what time it was, slowed down and enjoyed more of her first day back from vacation, a ten-day special to Saint John. But circumstances being what they were, she continued her mad dash toward the elevator. Wriggling through the nearly closed door, Claudia leaned back against the rail and drew a deep breath.

Surprise! The elevator was heading down to the basement. She managed a 'Hey, what the hell,' smile.

The doors opened; a maintenance man steering a trash cart got in. While doing so, his stuck-on name tag flashed past her face; Boris something or other. The terrible scrawl rendered the last name illegible.

His arm, and then the cart brushed her. "Sorry," the man muttered.

Claudia immediately felt the evil. The man was bristling with it. He glanced at her. His posture and nonchalance indicated Claudia wasn't his target. She shifted her weight from one foot to the other and then slid backward to the farthest corner of the cube. She bit her lip, hoping he wouldn't try to start up a conversation.

The doors closed and the elevator started its ascent. Stop at one she mused, and I'll get off. The first floor came and went, as did ten, fifteen, and then, twenty. At twenty – eight the doors opened and the man got out. He glanced back with a casual farewell from his dead-fish eyes. As the doors closed, Claudia breathed a sigh of relief. Her palms were sweaty. She even forgot about trying to get to her desk on time.

Floor forty lit up on the display. It was hers. The doors glided open and Claudia sped down the hall. The glass doors she pushed open were lettered 'Industrial Investigations, Incorporated' but that was not what

'Triple I' actually did. It stole secrets from those who had invented new and promising products for the benefit of those too dull-witted or lazy to create their own. Claudia was just below the rung of the ladder labeled Senior Investigator. One more successful 'acquisition' and the title would most likely be hers.

"Well, look who's here. Welcome back. Get enough sun?" John Drake asked. John was one of the good guys, a friend. "Hey, what's wrong?" he added. Though she didn't realize it, Claudia had paled; even her Caribbean tan couldn't hide it.

"It's nothing. Let's skip it," she muttered.

"Ah, she's back," a newly arriving Ted Wagner observed. "Uh, Claudia, would you mind coming with me, please?" Claudia followed Ted back to his office. After she entered, he shut the door.

"What is it?" Claudia countered.

· "One doesn't come back after ten days in Saint John looking as if they'd seen a murder. What's up?"

"The elevator–just a few minutes ago - there was a guy – he frightened me. You know I don't scare easily. This guy. . ."

"Did he make a move? He didn't assault you, did he?"

"Yes, he did–in a way! He scared the hell out of me."

Wagner didn't say anything else. He simply leaned back in his chair and surveyed Claudia.

Was it the lines etched in her brow or the unsteadiness of her voice that gave him the answer he needed?

Perhaps it was her manner. In any event, he didn't attempt to minimize her encounter. She had convinced him her experience and the reason for her fear were valid. Being tuned in to people was Ted Wagner's gift.

Over the years he had come to know that Claudia Morgan knew who she was. There wasn't any reason for her to create a persona for public consumption. What you experienced was the real deal. In addition, though Ted Wagner was her boss, Claudia annoyed him time and again by showing that she was his intellectual superior. Though she didn't flaunt it, this fact was evident to everyone in the office

Still, Wagner clung to his position tenaciously and did all he could to appear being the one in charge.

"Come on, I'll buy you a cup of coffee. It's good to see you."

Claudia replied with a smile. Wagner would be falling flat on his face as a manager if it weren't for her successes as an industrial spy. The other four 'investigators' under his control were inept, and he didn't have the skills or the will to enhance their expertise.

"What's that?" He said, pointing to her shoe.

"I don't know." Wagner plucked a few tissues from the holder and wiped something from Claudia's shoe.

"Looks like some kind of gel. Where have you been?"

"I haven't been anywhere. Wait – the maintenance man in the elevator–that's probably where I got it."

The cafeteria was almost empty. The woman behind the counter avoided giving the pair a glance.

She assumed their coming at such an odd hour had to do with romance. Claudia and her boss sat at the table farthest from the serving counter.

"What's the rush?" Claudia extended her hand. "Give me the envelope, please." She knew Wagner always delegated a new assignment in this way.

Wagner reached inside his jacket and produced it.

Beneath Claudia's name was written the word 'URGENT!!!!' in large type including the exclamation marks. Claudia had received perhaps twenty such envelopes, but this time she felt that the immediacy of Wagner's invitation to meet indicated that this might be 'the big one,' the assignment that might propel her upward. She started to tear it open. Wagner placed his hand on hers.

"Not here. Wait until you're alone. Read it and give it some thought. Call me on my cell."

Claudia nodded.

Wagner left. Claudia watched him pass through the cafeteria doors and then got her coffee.

"Cheapskate?" the cafeteria worker questioned. "You know it," Claudia agreed. Returning to her seat, she mulled over her superior's uncharacteristic behavior and the urgency he seemed to have placed on this assignment. It wasn't like him to appear so anxious. She could hardly wait to know more. Once inside her office, Claudia closed the door. She drew the shades and began reading Wagner's note.

Sergei Trasker is a microbiologist. He was fired three years ago from Becker Pharmaceutical because he told the government about some off–shore dealings the company had with terrorists. It seems the firm was selling medical supplies to them and channeling the money to a Swiss bank. To make the situation more complicated, it was rumored that he was on the verge of an astonishing medical discovery while employed at Becker. Fortunately for him, he kept his work to himself. When the firm made the decision to let him go, they intended to surprise him at his desk and access his research notes, but he left before the raid took place. Royalties from other patents stateside and abroad enabled him to set up a state-of-the-art lab on his 'estate,' somewhere in Westchester.

It's a good bet that access is limited to his trusted friends. I assume the place is fenced and maybe even guarded. I've racked my brain and can't come up with any way you can meet him 'accidentally' on purpose. Becker has offered us ten million if we acquire the research notes and twenty more if we can tell them precisely his research objectives.

Oh, yes, and Triple I will pay the agent, you, a two million dollar bonus and upgrade you to Senior Investigator upon successful completion of this assignment.

Call me.
W.

PS He has a brother, Boris, who was in prison, and has just been released. The story is that he was wrongly convicted of murder. Personally, I think it was a ploy to put pressure on Sergei to cough up the research. Prison personnel have said that the brother is very angry and might be thinking about getting even with his accusers. How he got out with an attitude like that I don't know. Most likely Sergei had connections. Now you know all I know. Be careful.

I wish they could see me now, Claudia mused. Pop and Mom would be proud. Who else is going to get a two million dollar payday?

Indeed, Bruce and Beatrice Morgan, Claudia's parents, would have been proud. All those discussions between the two at the supper table that spilled over into the living room and went on until very late in the evening had borne fruit, much more than they ever could have dreamed. Bruce, a CIA analyst, and Beatrice, a psychotherapist, often discussed issues relating to their interaction with superiors, uninformed associates, and dolts, all too often the same. Claudia, still a youth, was fascinated by their incisive discussions and digested all of it, even to the point where an exasperated Beatrice was forced to order Claudia to go upstairs, do homework, surf the net, anything, but just leave them alone.

Life tore Bruce and Beatrice away from her when their plane crashed somewhere in Russia near the Urals. It was an enormous shock, but the young woman, in her senior year at Vassar, survived the tragedy. She had a warehouse of wonderful times with her parents to assuage her grief.

Ted Wagner, unaware of Claudia's personal life, had inadvertently chosen well.

She folded the letter and put it back in the envelope. Before she met with her boss again, she wanted to script a plan, including a way to get into the estate of Sergei Trasker. The usual ways to meet a person 'accidentally' would not work. The scientist was unlikely to be appearing in public. He would also be on his guard.

Without a doubt Becker Pharmaceutical personnel were after him. The fact that they and other professionals were unsuccessful in obtaining his research and had to turn to outsiders was in itself an affirmation of the man's skill in eluding capture. Her meeting would have to appear unplanned, but how might that be accomplished?

A fly landed on her ankle and started making its way down to the spot where Wagner had removed the gel. Claudia shooed it away. She bent over and removed her pump. A trace of the fluid still clung to the instep. Carefully she wiped clean every bit she could find. As she turned to toss the napkin into the trash, she paused. Taking an envelope from her drawer, she placed the napkin inside and wrote a question mark on the envelope's face. Then she tossed it into the bottom drawer of her desk. Sometimes people do things for no reason. Sometimes there is a reason but it hasn't come to mind yet.

Mr. Fly returned. She swiped at him with a convenient file folder and the poor thing, stunned, spiraled to the floor.

"Thank you," Claudia whispered to the fly, "you've given me an idea." She slid a sheet of paper under the flailing creature, opened the window and tossed it out. "Thanks again," she said as she waved goodbye. She dialed Wagner's cell. "Got a few minutes? We should talk. Are there any restrictions on expenses? I'm going to need some money."

The twenty-eighth floor of the Gilbert Building was occupied by the State Judiciary. State Supreme Court and Court of Appeals Judges had their offices there. Judge Sanford Collins' office was room number twenty. His life was a catalog of public service, first to the federal government, then two tours representing the Judge Advocate General in Kuwait, and, finally, the practice of jurisprudence at various county and state levels. Collins had officiated in the trial of Boris Trasker, a man who repeatedly professed his innocence in the murder of Terrence Rosemary, a notorious drug dealer. Drunk, and in a stupor, he was found at the scene kneeling over Terrence's body. Boris did not recall picking up the murder weapon, a pistol, even though his fingerprints were found all over the barrel and grip. He didn't even remember being at the scene. Unable to function and barely conscious, it was at this moment the police came upon him. Because of the vagueness of his responses and his inability to remember pertinent details, the police were convinced they had their man.

Despite his claim that he had been framed, and every effort his brother Sergei made in his behalf, Boris was convicted and sentenced to the maximum. Good behavior shortened his incarceration; that's what Boris believed. Intervention by governmental others was the real reason. He was released on the first of the month.

Office number twenty was in use. A sign on the outside doorknob read 'Do Not Disturb.' Judge Collins was watching the live TV interview of the recently released felon Boris Trasker by celebrity talk show host Benton Topper. Collins fit well the historic colloquialism he had been tagged with; 'the hanging judge.' The jurist was tough on criminals; few escaped the maximum sentence provided by law. Though close to retirement age, he was still active. His docket was as full as ever.

"Mister Trasker, do you still maintain to this day that you are innocent?"

"I never killed that man; I said it then, and I say again, I was framed. Why, I don't know, but that's what happened."

"What do you intend to do?"

"I am retaining the law firm of Brackett and Moriarty. I intend to go after my accusers with the full force of the law. Your viewers and everyone else have to know I am innocent."

Judge Collins responded to the sound of a door opening behind him. "You!" He exclaimed.

He quickly turned to the television and then back to the person who had just entered his office.

"Wait!" He pleaded. The assailant took aim and squeezed the rubber bulb attached to a plastic tube. The rush of air it produced launched the dart that pierced the judge's neck. The venom it carried gave its victim perhaps a minute more of life. As paralysis spread through his body, Collins slumped over and, like a limp rag, he slid to the floor.

Near death now, the judge turned once more toward the television and then back to his assailant.

Instead of exhibiting anger or fear, the victim seemed perplexed.

After the assassin left, Collins crawled to his desk. Pulling himself into his chair, he dipped his finger in the blood trickling from his neck and managed to scrawl something on the desk pad. The end came swiftly.

"Who in the world would want to kill him?" Frank Santoro, Senior Investigator, Special Operations, City Police, exclaimed.

"There are plenty. He sent a lot of bad actors upstate during his time," replied his partner Bob McCann. Santoro and McCann examined the crime scene. Collins' remains had been removed but the forensic team was still there.

"Why now?" Santoro paced back and forth. "See if any people sentenced by Collins were recently released from prison."

"I'm on it." McCann left Collins' office. Alone now, Santoro began examining the room more closely. He knew it had been dusted for prints and any items deemed pertinent had been catalogued and taken away for further study.

He opened each desk drawer, turned over each piece of paper, emptied the waste basket and went through each piece of trash. His final effort was to closely examine the felt desk pad. He found that something had been written on it, but the characters were obscure. Santoro kept changing his position to take the best advantage of the available light from the window. Then, he saw it, but barely. Was it a 'B,' a '3', or something else? The forensic crew would have to tell him; the same forensic crew that supposedly went over this same room with a fine toothed comb – and did not spot the scrawl.

Santoro took out his cell. "Hello, Santoro here. What the hell are you forensic guys doing? Do I have to do all the work? Get back up here. I found something. Collins may have provided us with the identity of his killer. Finish your coffee? You're not telling me that your coffee comes before recovering a clue you missed, are you? You take the time to finish that coffee and you'll be doing forensic work on seagulls in Riverhead for the rest of your career. How the hell could you have missed this? What did you miss? You'll see when you get over here. It was right under your nose!"

McCann returned. "Boss, there were five men released since the first of this month."

"Any of them have a B in their name?"

"There were two; Alexandro Biconte and Boris Trasker."

"Both tried and sentenced by Collins?"

"Yes; Biconte took the red eye to Frisco four days ago. He's got family there. I think he's had it with New York hospitality."

"Where's the other one?"

"He's still around. He's got a brother and lives with him somewhere in Westchester. That's the only family he's got near here."

"Does he have a girl friend?"

"I couldn't find any mention of one."

"Find out where in Westchester the place is. We'll pay him and his brother a visit." Santoro sat down. He seemed relieved. Solving this might be easier than he thought.

"No!" Ted Wagner could hardly believe what John Drake was telling him. "Someone was murdered in this building? Judge Collins; how is that possible? That floor is crawling with guards and law enforcement people. How could they not have caught the murderer?" Leaving Drake in the hallway, Wagner changed direction and burst into Claudia Morgan's office. "Did you hear? Judge Collins has been murdered."

"That's horrible. When did it happen?"

"Yesterday; they think the murderer might have been disguised as a maintenance man. No other person was known to have been in the area. It had to be him, the one you mentioned."

Claudia fell back in her seat. "That guy I saw in the elevator; it was him."

"Maybe you should talk to the police. Should I call them?"

"I will - no, wait. No; my assignment, remember? There will be pictures, interviews; that won't help me with Sergei Trasker. I need to remain unknown to him, at least for now. I can talk to them later, after I'm finished with this job."

"You're right." Wagner agreed.

"Ted, I'll need ten thousand; I'm leaving tomorrow – on assignment."

"When do you need it?"

"I'll need it in cash, by three. The next time you see me, I'll have the goods."

Wagner sighed; then smiled. "Okay, by three."

Claudia Morgan swung her chair around and looked out of the window. It wasn't the view she was searching for, but answers. Who was this Boris? Why was Collins killed? But all that could wait. Her first order of business was getting in to see scientist Sergei Trasker. Would her scheme to get into the compound and meet him work? She needed time to sort it all out.

"I found out where the Trasker estate is. When do you want to go out there?" McCann was a bulldog, tenacious when it came to retrieving information. Short, muscular, and determined, he rarely came up empty. If information existed about anything or anyone, he found it. He could teach a Rottweiler a thing or two about ferocity and determination.

Santoro glanced at his watch. "It's rush hour; we'll go tomorrow, maybe ten or so. That okay with you?"

"Yeah; I'm still looking through Boris Trasker's psych evaluations; I don't find any markers that label him a danger to society. Come on, we aren't even sure he's killed anyone."

"They convicted him didn't they? Of course he was guilty."

"Should I say it? Yes, I will; Sacco and who was the other guy? Remember them; they were guilty too, until they found the real killers."

"Get off your orange crate. I get it; we'll interview the guy and size him up. I want to look at him eye to eye. After that, I'll know which one of us is right." Santoro was proud of being able to recognize reptilian behavior in a person; that part of the brain without conscience, where survival and predation are the principal motivators. Years of encountering and dealing with criminals provided him with ample evidence such a profile existed.

This never-ending back and forth between the two men was their insurance policy; it kept neither from jumping to conclusions while in the heat of pursuit. Even though Santoro was one rank higher than

McCann, the two men were equally intelligent and experienced. For some reason, he could never pass the exam. After four tries he stopped taking it, content to remain Santoro's partner. Rank or not, each man viewed the other as his equal.

Claudia Morgan was an athletic twenty seven years of age. She was the kind of woman that made schools like Vassar proud. Triple I was her first job out of college. Ted Wagner, her interviewer, assessed her qualifications. After reviewing her portfolio for a full three seconds and scanning her physical features for thirty, he concluded the following; she was attractive and reasonably intelligent. He hired her. But Claudia's new firm had much to learn about their new hire; she was formidable and ambitious. She accelerated through the ranks at breakneck speed. Some in management wondered just how far she might go.

In addition to all her intellectual prowess, Claudia Morgan was a jock. Beginning with the sport of volleyball in college in her freshman year, she moved to racquet ball for a time. By her junior year she had switched to tennis. She loved the game and was good at it. A strong upper torso, an ability to execute short bursts of speed, and deliver solid ground strokes enhanced by a technically sound backhand gave her game unexpected authority. Becoming an investigator at Triple I had also forced her to take a bit of karate. Though she never had to use it, she still continued the discipline for safety sake. Now she was about to put herself to another test. Hazardous perhaps, but, that being said, it was necessary; $2,000,000 necessary.

Ellenville, New York nestles just south of the foothills of the Catskill Mountains. It's a quiet, small community of perhaps several thousand. If one were to include it within the old Borscht circuit of the nineteen twenties; few would object. Just south of the village, Route 52 ascends the western slope of the Shawangunk Mountains before it levels off for a spell. Farther on, it winds down the eastern side of the hogs-back. The steep western slope alongside the road and the valley sprawling north to south far below makes it a perfect launching spot for the hang-gliding crowd. Enthusiasts from miles around come to enjoy the unique experience of flying through the air, held aloft by a king-sized kite filled with wind.

Jimmy Todd, a local hang-gliding instructor, notices that student Claudia Morgan seems nervous this morning. He tries to put a good spin on the situation. "Look, you can handle this solo flight. Go out there and get some air."

"Shouldn't I get more training? Is this all there is?"

"Some people never get the knack of hang gliding. I've watched; you're a natural. I mean it. I wouldn't send you up if I wasn't sure you could do it. Now go!"

Running along the short wooden ramp that jutted out from the highway, Todd's star student became airborne at just the right time. She straightened her legs. She felt the same as on other flights, but this time, Jimmy wasn't with her. Overcoming her reticence, she took command of the situation, searching for and finding the updrafts that would lift her upward in ever-widening spirals, farther and farther away from the highway and her excited and waving instructor. Soon, she found herself soaring above the nearest peak. The winds would be different up here and she cautioned herself to take care. An unexpected gust forced her to bank sharply, but she recovered without incident. What she needed now was to find a place to land. Spotting some hay bales in a field below, Claudia decided to land between the fourth and fifth.

Steering carefully, she descended slowly, deliberately. Sixty feet above the ground, she took aim at the spot she had chosen. The wind pulsed. Suddenly her kite lost its air. Heading for the ground, she recalled what was needed; an abrupt yank on the steering bar and air rushed back into her kite. She had resumed control. She landed within feet of her target.

I'm almost there. With a little more practice I'll be ready, Claudia tells herself. She hears her instructor's four wheeler bouncing across the field. Soon its brakes squeal and it comes to a stop. Todd runs over and hugs her.

"That was great, just great. I told you you could do it."

"How'd you like to earn a thousand bucks?"

Claudia's question causes her instructor to cut short his elation. "Is it legal? It's got nothing to do with drugs or contraband, does it? I'm not going to go to jail, no sir, not for a thousand."

"No, it's not illegal. I wouldn't do that to my favorite instructor."

"Then what's it all about?"

"I want you to show me how to fake a crash, a small one, in Westchester."

Westchester County is urban and crowded with business firms in the south, and residences and commercial establishments in the west along the Hudson River. It's residential and commercial in the east, and hilly in the northeast. Sergei Trasker's fortress estate is in the northeast. Protected by difficult terrain and wild, dense foliage, many estates such as his enjoy an uncommon and surprising solitude so near such busy surroundings. Westchester provides an uncomplicated access to the many pleasures life offers. As if that were not enough in itself, choosing the correct location also offers a modicum of privacy. For those who have the means to afford it, privacy can be improved to include a state of complete solitude and invulnerability.

The scientist personally interviewed and selected each of his security force. All were foreign born and none had ever lived for any length of time in the United States. Once employed, they agreed to have no contact with anyone outside the walls of his estate. Days off were spent within its confines. Those who for reasons of their own wished to leave *Zemlia Sviataia* (Sacred Land), were allowed to do so but not allowed to reenter. They returned to their homeland. Whatever they had seen or heard while in his employ was never to be revealed or discussed with others. Those were the terms of their indenture.

The estate was heavily wooded. Shaded, tree-lined paths were abundant. Situated on a prominent knoll, an enormous pool extended southeast of the main residence. An oval driveway gracefully curled through a formal garden and channeled visitors toward a six granite-columned portico where they could enter the main building.

The style of the residence was intended to be seventeenth century, but the windows in several wings displayed a strong gothic influence. Some might also have recognized a flair of the Byzantine here and there.

There was a courtyard, and at its center a building unlike any of the surrounding structures.

It resembled a World War Two German pillbox, one of the many that may still be seen along France's northern coastline. The cement-gray clam shell had no doors or windows. The entrance to this, Trasker's laboratory, was known only to him. If Becker Pharmaceutical personnel were ever to penetrate the estate, overcome the guards and accidentally find the entrance, all would be in vain. He had fitted the lab with a self-destruct mechanism, again, its location and design known only to him.

The red sports car raced up the drive and screeched to a halt. 'Boris' was returning from the city. Sergei already heard about Collins' death on the TV.

"You're back," the scientist commented sarcastically.

"And I'm fine, brother; just fine," Boris replied.

"Don't call me brother. You shouldn't be doing these things in my brother's name. Where is he?"

"We do what we do. You are in the game. And, like it or not, you will play."

"What have you done with my brother?"

"Do you wish to trade yet? I'll give you your brother if you give me your notes."

"We'll see what tomorrow brings. It's certain that the police will come and interview you. Don't think they are stupid; you'd better answer carefully."

"What do you think they will want from me?"

"Where were you during hours so and so; questions like that."

"I was being interviewed by Benton Topper on TV. I have five million witnesses who can verify where I was."

"You know that's not true," Sergei snapped back.

Claudia Morgan was spending her evenings researching her target, gathering a great deal of information about his career. It was impressive. Born in Riga, Latvia, he had been spirited away to Russia in 1980 after being lauded as one of those rare European youth of genius stature. There he experienced the finest education, and was allowed to access many Russian world–renowned academics and scientists. The literature also revealed that Sergei exceeded his captors' expectations. With such an intellectual force in their possession, she understood how the Russians might have expected to take a commanding lead in the field of microbiology. But it appeared one of his most important needs was not met.

Sergei Trasker must have been unhappy living in Russia. He must have never considered himself anything more than a prisoner incarcerated in a strange land against his own will. Favorable treatment notwithstanding, the young Latvian must not have forgotten his beginnings. The detailed account ended there. Covertly, and obviously with someone's help, he had escaped and made his way to the United States.

Though no record could be found of the event, Claudia believed the State Department or other agency became aware of the scientist's discontent and helped him escape. When he arrived stateside, government 'friends' immediately saw to it that the young genius had everything he needed to continue his work. While the Russians fumed, there was little they could do. Sergei requested and was granted political asylum. For the Soviets, it seemed they had lost.

Becker Pharmaceutical was under contract with the government and engaged in a number of long term projects. The record showed that the brilliant young political refugee went to work for the firm.

Hidden were the machinations of a federal government anxious to first, deny Trasker's expertise to the Russians and, second, to nurture it for their own benefit.

Claudia's review of the events that marked the scientist's life had an unexpected effect on a personal level; she desired to meet this man who staunchly refused to surrender his work to his superiors at Becker Pharmaceutical, a firm that operated facilities in 15 countries and most likely had other, more onerous ties.

'Boris' Trasker reached into his topcoat and pulled out his phone. There were several names arranged in anagrams. Collins, the first, was in bold. Jim Peters was second. He was the arresting detective whose detailed testimony did much to sway the jury and secure the real Boris' conviction.

As the imposter drove through the Borough of Queens, he looked to his right and surveyed Queens College. Peters' home was just five blocks from the Institution. From his surveillance he knew the detective would be coming home shortly. Today, Friday, was bowling night. An assassin has his own perception of time; to him, waiting for his prey may seem like a thousand years.

About eleven, a car turned the corner and headed down the street. Boris had moved his near Peters' driveway, opened the trunk, taken out the jack, and tire iron. He already extinguished the streetlight at the corner with an air rifle. Aided by a moonless night, the fedora he wore obscured his face.

Peters pulled up alongside the car. "Trouble?" He asked.

"Damned tires; they blew, two of them. Can you imagine? Is this your place?"

"Yeah. I'll park; then I'll give you a hand."

"Thanks."

"Sorry for the inconvenience."

"That's okay; it's just another letdown."

"What's that all about?"

"I bowled tonight; I bombed, rolled twenty pins below my average. It was a disaster. And now this. It's just not my day." As Peters was gazing down at the front tire, his assailant approached from behind and hit him over the head with the tire iron. The detective slumped to the ground. Boris placed him in the trunk, inflated his tires and sped off. No one had driven or walked by during the abduction.

Up at five, at Ellenville by nine, in the harness by nine-thirty, and aloft minutes later. This was Claudia Morgan's regimen three days a week. She was well on her way to becoming a competent hang glider. She was forced to maintain this schedule because she still had not found any place in Westchester to actively pursue her training closer to the estate. The other two days she scouted the countryside looking for Sergei's lair; Armonk, other small towns, then Route 22, from Brewster in Putnam County, then south, and west along the tributary roads that paralleled Interstate 84, as well as a host of other would–be hideaways. Claudia was getting to know the county as well as the wildlife that lived there. Still, day after day she marveled at the new roads she found by taking an unscheduled right or left turn.

It was her practice to stop in at local diners for coffee breaks. Perhaps a truck driver might inadvertently mention some fact that would help her find his estate. Sipping her coffee at the counter on this particular day, she overheard one complaining about 'the hoops he had to jump' just to deliver fuel oil to this one customer. Not an uncommon event in Westchester, the driver's conversation nevertheless piqued her interest. When the trucker got up to go, She followed him.

The fuel truck took many of the roads she had already reconnoitered. So far, there was nothing new about his route. Suddenly turning right, the truck entered an unmarked one lane road. If the road was intended for two cars, they would need to be Nash Americans, those Lilliputian roadsters manufactured in the mid 1950's.

The truck slowed and eventually stopped. The driver slowly maneuvered his vehicle left onto another well-hidden lane. Within seconds, the truck was swallowed up by the thicket. Claudia pulled ahead, turned into the lane a bit, and then performed a perfect one point turn. Now pointed toward the main road and positioned for a quick getaway, she followed on foot the path the truck had taken. The distance to the gate might have been several hundred feet, but in heels it seemed more like a mile. Hidden from view by a large oak tree, she watched the iron gates swing open and the truck enter the grounds. Three men dressed in camouflage uniforms and armed with weapons inspected the driver and truck. Even at a distance she could see that the driver, now having dismounted and standing alongside his truck, was nervous. His too loud jokes, an attempt to defuse the stern attitude of the guards, were useless. A tense quarter hour elapsed. Finally, he was waved on.

Claudia reached into her bag and retrieved her digital camera. She began photographing everyone, hoping some might show up on one of the many criminal databases and thus provide her with an idea of who owned this property. A few moments later, she heard several twigs snap to her right. A guard was picking his way through a patch of windfall and making his way toward her.

Westchester is hilly, and this time that attribute worked in her favor. As the guard descended into a steep gully, each lost sight of the other. Claudia ran. In the time it took for the guard to climb up the other side, she was already back in her car starting the engine. She had her answer; the property owner's name. The emblem on the guard's uniform had two letters, ST, inscribed on it; it had to be Sergei Trasker.

Mrs. Peters awoke to an empty bed. Her husband had not come home. She was not concerned. It was not that unusual in the life of a law enforcement officer to have gotten a call from the precinct to report for duty at some ungodly hour. She looked out the window and saw her husband's car parked at the curb. That was unusual. As noon approached, Peters still had not contacted his wife. She called the precinct desk sergeant. "Hi, Charley, it's Kathy Peters; is Jim there? He didn't come home last night. I think he might have been called out on a case."

"I don't see him in the house. I'll ask around."

As minutes became half an hour, the wife had the growing sense that something was wrong.

Finally, the desk sergeant called back. "He's not here, Kathy. Nothing's come up that would have required him to come in."

"Thanks." This was not right, she mused; Jim always calls. The phone rang. "Hello?"

"Kathy, it's Charley again. We're sending someone out there to be with you."

"Why, what's wrong?" She felt that same tug in her stomach when she found out that her husband had been shot by a bank robber. "Charley, what is it?"

"It's Jim."

Kevin Moriarty of Brackett and Moriarty glanced at his Rolex; it was late, nine o'clock. "Are we done, Mr. Trasker? You've been here four hours and all you have succeeded in doing is convincing me that you really hate the people who put you in prison."

"Oh, I do, yes, I do. And I want you to make them pay for it. You have a reputation for being a Doberman. That is the kind of lawyer I want. Will you take my case?"

"Let me think about it. I have many clients. They also require my attention. Your case looks complicated and your assertions are going to be difficult to prove. Establishing your innocence after a jury has found you guilty will not be easy."

"Here's a check for $50,000 as a retainer. Will that help?"

"Where did you get this kind of money?"

"I have a wonderful and generous brother. By the way, what time did I come in this evening?"

"You came in at five; five minutes after five, to be precise. Why?"

"Remembering what time it is, is important. Have you made note of it?"

"Yes; with the hourly fees we charge, we have to. Your session tonight, for example, has cost you $1,200."

"It's a bargain," Boris replied.

"What a place. It's taken me nearly an hour to find the entrance," McCann complained.

"Get out and ring the gong or whatever that contraption is over there."

McCann walked over, swung open the box and picked up the phone. "Hello? It's Investigator McCann, police. We're here to talk to Boris Trasker. Open the gate." McCann listened for a moment, and then returned to the car. "They're coming down. Our car is not allowed inside. They're sending a vehicle to get us."

"What kind of crap is this? We're the police."

"Trasker crap I guess you could call it."

Soon, two armed men in an all-terrain vehicle came over the grassy knoll and pulled up in front of the gate. A second, carrying three armed men, observed from a distance.

"They aren't taking any chances," McCann observed.

"Nope, they're not. I would say this place is well–guarded, wouldn't you?"

McCann gave Santoro one of those 'are you kidding' glances.

There was no talk during the ride from the gate to the mansion. The armed escort followed at close range, but not too close.

As the mansion came into view, all McCann could say was "Jesus." It was indeed very large.

"What's that thing," McCann asked as the vehicle passed by the pillbox. No one offered an answer.

Sergei Trasker met the two policemen at the front portico. "Good morning; I understand you want to see my brother?"

"Yes; police business."

"Police business?"

"Yes, about the murder of Judge Collins," Santoro muttered.

"Please come this way." The scientist led them to a large drawing room. 'Boris' Trasker was engaged in speaking to an enormous Great Dane named Basil.

"Yes, you are a good boy, Basil, a good boy," The imposter purred.

Detective Santoro opened the conversation. "Mr. Trasker, we'd like to talk to you about. . ."

"That judge who sent an innocent man to jail," Boris made no effort to camouflage his cynicism.

"I didn't come here to discuss your sentencing. Where were you on the morning Judge Collins was murdered?"

"Being interviewed by Benton Topper; live, on television. Millions of people. . ."

Sergei stared at the man. Boris stopped talking.

"Sorry about Judge Collins," Sergei offered. Santoro did not reply.

"Is there anything more?" Sergei asked.

"We'd like your brother to come down to the precinct for some more questioning. Would tomorrow be all right, say ten?"

Sergei nodded. "That's fine; I'll have him there at ten."

The guards escorted the detectives back to their car.

Once on their way, Santoro told McCann "Make a list of everyone involved in Boris Trasker's trial. If he decides to strike again, I want to know the people he'll be targeting."

"He's got an airtight alibi, Boss. It couldn't have been him."

Santoro had interviewed many suspects in his twenty-nine years with the Department. The guilty ones always had that serpentine gaze; dull and seemingly detached, yet acutely aware of current events as they unfolded. He coined it the gaze of the predator. Boris Trasker had it. "Just do it. I'll bet you a steak at Barney's it's him."

"You're on."

"I want to glide right into here, this place," Claudia was showing Jimmy, her instructor. Sergei's mansion, shown on the map, was partially blotted out by her finger. Jimmy gently moved it aside.

"If that's where you want to go, you can't. There's no place around high enough to launch a hang glider. And I'm not doing anything risky."

"You're not doing anything risky; like what?"

"Like what happened last year to that jerk in New Jersey. Some coconut got it into his head he could launch from the boom of a crane, and he wanted me to set it up."

"Did you?"

"Do you think I'm nuts? No."

"What happened?"

"He hired a crane with a hundred twenty foot stick. He climbed up about a hundred feet and got ready to launch. But he didn't run and let the wind fill the parasol, he jumped. The pressure of all that air hitting the kite at once tore the fabric from the frame. He got off all right, straight down to the pavement.

When I heard about it, I was glad I didn't have anything to do with it."

"So you're saying he might have been successful if he had launched from a platform?"

"Maybe, but who's going to build a platform a hundred feet in the air? How could anyone keep it from swaying in the wind?"

Claudia smiled.

"Oh, no; you're not thinking of. . ."

"Get in the car. We're going shopping."

After visiting the Traskers that morning, Santoro and McCann stopped off at Ted Wagner's Triple I office. It was at his behest; he intimated he had information about the Collins murder. Of course Claudia Morgan was the one who might have been able to help them, but Wagner enjoyed being at the center of the activity, even if it required telling a few white lies.

"What do you have for us," Santoro asked.

"Actually, I didn't say that I had the information. I said I knew someone who did."

"And, actually, I didn't say you were obstructing an investigation, but I'll take you downtown if you want to continue playing games."

"It's my associate; she's the one who saw him, the maintenance man. She's the one you should be talking to."

"Why hasn't she come forward?"

"Because she didn't know about the murder before she left on assignment. By then, she was committed. Actually, she intended to get together with you when she returned."

"Find her and have her at the precinct tomorrow – at nine-thirty or I'll have both of you in a cell by evening. You can count on that – actually." If it was possible to put a sneer into a statement, Santoro just did. Wagner's face reddened, but he still managed a smile. Santoro left the office with McCann in lockstep.

"Hello? Claudia? Can you come off your assignment just for tomorrow? Yes, it's urgent. The police need to see you. Yes, I told them you couldn't come, but they insisted. You should have heard the argument I gave them. You have to be at the precinct tomorrow at nine-thirty. Yes, I have to go, too.

Claudia. . . don't be that way. . . there's nothing we can do about it."

Assistant Chief John Mason tapped lightly on Chief Davis' door. "Come," was the reply. As Mason stepped inside the office, both men glanced at each other. Sadness mingled with anger was etched on both their faces.

"Are you going out to see her now?"

"It's as good a time as any. Why, keeps running through my mind. Why would anyone want to kill Jim Peters?"

"The reason doesn't matter. What matters now is getting the one who did. I'm sorry I have to send you, but you were his best friend. It would be better coming from you."

Kathy Peters opened the front door of her home and stepped out into the sunshine. John Mason had just arrived and was about to ring the doorbell. Mrs. Peters asked him in. His breathing was labored and she quickly sensed something was very wrong. He took a seat in the living room. She sat in a chair close by. The furrows across his forehead were distinct, like the cracks in the face of a granite cliff. He was dealing with enormous and undeniable realities: Peters, his longtime friend, was dead, and it was his task to tell his friend's wife.

"Jim is gone, Kathy. We'll get whoever did this, I promise you. On my mother's grave, I promise."

"Where is he? Can I see him?" Mrs. Peters seemed extraordinarily calm. Mason suspected that she might have been in shock.

"Not now. I've got one of the badges outside. He'll stay with you for right now. I'll call someone to come and stay with you. A grief counselor will be able to help with calls and anything else you need."

Suddenly bursting into tears, Mrs. Peters embraced her husband's friend. It was a clinging-to-life desperate hold, as if hugging him could somehow erase the reality of what had happened. "I don't understand why someone would do this. Oh, why was it him, why him? He was a good man. . ."

Mason returned her embrace. "I know. The other night he was crabbing about his bowling score.

He promised himself he was going to practice between league nights so he could improve his average."

"What will I do without him?" Mrs. Peters cried.

Mason had no answer.

Returning from Triple I later that afternoon, Santoro and McCann entered the precinct. They sensed a difference. Making their way to Mason's office, Santoro rapped on the door and they entered.

"What's going on? The whole precinct has a sad face. Who died?" Santoro asked.

"Jim Peters has been murdered; and tortured to boot. First, it's Collins, and now, Peters. Have you come up with anything?"

"The two may be connected with this Boris Trasker's recent release from prison. Even though he repeatedly claimed he was innocent, the jury still found him guilty and sent him upstate. He got out the first of the month. Now all hell is breaking loose. I think he's the one but I can't make the case yet. He has an ace in the hole. He was on live television when Collins was murdered. The TV studio people confirm he was there. I can't figure out how he did it, but I will. He's coming to the station tomorrow. I'll ask him where he was when Peters was killed."

"Are there others this guy might target?"

"The way I see it he's after the people who judged him guilty and sent him to jail. The rest of the world doesn't matter. We've got to identify the key players and keep an eye on them. He'll make another move soon, I'd bet on it. He's waited a while to get even; he's anxious."

"What do you think, McCann?"

"Looking at the guy, I'd say he did it. But how do you get around the being two places at one time thing? My gut says it's him, but my head says keep looking for another guy."

"What do you have to say to that?" Mason asked of Santoro.

"I'll bet six month's pay it's him. I don't know how he's doing it, but it's him."

"Bring him in when you get the goods. I'll contact Chief Davis and bring him up to speed."

"When he comes in tomorrow, we're bringing in a surprise witness who might have seen him in the Gilbert building when Collins was iced."

"Does he suspect we have this person?"

"I don't know, but we'll take precautions and make sure he doesn't see her."

Claudia Morgan and Ted Wagner arrived just before nine-thirty and were ushered into a room at the rear of the precinct. The frosted glass panel on the door and the one way window prevented anyone from peering inside and identifying the occupants.

"Stay here until Sergeant McCann comes for you, Miss Morgan," Detective Santoro instructed.

"And you Mr. Wagner, are to remain in this room until we finish our interrogation."

"Don't worry about me, I'll be careful and stay out of sight."

"We don't care about you," Santoro replied.

Late, Sergei and Boris entered the precinct house shadowed by two 'companions' in camouflage uniforms. Since the duo carried side arms, they were disarmed and escorted to an anteroom. Kevin Moriarty Boris' lawyer was already at the precinct. The three were escorted to the interrogation room. A one-way mirror lined one of the walls. Santoro had placed Wagner and Morgan in one farther down the hall, away from the one Sergei, Boris, and his lawyer were in. He thought it would reduce the chance of Boris accidentally running into his star witness.

Santoro stayed in the room with the brothers and their counsel and engaged them in conversation while McCann retrieved Claudia Morgan and led her to the room where she could view the three without being seen.

"Recognize anyone?" McCann asked.

"That one, him; he's the one I saw in the elevator. He's the maintenance man."

"Are you absolutely sure?"

"I'd bet my life on it."

"Stay in here; don't leave this room for any reason."

McCann left Morgan, walked down the hall, and reentered the interrogation room. Santoro glanced up at his partner. He raised his thumb and said, "Bingo."

"Shall we begin?" Santoro suggested.

"Let's," answered Moriarty.

"We know you murdered Judge Collins, Mr. Trasker. We have a witness who has identified you entering the Gilbert Building about the time of his death."

"I was at the television studio. I have millions of people who saw me being interviewed. How could I have murdered the judge?"

"It's a case of mistaken identity. It happens all the time. Someone sees a chance for getting a little notoriety and takes it," Moriarty opined.

"We'll see," Santoro fired back. "And where were you when Jim Peters was murdered?"

"And when was that?" Boris asked.

"It was yesterday evening, about eight; let's make it between seven and nine."

"He was at my office from five until a little after nine," Moriarty answered.

"So, you have ironclad alibis for the two murders, is that it?" Santoro growled.

McCann interrupted. "You're guilty. It's written all over your face. Save us all some time and come clean. We're going to figure out how you did it. We'll get you."

"We want to get a DNA sample," Santoro injected. "You can do it now, or we can get a court order and get it done in a few days. Which do you prefer?"

"Do it now. I have nothing to hide."

Boris Trasker arose and Investigator McCann escorted him out of the room. That left the scientist, the lawyer, and Santoro to pass the time of day.

Claudia Morgan had been observing all this from behind the one-way mirror. She had not been mistaken. Boris was the one she had seen at the Gilbert Building. The predatory aura she had observed in the elevator was still there, bristling just below the surface of his skin. She marveled at how a person could sense such things, even from another room. But now her attention was drawn to Sergei. He seemed uncomfortable with the situation, with whatever his brother might have been doing. She watched him squirm when Detective Santoro accused his brother of murder. Older brother Sergei was a good man in a bad situation, she concluded. What harm would there be if she were to meet him, accidentally of course, and right now. Claudia Morgan spotted a folder on one of the nearby seats. She picked it up, shoved a few leafs of paper into it and went out into the hall.

"How long will this take?" Moriarty asked, "I have another appointment this morning."

"A few minutes more," Santoro answered.

The door opened. "Here are those profiles you wanted, sir," she said as she handed the folder to Santoro. Attorney and scientist immediately reacted to the attractive woman suddenly in their midst.

Disregarding Moriarty who was closer, she reached over him and shook Sergei Trasker's hand. "Hi, I'm Claudia Morgan."

"Hello," a pleasantly surprised Sergei responded.

"Thank you." Santoro's stern response conveyed only one message; leave.

"Yes sir." As quickly as she had appeared, Claudia was gone. She rushed back to her previous location to monitor the responses to her unexpected intrusion.

"Do all of your secretaries look like that?" Moriarty asked.

"No, not all," a shaken Santoro responded. "Doctor Trasker, I notice you are grinning. Have you anything to say?"

"No."

Claudia was pleased with the effect she had had on the scientist. It was good, no matter the cost.

She knew that Detective Santoro wasn't pleased, but she would deal with that later. She had made contact with Trasker without having to hang-glide into his estate. They weren't strangers any more. She counted that as an advantage. Now, some inept woman falling from the sky wouldn't be viewed as a spy, instead, a secretary pursuing an avocation on her time off.

"All done," McCann said as he returned with the suspect.

"We'll be in touch," Santoro remarked as the group stepped out into the hall.

"If they call you again, let me know. I want to be here," Moriarty instructed. Boris nodded.

Just then, the ladies room door opened and Claudia emerged. She nearly ran into 'Boris.' She muttered a "Sorry," backed up, and closed the door.

As the two investigators watched the trio leave, McCann turned to his boss and noticed the grimace on his face. "What?" He asked.

"That Morgan woman burst into the room; she shook Sergei Trasker's hand, even told him her real name. And now, Boris has seen her; shit."

"What's wrong with her? I told her to stay in the observation room."

A moment later, the rest room door swung open again and Claudia emerged. Scanning the expressions on the men's faces, she smiled and said, "It's not that bad. So, he saw me. Don't look so worried."

"I'm not worried, I'm mad! You may be a material witness to a crime. Do you know what murderers do to material witnesses?"

"Nothing's going to happen to me."

All Santoro could do was twist his head back and forth. The words he had for the woman he refused to utter. "Follow me," he commanded. McCann and the woman followed.

"Bad move," McCann whispered to the woman, "You really got him mad."

"Come on, we'll go and get Dooley," Santoro grunted. The three headed for the room where Wagner was waiting.

"Who is Dooley?" Claudia asked McCann.

"Schultz and Dooley; they're two dumb beer cans that advertised Utica Club beer on TV years ago. I guess Frank doesn't think much of your antics."

"He's right about Wagner, anyway."

"How'd it go? Do we have our man?" Obviously Wagner expected Claudia's identification to wrap up the case. Life was black and white to him. That was why he was still single. He couldn't deal with the complication of having another human being sharing a life with him.

"No, we don't," Santoro replied. "Go home and don't play any more games. I'm on a short fuse; fair warning."

"Sure, fine, okay; I hope we have been helpful." Wagner grasped Claudia's arm and made a swift retreat.

As Wagner and Morgan were getting into his car, Sergei and Boris drove by. The scientist noticed that the woman, supposedly a clerk, was leaving the precinct and with a male escort. He thought that odd.

The man opening the car door for Morgan had his back to them. Sergei couldn't see who he was.

Santoro and McCann were stumped. Boris Trasker seemed to have unimpeachable alibis for both murders. Even Occam's razor didn't help. In this case, the most obvious one might not be the correct answer. There would have to be two, perhaps even more identical Boris Traskers, but how? The premise seemed so preposterous Santoro didn't even consider it.

Quandary

"Home early?" Mimi Santoro asked as her husband opened the door. He met his French wife while serving in Army Intelligence during Desert Storm. She was a correspondent for a news service and he a Major, recalled from civilian life for the duration.

"I'm bushed. I've used up every ounce of brainpower and nothing good has come of it. I've even lost ground. This case has got me running around in circles."

"Oh? What's the problem?" Mimi placed a cup of hot coffee on the table. "Do you want a piece of cake to go with that?"

Santoro shook his head.

"This guy is laughing at us, daring us to find out how he does it."

"How he does what, exactly?"

"Murder someone and then seem to be in another place at exactly the same time. I've racked my brain and can't seem to come up with an answer."

"It's simple. There are two of them," said Mimi.

"Two men that look exactly the same; I doubt that very much."

"You haven't seen the pair together, have you?"

"No, I haven't."

"So how do you know how closely they resemble one another?"

"I don't", Santoro slapped himself in the forehead, "that's right, I don't."

"Are you hungry?"

"Now I am. Let's go out and eat."

"I'll get my jacket."

As Mimi went to get her wrap, Santoro called after her, "Hey! Ever think of becoming a cop?"

She replied, "One in the house is enough; too much."

Rue Madeleine was a restaurant the pair frequented several times a month. The candled ambiance and quiet suited them. Ever a romantic, Frank loved holding Mimi's hand across the table. It reminded him of bygone days, when he was stationed behind the lines and living in relative comfort in Kuwait. He never discussed even with his wife, why he had been stationed so far away from the Desert Storm War.

There were reasons, and good ones, for his being in Kuwait.

He met his wife at a press conference, one of those much talk-no information military updates the Army Public Information officers gave to the media. Leaving the building, Mimi attached herself to Frank and, for the next two hours over lunch, tried her best to extract information from the tight lipped Major.

During the thrust and parry between the two, something else came into play. Mimi noticed how attractive Frank was and that he was not wearing a wedding ring. Frank, in turn, noticed that he was sitting across the table from a beautiful and irritating woman; irritating because on several occasions her questioning had almost caused him a slip of the lip. It peeved him that she was so skilled. Still, his impression of her was highly favorable. Risky as it was, he found himself enjoying this battle of the wills.

They met again and again, the presumption being she was still attempting to extract information about the war for her magazine. Eventually, a truce was called to the farce and more serious negotiations began. Frank found Mimi tender and true, smart when she had to be, and incredibly aloof when Frank needed that from her. As intimate as their relationship had become, Frank still withheld the information he needed to from her. Mimi never challenged that need.

As dessert was being served, Frank revisited his wife's presumption. "So, you think there might be two of them?"

"Let's put this on a personal level. Here we are, eating at Rue. A bank robbery occurs in White Plains; the thieves are photographed on the cameras in the bank. Their pictures appear tomorrow on the front page of the paper. Someone we know identifies one of the robbers and says to the police, 'that's Mimi.' When the police come to question us what do you tell them?"

"There's someone else who resembles you."

"How's your appetizer? Mine's delicious."

"Mine, too."

"I hired a crane with a one hundred-twenty foot boom and a platform. The operator agreed to lift it to a hundred feet. He wanted ten grand. Then I told him the location. The Hawthorne Circle area is very busy and he's afraid of being sued. We're looking elsewhere."

Claudia Morgan and Jimmy Todd her instructor were of one mind. Skeptical when the project started, Jimmy had come to respect Claudia's chutzpah; she was not like anyone he had ever met. He admired her courage and determination and was moved by her complete trust in him. He might have even loved her, but he recognized early that the gap between them on many levels was too great.

His student on the other hand, was getting cold feet. She vacillated between being sure of her ability to fly and the vision of crashing on a heavily travelled parkway or into some remote hill. She had already learned that the direction and strength of the wind were the only forces that mattered. Her skill in making them work for her was subordinated to their being present and strong enough to keep her aloft.

Still, Sergei's situation motivated her. Yes, she was after the Triple I incentive, but that goal seemed to be fading, taking a more and more distant second to her being able to help the troubled man she met at the precinct.

"When do you want to do this?" Jimmy asked.

"Let's look at the weather. That should give us a clue."

"I'll look into the long range forecast. Do you want to know today?"

"I don't need to know today."

"Getting cold feet?"

Claudia let her chin drop to her chest. "Oh, you noticed."

"It's not the first time I've seen one of my students freeze up. It happens a lot. You can do this.

The big question is whether Mother Nature is willing to help."

"I don't want you picking pieces of me out of some tree."

"You'll be all right. It's fall now; the winds are strong most of the time. October is a good month to fly, but not for novices. You're not one of those anymore."

"How far do you estimate I need to fly?"

"I make it no more than five miles. If we find a good launch site, it should be somewhere between one and two. Your big problem will be going over or getting around that one tall hill near the estate. If the winds are strong, the updraft will make it a piece of cake. If they're not, you'll need to find the thermals."

"Thanks for that."

"It's not that gloomy. You can do it. Go home; I'll call you in the morning."

Having returned home, Mimi and Frank were just getting out of the car when his cell phone vibrated. "I thought this was going to be our night," Mimi whispered into his ear. Frank shrugged his shoulders and countered with, "I know, I know; what's up, Bob?" Santoro's countenance soured as he listened to what McCann was describing.

"And what was the TOD? Let me guess. He's got an alibi? How could it be any other way? Give me an hour; I should be able to get over there by then."

"What? Mimi asked.

"It's him again, our two-places-at-one-time killer. He's done it again."

"There are two of them, I tell you."

"Forget it; let's go upstairs. I told Bob an hour; that could stretch to two."

Mimi smiled. "I'll see what I can do."

Beacon flashing, Santoro arrived on the scene two hours and thirty minutes after he had received McCann's message.

"Sorry to call you at home, boss."

"I'm used to it."

"Yeah, you're right. But this time, it might be worth it. The victim battled with the guy. We got some DNA."

"Jesus, finally we're breaking through. Did you send it to the lab?"

"I took the shirt and jacket; hand-delivered it myself. I wasn't going to let anyone screw this up."

"It better produce results, it's all we've got."

"I know how you feel Frank. It's been a tough one, losing Peters."

"We've been through a lot, Bob, but this one; I'm not sure where we're going. There are so many angles. The case seems open and shut; the convict is seeking revenge for being put in prison unjustly.

That's what it looks like. But I get a creepy feeling. This cold chill down my back tells me that there's something else afoot. I can't shake it."

"I have the same feeling. I was going to mention it, but I decided to let it pass. What do you think we've got here?"

"I can't put my finger on it yet, but there may be more than just the assassination of the few people who participated in that trial. My gut tells me we're standing at the edge of something bigger than a pissed-off prisoner bent on revenge."

This time the deceased was Rodney Pearlman, Boris Trasker's defense attorney. Santoro would never have expected Pearlman to be a victim. He had done everything in his power to exonerate his client, to convince the jury he was innocent. He even visited his client in prison and tried to convince him that mounting an appeal would be in his best interest. Why then would he want to kill the only person that vigorously defended him before, during, and after the trial? Santoro noticed that this victim had been slain differently than Collins or Peters.

Santoro's experience in Army intelligence provided him with that sixth sense most spies need in order to survive. Of course he wasn't a spy, but he regularly dealt with them. The good ones remained alive by anticipating events before they occurred. The others never saw their demise approaching. The part of this drama that annoyed Santoro most was the arrogance shown by Boris Trasker; he was daring the police to expose him. Santoro made himself a promise to collar the bastard. He hoped the DNA would give him what he needed. Calling Boris Trasker in right now would be counterproductive. Doing so would just make him more cautious. Santoro decided to let the murderer believe he had succeeded again.

The scientist sat on the bench at the big bay window in the great room. Basil the Great Dane sat at his feet. The room overlooked the huge swimming pool. At the moment two merganser ducks had landed and were splashing themselves with water. Sergei smiled; it reminded him of his days as a youth in Latvia, the happy times before the Russians spirited him away to 'a better life.' He stroked Basil's enormous head. As the sun's rays advanced across the room, his thoughts turned to the beautiful woman he had seen at the police precinct. Whether through sexuality, appearance or intellect, Claudia Morgan had indeed achieved the response she desired. The scientist could not get her out of his mind.

Unknown to him, Sergei had affected her in the same way.

"Thinking about that girl at the precinct," 'Boris' asked.

"Yes, I am. She is the most beautiful woman I have seen in a long time. And her mood seems very pleasant."

"And you saw all of that in just the few moments you were with her?"

"You would not be making so much fun of it if you had seen her smile at me."

"Forget about her. Remember your brother Boris; he's depending on you. You know what will happen to him if I am not successful."

"Who are you? All of this is about my research, isn't it? I will never give that to you."

"Oh, you will." Boris attempted to place his hand on Sergei's shoulder, but he shrugged it off.

"I see you're not friendly today."

"Leave me alone."

"We will stop when I say so; when you give me what I want."

"Boris already went to prison because of you. I didn't yield then, and I won't now."

"It will be life in prison this time, Sergei. Think well on this; your brother's life is in your hands."

Santoro entered his office and threw his hat on the chair. He hardly had time to get seated before Bob McCann burst through the door clutching the lab report.

"Bingo, I got the results; but there's a problem."

"Well, what are we waiting for? Let's go get him." Santoro jumped up from his chair, squashed his Fedora on his head, glanced at Bob McCann - and stopped. "What kind of problem?"

"You're not going to believe this"

"What?"

"It's DNA, all right, but there was fluid with it?"

"What kind of fluid?"

"Amniotic fluid; the fluid from a mother's body, a pregnant mother's body."

"It's his DNA, though, isn't it?"

"Maybe, if he's a baby. It's crazy, Frank, I can't make heads or tails of it. I'm stumped."

"What do you think; call him in?"

"What's the point? The DA will laugh us out of his office if we try to pin something on him with this stuff. I say let's wait. We just need a few more pieces of the puzzle, that's all. It'll all fit together, you'll see."

Santoro sat down in his chair, turned to the window, and tipped his Fedora so that it shaded his face from the sun. Bob McCann knew what that meant; the boss was going to engage in some powerful thinking. He slipped out of the office and gently closed the door. Santoro was deep in thought.

In contrast to Peters' torture and murder, Pearlman's was quick, clinical; the small caliber projectile entering just behind the left ear. A person standing ten feet away might not have been able to discern the noise of the shot from the din of passing traffic. Collins murder was also swift, but silent.

Circumstances and location dictated that it had to meet those criteria. Santoro delved deeper; three deaths- two, professional and swift, and one, gruesome and protracted. Was there a reason for the difference?

Boris could have dispatched Peters just as easily as he had Collins. He did Pearlman. Why was Peters different? The street was empty; there were no passersby. Why kidnap him? *Because Peters had something that his killer needed to know. That's why he didn't waste the detective right there in front of his home. But what?*

Santoro jumped up from his chair and called out. "Bob! Bob!" McCann rushed into Santoro's office.

"Dig into Peters' background. I need to know what he did before he joined the force. And look into the other two, Pearlman and Collins. We might be on to something."

"Sure, Boss; just one thing."

"What?"

"Take off that ugly goddamn hat."

Could that be what this was all about? Was there another reason that controlled the way Boris Trasker was behaving? The more Frank Santoro considered the possibility, the more he liked it. And Mimi's idea added the answer he had dismissed; two of them. The amniotic fluid issue puzzled him, but now that he felt he was on track; somewhere, there was an answer for the DNA paradox, too. Santoro knew that most crimes were solved by evidence; many times from research carried on far from the actual scene of the crime. His intuition suggested that now this might be the case.

Claudia Morgan hurried along the windy cross street; October was well-known for its bursts of wind and bone-chilling cold. It had been a while since she had visited the Big Apple; and because of that, she had planned poorly and not donned the heavy coat left at home. She braved the surges of cold wind, but she stepped into nearby doorways when they left her shivering.

Professor Constantine Potemkin was the man she was looking for. A United Nations symposium on matters biological was the reason for the Russian scientist's presence in New York. From her research Claudia had learned that he had been Sergei's mentor, as well as an acknowledged giant in his field: the development of the fetus and the constantly-changing nutritional value of amniotic fluid. He spent over a decade documenting the behavior of several hundred pregnant women and their development of the fetus throughout the process of gestation.

Claudia read the published papers that detailed his findings and the experiments he conducted on the changes that occurred in amniotic fluid as pregnancy progressed. For some reason, after releasing several papers to the scientific world for their review and acclamation, the Soviet government began to heavily censure his works. Eventually, they stopped him from publishing any other whitepapers.

She had arranged an interview with the famous scientist through her contacts in the United Nations. She had managed to get an hour with him at his quarters in the Dakota House, an impressive residence on pricey Central Park West. It seemed the Russian gentleman had friends who offered him their apartment while he was in town. As she approached the entrance to the building, a formidable doorman greeted her.

"How may I help you, Miss?"

"I'm here to see Professor Potemkin. I believe he's on the 8th floor, but I don't know which apartment."

"Ma'am, there's only one apartment on the 8th floor; it belongs to Professor Potemkin's cousin Mr. Vollmer." The doorman turned and picked up the in-house phone. "What's your name ma'am?"

"Claudia Morgan; I have a 10 o'clock appointment."

The doorman repeated Claudia's name over the phone. "You can go up now." He escorted her to the elevator and wished her a good day.

The ancient lift, regal in its own time but desperately outdated in this, limped its way upward.

Claudia reminisced about the building's history and how long it had been a mainstay of New York City architecture. Before she had time to finish her thoughts, the elevator bumped to a stop and the doors opened. The entire landing including the ceiling, were faced in granite or marble, she couldn't tell which.

At the farthest point from the elevator was one large, shiny, copper-clad door. Claudia walked up to it and pressed the mother of pearl doorbell.

She heard someone approaching. The door swung open and a very elegant looking snowy-haired man bowed slightly and half-whispered "Miss Claudia Morgan?"

The woman smiled her reply and entered. "I am James, the professor's valet, ma'am," he announced. "Professor is in the sitting room. Would you care for some coffee or water; something stronger, perhaps?"

"I'm fine, thank you." Claudia reviewed her reasons for visiting the professor; surely it was about Sergei and his research, but she wanted to know more about the man and felt that speaking to Potemkin might help. Her research told her that this man had been associated with him for years. Certainly he could give her some insight as to his character. But would he?

The white-haired elderly man rose and bowed slightly. Claudia was pleasantly surprised.

Although the good professor was well along in years, about 75 to 80 she judged, hc was in remarkably good condition. His warm smile and genial manner announced a person who was still viable, both intellectually and emotionally.

"And you are Miss Morgan I presume. How are you? Well, I hope. Your message over the phone indicated that you had some questions about Sergei. That interested me. I have spent many years working with the brilliant man, you know. I miss him greatly and I am sad that he defected. Regardless of what you have heard, Russia is not a bad place for scientists to work - to do research I mean - the rest you heard about other things may be true." Potemkin winked. "There is definitely a hierarchy in Russia; there is no Czar, but many Czar-like people." Potemkin motioned for Claudia to sit.

"Now, Miss Morgan, what is your interest in Sergei Trasker? Have you met him? Are you interested in stealing his research? Are you a corporate spy?"

While the professor fired question after question at Claudia, he was observing her reactions. What he concluded surprised him; there was more than one reason for Claudia's meeting the professor. Still uncertain of her main reason for coming, his instincts told him that this was a person he could trust.

"You care for Sergei. Still, I see something else, but I have no idea what it might be. Can you please help me? I care a great deal for him, but I will not reveal anything I know about him unless I trust you. Are you a Russian spy?"

"I am not!" Claudia indignantly replied.

Potemkin grinned. "That's what I wanted to hear; righteous anger. Would you like to take a walk in Central Park? New York is lovely this time of the year, and I never fail to do so when I am fortunate enough to be here."

His was a strange request. Why would a man she hardly knew be asking her to take a walk in the park when it was so private in the apartment? Privacy; who else might be listening? Claudia had forgotten that she was talking to someone whose every move was most likely being monitored by his government, spies, or whomever. Her realization seemed so obvious that she smiled inside.

"I'd love to."

"James,"

"I have your hat here, sir. Will you need gloves?" The professor nodded.

As Claudia and the professor left the building, she noticed James the valet followed at a distance and that he was carrying something she would've never expected to see under the circumstances; a large boombox. Its presence piqued her curiosity. Making their way across a still well-forested Central Park West, the professor engaged in small talk: the leaves starting to fall, the sudden gusts of the wind, the sunny day, the wellbeing of his children and grandchildren who still lived in Russia. Once in the park proper, he suddenly became silent. He glanced to the right, left, and around; he seemed to be looking for something. Claudia wondered what in the world it might be. Success; the professor spotted a lone bench, far from any other structure. "Please," he indicated with the swoop of his hand. She sat. Potemkin glanced at James. The boom box was energized. It bombarded the atmosphere with brutally loud contemporary music. It annoyed her.

"Now we can talk. What do you want to know about Sergei? I have much to tell you. I miss him greatly, you know. He was a wonderful collaborator; we accomplished much together. Still, he was a slave, but a very well-treated slave, I might add. His life was not his own. I cannot imagine how he must have felt living in Russia and never being able to see any of his relatives, never being able to write them or receive their letters. One might say he had no family. That's what drove him away, that's what made him defect."

"What about his brother?"

"When Sergei wouldn't agree to come back, they threatened him. Finding they couldn't break him, they resorted to other measures. They murdered a man, drugged Sergei's brother, and had him jailed. Still, Sergei would not yield. So they started again. This time, they are building the case to have Boris incarcerated for life. The man you saw, the man called Boris, is not Sergei's brother. The real Boris is being held, here, in the United States. They call the place Lubyanka, after an infamous Russian prison.

Everyone who survived being there came out with horrific stories about the treatment. I'm sure Boris is well treated. They wouldn't want to anger Sergei. That would close the door for good." The professor swiped his chin with his fingers. "That is Sergei's dilemma; how to rescue his brother without giving them the research."

"But why do they want it so badly? Is it that special?"

"You have no idea. Sergei developed a stem cell protocol that is eons ahead of the most advanced research here in the United States. Adding that to what he already knows; I must stop - I am beginning to say too much."

The noise from the boom box had ceased. The professor looked toward James, who nodded slowly but perceptibly. Someone was approaching. The professor got up and took Claudia's arm. "That is all for now. Shall we walk?" The pair, with James trailing close behind, continued. The professor returned to his former topics, his children, grandchildren and the weather. Before their parting, he asked, "Do you have a card?" Claudia reached into her pocket and produced one. After perusing it, Potemkin bowed and wished her a good day. She watched as the pair made their way down the path.

When she returned to her apartment Claudia was confused. What had she just experienced? What message did Potemkin convey? It was clear he respected and admired Sergei. It was also clear that he, the professor, was under constant surveillance. Perhaps the Russians hoped he might try to contact his former colleague during his stay. They were mistaken. She had received the impression that the professor, acutely aware of their tactics, would die before he helped them bag Sergei. Another perspective also seemed plausible; with Sergei's research being so valuable, could Becker Pharmaceutical and perhaps Potemkin also be acting as agents for the Russian government? Several million dollars is quite a prize for obtaining industrial espionage data. The amount far surpassed anything Claudia received for an assignment. Might Becker be playing both sides, and might Sergei's discovery truly be significant enough to justify all this competition?

What discovery is so important to justify incarcerating someone's brother for life as a bargaining chip? And, how important must it be for Sergei to resist when his brother is being placed in jeopardy for a second time?

Claudia plopped into her favorite chair. The information she had gathered so far was complicated.

She considered where or how to move next. There were too many unanswered questions and she needed time to mull them over and perhaps find some answers. A visit to Morpheus might help. She shut her eyes and dozed off.

"You're going to flip when you here this." McCann seemed excited.

"What?" Santoro replied.

"The service records for Peters, Collins, and Pearlman are phony. They were doctored; all three."

"Doctored?"

"Many entries don't jive; there are postings about service here or there, this theater or that. But when I dug deeper, I found it was all fluff. I couldn't cross reference times and locations. Disbursements made to the three were continents away from where they were supposed to have been. The entries seemed an afterthought, as if someone was trying to cover something up. If you asked me where these guys served, I could tell you where the records said they were. If you asked me to verify where they were at a certain time, I couldn't. The rest of the paper trail doesn't hold up. I've looked at enough of these over the years to be able to detect false documents."

"I've known Peters for years; it can't be."

"Did he ever discuss his service with you?"

"Sure, plenty of times. He even told me about his secret mission in China."

"And when was that?"

"It was 84, 1984."

McCann thumbed through Peters' folder. "It says here he was in Washington in 1984; special assignment. Collins and Pearlman were also in Washington during the same period."

"Where were they supposed to have been?"

"China, but all had liaison positions and get this, to the Combat Readiness Task Force."

"Bull; I bet that's a code word for some kind of op."

"So there was a connection between the three victims unrelated to the Boris Trasker case. What could it be?" McCann posed the question.

Santoro didn't have an answer.

"Drug murders seem a cinch when compared to this."

"Expand your search. We need to know what activity connected these men."

McCann left.

The doorbell rang. It rang again. Having risen at ten and worked all through the night, she intended to sleep in. Now someone was at the door. She glanced at the clock; 7 o'clock. Who could possibly be here at this time in the morning? She put on her robe and headed for the front door. Claudia was not at her best. Glancing through the peep hole she thought she recognized James, Potemkin's valet.

He was wearing a fedora pulled down over his face. It made him virtually unrecognizable. She opened the door and asked him in. To her surprise it was the professor who greeted her.

Seeing her confusion the professor explained, "We have to do these things Miss Morgan, Many people are watching me. I am under constant surveillance. My benefactors would be very happy if I tried to contact

Sergei. I will not do that. You, however, may be the way I can get a message to him. Are you willing?"

"Yes."

The professor began moving his lips as if he wanted to say more. She watched with fascination as his lips continued to move but made no sound. After a short while the professor spit a tiny object into his hand. The tiny pod contained a microchip. "Give this to Sergei. It's a synopsis of my latest experiments and the conclusions I have drawn. There is also a surprise; no need to explain because you wouldn't understand. He will. Under no circumstances are you to allow anyone else to see this chip or let them take it from you. If you are in any danger, destroy it. The fact that you know nothing about its contents will probably save you from being tortured. You don't have to do this. This is not a game. The people involved are very serious about their work and the fact that Claudia Morgan has the chip will have no bearing on what they will do to retrieve it. Do you understand what I am saying?"

"I do. I can't say I'm not afraid. I don't even know the man that well and here I am doing this espionage work. It's crazy."

"Do you think he is a good man, Miss Morgan?"

"I believe he is."

The professor headed for the door. "I must return, otherwise my friends might become suspicious why James has left the professor for so long."

Claudia watched the old man as he disappeared behind the closing elevator doors. What a life, she thought; hiding, deceiving, weighing the consequences of every step, every movement. I could never live like that, she thought. Why am I doing this? This is not for amateurs. And, make no mistake, in this situation, I am an amateur. Still, I want to help Sergei; how? There must be a way, something; of course.

Why hadn't she thought of it before? That tissue she deposited in her desk drawer. Claudia put on her coat and headed to the office.

"Anything?" Santoro asked as Bob McCann entered his office.

"Not yet, but I have some calls in to some old friends. I'm hoping they can break down this wall of silence I've been up against. Whatever these guys were doing, the project was top drawer, it was super- secret."

"Keep trying." The buzzer on the intercom sounded. Santoro pressed the talk button. "Who?

Claudia Morgan? Send her in." Santoro looked at McCann. "I wonder what she wants."

"She gave us a little trouble at the interview, but she's pretty smart I think. Maybe she's got something for us that might help."

Morgan entered the office beaming.

"What are you so happy about?"

"Well, Chief Investigator Santoro, I may just have busted your case wide open." She said as she extracted the tissue from the paper bag she was carrying and placed it on Santoro's desk. "When I was in the elevator, that Boris cleaning guy brushed up against me and deposited this stuff on my shoe. I meant to give it to you sooner, but I was busy; one thing led to another and I just forgot. I'm sorry about that."

Santoro glanced at McCann. "Get this to the lab."

McCann retrieved the paper bag with tissue from Morgan and left.

"Do you have anything else?" Santoro asked.

"I spoke to a professor Potemkin, Sergei's former colleague. He told me that all these murders are ways to ransom Boris Trasker so that Sergei will give them information on an important discovery he seems to have made. The first murder that sent Boris to prison was also contrived. The Russians tried to use him as a bargaining chip to get Sergei to give in. So far he hasn't. So, they're trying again. This time, it will be life for Boris if they don't get what they want."

"You expect me to believe all that? That's the craziest story I've ever heard, and I've heard a lot of them. What discovery can be that important? It doesn't make sense; it sounds like science fiction to me. I'm not buying it."

"I've done my duty; and now, I'm on my way." Morgan seemed restless. Santoro thought he'd ask why.

"Going somewhere?"

"Yes, back to bed. I didn't get much sleep last night. But, tomorrow, I'm going flying. I'm a hang gliding enthusiast; didn't you know? It seems like it will be a good day for it."

"I didn't realize you liked Central Park that much," Grigorev a Russian agent observed as he entered Potemkin's living room.

"Yes, it reminds me of my youth, when I used to frequent places like that," Professor Potemkin replied.

"And the woman, who is she?"

"New York is filled with young women trying to prey on famous old men. I think she was one."

"How was she able to see you? What story did she use to get an appointment?" Grigorev was sly; many times he knew the answers to the questions he was asking. Potemkin needed to be careful.

"She told me she had a message from Sergei Trasker. Of course I believed her. I do look forward to meeting him at some point. But, after questioning her, I concluded she was lying. I thanked her for her time, she gave me her card, and that was the end of it." Potemkin glanced at the Russian agent, trying to fathom his reaction to the tale he had woven.

"If she did have a message from Sergei, I am sure you would have rushed over to my apartment and told me," the sneering agent replied.

The professor returned the Russian agent's sneer with a smile. Theirs was a chess game. The stakes were high and the future of Sergei Trasker and his astonishing discovery hung in the balance.

Potemkin's wife had just this morning told him she had discovered where the real Boris Trasker was being held. He needed the Morgan woman to convey that information to Sergei, but how could he dare meet her again? Already certain she was not a Russian operative, he could only wonder at her real purpose in seeking him out. He decided to take the risk.

"Enjoy the rest of your day," Grigorev suggested. "I know you are a faithful citizen, and, I am sure you will let us know when you have contacted him." The agent's meaning was all too familiar. Do as I direct or suffer the consequences.

Showing the agent out, James the valet returned. "What now?"

"Elena contacted me this morning. She found out where they are holding Boris. I must get that information to Sergei. Even in Russia they know what is going on here."

"That will be risky. I heard what you told him. You gave him the impression you wouldn't be seeing the woman again. And now you are going to see her again. Even I would be suspicious. By the way, how is it that they have not been able to break your code? Your wife e-mails you every day. I have read them; they are nothing I can understand. How could anyone get the information you get from them?"

"Turn up the radio."

The boom box began to saturate the room with guitar-driven noise.

"It pays to be a scholar, you know. Science was my primary interest, but I also loved to study the ancient languages that preceded the Russian; Elena communicates in an Ossetic dialect, an inheritance from the Scythians. It was used by ancients, the ones who lived around the Caspian Sea, and Lake Aral.

Some say the civilization extended all the way to the Black Sea. Even if someone were to break the code, they couldn't understand the words unless they had this background. The espionage community, I am sure, does not teach its agents Ossetic."

"Can I contact the Morgan woman? When do you want to see her? I suggest you wait several days. Grigorev is sniffing around too closely. You must be careful."

"I have five meetings in the next two days. That will convince our good agent I am not doing anything unreasonable. You too, James, must be careful. Everyone knows you are my arms and legs.

They will also be watching you. Do nothing about the Morgan woman until I tell you. Go about your regular duties. Perhaps that will ease their anxiety."

"I understand. Do you wish to take another walk in the park?"

"Yes, I think I should do that regularly; every day, perhaps twice a day. That way, when I meet the Morgan woman again, it will seem accidental."

"Do you wish to have your tea now?"

"Yes; and put something in it – something strong. After meeting with that apparatchik, I have earned it."

James was a faithful servant. His employer had informed him of the whereabouts of Sergei Trasker's brother, and now he, too, felt a burden to get the message to Claudia Morgan as soon as possible - despite Potemkin's warning.

Still, he had to consider being intercepted by Grigorev's agents. He needed a plan. His first concern was, in what form should the information be? That was easy; some sort of code. His second; where could he place it on his body so that it might be easily accessible? The third was the most crucial.

To make decoding possible, the cipher needed to appear complicated, yet be easily decipherable.

James retrieved an entrance pass to one of Potemkin's roundtables from the desk drawer and scribbled the array of ciphers and letters on the back. What professor would go to commiserate with his colleagues without taking reminders? Absentmindedly, Potemkin forgot his. That was the reason James would be hurrying across town; to give him his reminder. Perfect; what could be less onerous than that?

Full of himself at what he had accomplished, James headed directly but very indirectly for Claudia Morgan's condo. Hardly glancing back, the valet took note of a lesser apparatchik who fell in behind, but at a respectful distance. He did not try to elude him. That might be taken as an admission of guilt.

Claudia Morgan was suited up and ready. She wondered what it would be like, soaring into Sergei's courtyard. What would he say, and how would she reply? She sensed the compression as the elevator slowed to stop. The doors opened and she stepped out into the lobby. The raincoat she wore hid her jump suit. Embedded in the flow of people heading toward the elevator she saw James approaching.

Twenty feet behind, she spotted his tail, a short man in a too-large topcoat and a too-wide brimmed hat.

He was speeding up, hoping to enter the same elevator that James would be using.

Claudia changed her direction to intercept the valet. As they brushed past one another, he thrust the pass into the palm of Claudia's hand and continued on his way, his shadow in close pursuit.

Absolutely the last passenger, the apparatchik muscled his way between the closing doors into the over- occupied conveyance.

Claudia sped off to the launch site. She opened the palm of her hand and looked at the pass. Just a ticket to a meeting, that's all it is, she observed. But what were these letters and numbers scribbled on the other side? James wanted me to have this. It must be for Sergei, she concluded.

The trip to where she was to meet Jimmy Todd took longer than Claudia Morgan anticipated. She used the extra time to pump up her courage. I can do this, she kept telling herself, I can do this.

"The winds are coming from the right direction, westerly. It should be an easy ride over that hill we talked about. Watch out for lulls in the wind; you'll drop a hundred feet before you get air again. Be careful about that, real careful," Jimmy Todd warned Claudia.

"Thanks for the encouragement. Don't worry about the lulls; I'm on it. All I want to know is whether you think I can pull this off. You're the experienced one. Can I do this?"

"Yes. There might've been some question if the front was coming from the other direction, but as of right now, everything is in your favor. It should be a piece of cake." Claudia didn't catch the flash of concern that darted across Jimmy's eyes.

The pair drove to the launch site, an abandoned parking lot of a firm that made cold cuts and hot dogs. Its color-faded sign still adorned the bricked, window-shattered main plant. The crane operator watched as Claudia mounted the platform, maneuvered the kite into place and braced herself for the lift. Leaning over the controls, he glanced at the woman and asked, "Ready?" Claudia nodded. The crane's engine roared. A slight jerk from the platform indicated the craft was on its way up to launch position. The view got better and better the higher the launch pad rose. Northern Westchester was a beautiful place, a mixture of uneven wooded hills with civilization tucked into the valleys and spilling out into some of the fields. The breathtaking panorama encouraged and bolstered Claudia's courage. At the same time it caused her concern. She knew the strength of the wind would allow her to rise to great heights, high enough to clear the hill in question. But it would also make any changes in wind velocity more severe. A slight bump as the platform stopped brought her back to reality; she was now at launch height.

Waiting for a lull in the wind, she quickly positioned her kite. As a blast of wind started to push her forward, Claudia looked down at Jimmy, then ran five paces and launched. Turning into the wind, she had no trouble in gaining elevation. Now all she needed to do was orient herself and head for Trasker's estate. Several high-voltage electric towers crossed the path she had to take. She worked the wind and gained more elevation than she needed, making sure that any sudden change would not drive her into the lines. In a short time she passed the wires.

Now she had to concentrate on attaining enough height to surmount the single obstacle that remained; the wooded hill. Its slopes were severe, and Claudia marveled at how the trees were able to gain a footing and thrive on the steep, rocky slopes. This was the time she had to be the most cautious; while the wind on one side of the hill would carry her upward and over it, the decrease in pressure on the other side might result in the changes that she and Jimmy had discussed. As she approached, she could feel the wind velocity increasing. It was as if an invisible hand was lifting her up over the hill. Under different circumstances, this segment of the trip could have been fun. She didn't have to do anything; the wind did all the work. To her surprise, the other side didn't present a problem either. Now she could concentrate on finding the estate and devise a not-so-graceful landing in his courtyard.

A short time later she spotted its tiled roofs in the distance. It had been a good flight. As she approached, the kite seemed harder to control. Glancing up, she noticed a small tear in the fabric on the left side. She watched in alarm as the rip started to grow. At the moment the problem was not catastrophic, but soon enough the small tear in the fabric could become a large hole. Claudia was now in a race: land very soon, or fall out of the sky.

Wind velocity increased and gusts became more violent. That put more pressure on the fabric and Claudia watched with horror as the tear started to gain momentum and travel more aggressively across the entire left side of the wing. Close to the estate now, all she needed was perhaps two minutes - two precious minutes. The loud tearing sound above her head told her she was out of time. The kite fabric near the tear folded, much like an umbrella when exposed to the wind from underneath. As she plummeted earthward, all she could see were trees with large, ominous brown and green tentacles, all waiting to catch her falling body. As she smashed into the first one, Claudia covered her face. Moments later, an intrusive branch ripped portions of her jumpsuit, battering one arm, de-fleshing it shoulder to wrist. Compound fractures and broken ribs seemed inevitable. As if a thousand years had passed, she finally came to rest at the base of a large oak tree.

She heard a vehicle engine, and then footsteps approaching. Opening her eyes, she found one of Trasker's armed guards kneeling beside her. The expression on his face told her that she was in crisis.

In what seemed like an instant the man reached into his pack and produced bandages, splints and a handful of pills. From his canteen he poured a bit of water into its cup and told her to swallow the pills in his hand. After several gulps of water she did. The spurting sensation she felt was without a doubt a burst artery, somewhere down there, below where she could see. Claudia felt pressure being applied; the spurting stopped; a tourniquet, she reasoned.

The call on the guard's cell phone soon brought others. She could hear several more vehicles approaching . It wasn't long before the man she sought was looking down at her. Gently, he removed her helmet. Her auburn hair rolled out in soft folds to the ground. Claudia looked into Sergei's eyes, and smiled. "Hi," was all she could manage. Then everything went black.

Santoro was screaming over the phone to McCann. If it could have melted it would have. "Where is she? You've checked everywhere? What about Wagner, does he know where she is? I don't trust him.

He's coming in? Good I'll speak to him then. When can I expect him?" Santoro glanced at his watch.

"That should be right about now." Just then, someone gently rapped on Santoro's office door. He put the phone back in its cradle. "Yes?"

"It's Ted Wagner." His voice was trembling a little.

"Come," Santoro replied. As the man took a seat, the detective scrutinized his demeanor. He seemed unusually nervous. Santoro took that to mean Wagner had not been completely honest with him during his last visit. He also believed Wagner knew what Morgan was doing, but for some reason did not want to tell the police.

"Mr. Wagner, I think your friend is in trouble, deep trouble. Bob McCann has been trying to find her and can't. Can you help us?"

"I don't know where she is either, I swear. She had an assignment and she was working on it.

That's all I know."

"Did her work have anything to do with Sergei Trasker?"

"Yes, it did. Becker Pharmaceutical was paying our firm to spy on him."

"So, she was after him all the while. Her spotting Collins' murderer was just a coincidence?"

Wagner nodded.

"Becker offered Triple I a great deal of money to find out what he was doing in his experiments.

Claudia was going to get a large bonus when she brought back his notes. Collins' murder and her meeting Boris Trasker in the elevator was, as you said, a coincidence."

Santoro knew more now. Still, Wagner had not given police the information they so desperately needed, her location. While everything he had heard explained the reason for her behavior, he was still concerned about the woman's safety. The phone rang.

"Santoro; yeah Bob - you don't say. A crane was involved? Bring in that Jimmy Todd, I'll be wanting to talk with him. You'll be here in an hour? Good, I'll see you then." Santoro addressed Wagner,

"In a little while we'll know more about Miss Morgan's whereabouts than you. Stick around, you may find this interesting."

The light from the sun was brilliant. She could hear the seagulls. She recognized the scene immediately, the sand was the same as she remembered; Cape Cod's Marconi Beach. It had been so long since she visited there. She was in the water up to her chin and could feel the waves lapping against it.

Her father and mother were nowhere to be seen, but that didn't bother her. She would find them as she always had, by walking along the beach and spotting the family's black, white, and red tartan blanket. It was simply a matter of being diligent and walking along the beach for a while, that's all. She came out of the water and the sun quickly dried her. She began her trek. The gently blowing wind caressed her face and dried her hair seemingly in an instant. The pale blue sky was empty except for a few puffs of snow- white clouds making their way toward the eastern horizon. The day was coming to a close.

Families and bathers were picking up their blankets and calling it a day. She became concerned; she could not find her parents. Still, she remained confident she would. Soon, the beach was empty and she was alone. In the distance, she spotted someone approaching. He seemed vaguely familiar. As he came closer, she became excited because she recognized him. It was Sergei Trasker. He kept whispering in a very gentle voice, "Miss Morgan, Miss Morgan. . ." He reached out and touched her cheek.

"Miss Morgan, Miss Morgan, it's Sergei Trasker. You'll be fine; it will just take a little time."

Claudia Morgan was in the scientist's laboratory. Immersed in lukewarm fluid, she could feel it lapping up against her chin. The last thing she remembered was saying hi to him after taking that terrible fall from the sky. As her mind and vision cleared, she noticed that not only was she immersed but totally immobilized. Her torso, arms, and legs were held in place by an array of soft cloth restraints attached to metal rods. She felt no pain. The fluid circulating around her body was gentle, nurturing. But it felt like more than just warm water.

"How long have I been here?"

He smiled, then whispered, "You've been here six days."

"Am I in a hospital? I think I broke both legs, and something happened to my arm. Am I going to make it?" Claudia's voice was trembling.

"You're in my laboratory; and, yes, you are going to make it. In a little while, you'll be fine."

"What's happening to me? I'm feeling drowsy." She was preparing to say something more, but drifted off into slumber.

The scientist failed to mention her recuperation might take six weeks or more. He had other business. Faux Boris had just returned from seeing Sergei's real brother.

"So you're a hang gliding instructor, Mr. Todd, is that it? What were you doing with that crane? A few passersby said someone launched from its platform. Do you allow that? Isn't that dangerous? Who was it that took off? Was it Claudia Morgan? What's going on?" Santoro was pressing Todd for answers.

The instructor was frightened. "I don't know anything. After the woman paid me a couple of thousand bucks to teach her how to hang-glide, the rest of it was her doing. She wanted to fly into this estate she claimed was all bottled up with guards, fences, and maybe dogs. That's all I know. What I did isn't a crime, is it?"

"Tell me more. You're not getting out of here until you do."

"Ever been in jail, Todd," McCann chimed in, "it's not a good place to be."

"She wanted to meet this really smart scientist guy. She felt this was the only way to do it. I told her it would be dangerous, I told her the winds in this part of the county were unreliable. Now she's out there somewhere, maybe down in some trees or a ravine, or worse yet, in some swamp. There's no way to tell where she is. The winds got stronger after she launched. She could be anywhere. I shouldn't have let her go. It was the damn money."

"It's not your fault; that Morgan woman is ambitious, if you didn't help her she would've found someone else. That's just the way it is. You can go." Santoro could see that Jimmy Todd had become a pawn in a game he knew nothing about. Now he had to deal with the burden of perhaps sending Claudia Morgan to her death. Finding the woman had just become doubly important.

"What do you think, Bob?"

"Maybe I'll transfer back to traffic, I want to be a cop on the beat again. All of this is insane.

People risking their lives to meet other people, juice that rubs off of people that really belongs to a baby, murders intended to convict innocent people just to get some damn information; it's all nuts."

"Bob, you just nailed it."

"What now?"

"The DNA, that's the key to the 'why' of this case. How many murderers do you know carry around and randomly drop off their DNA at the scenes of their crimes?"

"I get it."

"I think that Morgan woman was spot-on. The bad guys are trying to pressure Trasker to give them what they want. And, if that's so, then Mimi might also be on point; maybe there are two of them; maybe there are three - or five. The DNA is to implicate Boris Trasker, the real one. Having him sent to prison for life is their ace-in-the-hole. Have the crew go back to Collins office. Tell them to look for DNA. I bet they'll find some, and maybe some of the gel that rubbed off on Claudia Morgan's shoe."

"I'll go with them."

Both the Russians and Becker Pharmaceutical were correct in their assessment of Sergei Trasker; first as the youth, and then, the man. A medical doctor, microbiologist and software designer, he also held several other advance degrees in unrelated disciplines such as electronics and information technology. His interests and skills were beyond the pale, as only the world's foremost scientists could appreciate.

Currently, he was engaged in birthing Pong, the last of his three Yorkshire terriers. As he removed her from the gelatinous solution she had occupied for the last month, she made no sound. He wrapped her in a warm blanket. She seemed so serene, as if she were resting, asleep. Her journey, which few could have envisioned a decade ago, was remarkable. If she could have told someone of it, and she most certainly couldn't have, no one would have believed her. Sergei gently placed the stun pencil against her fur. He energized it. Pong whimpered. The tiny canine became conscious. She crawled out of the blanket. Sergei hugged her. Pong welcomed the warmth his body provided. Eagerly awaiting the new arrival were her two mates, Ping, and Pang. Surveying the three, "Nice," was the only word Sergei could manage. Now, he had three identical Toy Yorkshire Terriers. He named them after the three ministers in Giacomo Puccini's opera, Turandot. Sergei loved opera.

"Play," he commanded. As the three ran off to cavort, the scientist focused on his most recent innovation, so small it could barely be seen with the naked eye. He created it to find Boris. Sergei swung the powerful magnifying glass over the work table and 'Blaha,' the flea, came into view. It resembled a fruit fly more than a flea. The construct was about 30 percent larger than its real life counterpart. It was, in fact, a nanobot. Equipped with a camera and transmitter, the device made its whereabouts known by a pulse, detectable to two miles. The scientist also designed it to emit a pulse for satellites, but that one occurred only once every twenty minutes.

He picked up the control module and turned it on. Blaha stirred, and then fluttered its wings. In an instant it was airborne, hovering. Moving the control stick carefully, the scientist made the flea dart forth and back, up and down, and then in a tight circle. Now, the final test; the scientist turned the bot in the direction he wanted and then thrust the control stick forward as far as it could go. Blaha made straight for the thick Lucite panel erected specifically for this moment. The tiny machine rammed it, and, in doing so, became embedded so deeply in the plastic that it nearly breached it. A nine millimeter slug would not have penetrated as deeply. Had the target instead been a person's skull, they would have been killed. The test was a success. The scientist opened a drawer. Inside were a number of boxes, each containing one flea. He put two of them in his pocket. Faux Boris was upstairs in the reading room, expecting to see him a half hour ago.

"I don't like waiting," faux Boris complained.

"You've seen my brother?"

"Yes, he is fine. I told him he should be coming home soon; that is, if you cooperate."

"My brother has a condition. He didn't take his medicine with him. I would like you to take him some."

"I'll make a special trip tomorrow. We must keep him in good health," Faux Boris smiled wryly.

Sergei Trasker returned to his office and filled a bottle with pills. He dropped the two fleas inside and twisted the cap closed.

Returning, he handed it over to the imposter. "He must have these soon. When can I see my brother?"

"That's up to you. But don't wait too long, or he'll be spending the rest of his life in prison. Then you can visit him whenever you want."

Sergei Trasker watched his foe saunter out of the room. It was not the first time he had considered a violent response.

Faux Boris drove down the highway toward White Plains and the Interstate. He opened the window, reached into his pocket, and tossed the bottle of pills into the ditch.

Late the next morning, the Sergei retrieved it. The signals from the fleas were clear and strong, easy to pinpoint. The scientist decided that a more direct approach was in order.

"What is happening?" A tense Faux Boris asked, "He looks sick."

"I don't know. He was all right this morning. He started to get this way right after lunch."

Dimitri, senior apparatchik of the two men guarding Sergei's brother answered. "I don't think it was the food."

"Those pills; I should have brought them," the leader shouted as he slammed his fist into his palm. "Get him to bed. I'll call Sergei."

The situation seemed to be spiraling out of control. For all his careful planning, the imposter had not anticipated this crisis. Who could have suspected the brother had a condition? It didn't show up in any of his medical records, prison, or elsewhere. Sergei must have been treating his brother's condition himself. That's why it never surfaced. What was he to do? How serious was his not getting the medication on time? The captor had no choice but to return and get more. What if Boris needed it sooner? Could he risk bringing Sergei here? It was out of the question.

Sergei answered his cell. "You what! Why did you throw them away? He needs that medication.

You are the king of fools! Yes, I have more. Come and get them as soon as you can. He must have them or he will die, do you understand? How bad is he? When can you come?"

"I'll be there later this evening; I'm two hours away now. I have to stay away from the Tappan Zee Bridge during rush hour. The traffic is horrendous. Besides, I have something to do."

"Can't it be sooner?" Faux Boris had already hung up.

The scientist evaluated what he had just heard. Two hours, that's how far away Faux Boris was.

He had to cross the Tappan Zee so he must have been the west side of the Hudson River. His brother's crisis had given him some of the information he needed. Now he had a general location; how could he further refine what he already knew?

Sergei Trasker returned to the laboratory. He needed to monitor his most recent patient's condition.

Rescue

A not-altogether conscious Claudia Morgan watched Sergei Trasker approach. "Hi," she meekly offered, twitching her index finger for emphasis. "How am I doing?"

Trasker surveyed the woman's arm. His gel and its ingredients had already begun to regenerate the flesh on her arm; the broken ribs would take the most time. Two, perhaps three more weeks and the gel will have completed its work. She would be restored to the state of health she enjoyed before her fall from the sky.

The scientist inserted a needle into a port and several drops of a stimulant flowed into her arm.

His patient needed to be fully conscious; he had questions.

The drugs resurrected the old Claudia. "Well, that feels better. What did you give me? Can I take some of that home when I leave?"

"I need information."

"Professor Potemkin gave me a chip and said to see that you got it. I assume you found it, and the scrap of paper. His valet, James, gave me that. I think it was for you, too. He wouldn't have risked coming to me if he didn't feel it was important. Some creep in a topcoat and 1920's gangster hat was shadowing him. I read James' scribbles; but I couldn't figure out what it meant."

"It's not that hard. Letters mean numbers and numbers the reverse. As boys we used to give coded messages to each other - especially about the girls we liked." Trasker grinned. "No need for that now." Turning serious once more, "Lake Mohonk was the first group. I don't know where that is. The second array was two groups of six numbers, each group preceded by a letter. The pattern is familiar, but I can't seem to decipher its meaning."

"Were any of the letters N, E, W, or S?"

"Of course, they're coordinates; how stupid of me. Potemkin is telling me where my brother is.

The coordinates define his location exactly."

"See, two heads are better than one; mystery solved." Claudia smiled at Sergei. "When do I get out of this?" Claudia asked again as she surveyed the bubbling pool engulfing her.

"I think your recovery will take a few weeks more, perhaps three. It all depends on what that little gauge near your left foot shows. When you have achieved the necessary alkalinity, we will be able to move ahead and finish the process of restoring you to full health."

"Am I that full of acid? What's going on?"

"The treatment you are receiving cannot be found elsewhere. When you get better, I will explain what I have done. Can you wait?"

"Do I have a choice? My arm looks great. I don't see any scars. Don't tell me you're a witch doctor or a magician, I just won't believe it."

"Reserve your judgment until after my explanation," a grinning Sergei replied softly.

Just then, Ping and Pang began cavorting around the foot of Claudia's tank. Pong sat and watched, this time the spectator.

"What's that?" Claudia asked.

"It's, nothing, just two Chinese ministers having some fun with a third watching," He replied.

"Oh," Claudia replied. She was too tired to carry the conversation further. The room's light seemed to fade. It was time for Claudia to return to Marconi Beach and her youth. More rest could only benefit her recovery. Even under these circumstances she enjoyed being with Sergei.

The scientist turned his thoughts to rescuing his brother. Sometime this evening his brother's captor would be returning. What kind of scenario could he construct to convince his enemy to take him along to see his brother?

Sergei had eight men at his disposal. All were well-versed in the art of warfare, and each faithful to their employer. This would be a five man mission. Those remaining at the estate would remain at their post and guard against intruders.

"Lev, please come to the house." Soon, there was a knock at the door. "Come," Sergei Trasker replied. The lead guard entered. "Tonight, we are going to rescue my brother. I know where he is. You and four others will take positions around the location I indicate. I am assuming our imposter friend doesn't have many men guarding him. He is no threat, so there is no need to take extra precautions. Also, they do not suspect I know where they are keeping him. You must get your people together and leave within the hour. I want you in position before he and I get there."

"You, and he, how will that happen?"

"My brother's condition is serious and I must be there in order to treat him. That should be reason enough for him to take me along. Take what you need from the armory. Try not to kill anyone."

"It will be like shooting diseased horses, a mercy killing."

Lev left to inform his men of the mission. He returned as others were making preparations. He and Sergei went over his plan. It was simple; Sergei would carry a homing device and a transmitter. In this way, Lev and his group would know exactly where he was. Once in position and ready, he would transmit the word "Davai," 'give.' If all was favorable at Sergei's end, he would respond with the same word.

"Don't worry, we will rescue him. Tomorrow, you two will be having breakfast together."

"Thank you," Sergei half-whispered. He could barely utter the words.

Faux Boris arrived earlier than expected. Fortunately, Sergei Trasker had already dispatched Lev and his crew. In the interim, the scientist armed himself with six fleas, two in the new bottle of pills and four at different locations on his person. A case containing a hypodermic needle and serum in the inside pocket of his jacket caused it to bulge. The serum injected directly into his brother's bloodstream would act more rapidly than pills.

"Where are they? Where are the pills?"

"I'm going with you. If he is more ill than you think, he will need the serum I am bringing.

Don't fight me on this. He could die."

Faux Boris, already concerned about the brother's failing health, agreed. "Come on, I need your brother as much as you do. He's my trump card."

Not for long, Sergei thought.

The ride to Mohonk Lake House was breathtaking. Fortunately, there were no speed traps or troopers on the New York State Thruway to arrest Faux Boris and his passenger on their 95 mile per hour ride. The imposter slowed as he approached the Lake House, not wishing to draw any more attention to his arrival than necessary.

He called in. "Hello, I'm here. Is everything in order?" The voice on the other end assured him it was. "Come," Boris gestured to Sergei, and soon the two were climbing the elegant wooden stairway to the room where Sergei's brother was being held captive. The scientist's concern was that his brother might be more seriously ill than expected. If regressed beyond a critical threshold, the real Boris would need more extensive treatment. And that could only be given at Sergei's laboratory, The imposter knocked; a voice inside answered "Da?"

"Eto ya," it's me, Boris answered.

The door swung open and Dimitri, a large, broad shouldered man, eyed the pair standing before him. Sasha, the second captor, was standing several paces to the rear, gun drawn. "How is he?" Boris asked.

Dimitri glanced at his boss and shook his head. "Not so good," he muttered.

"Where is he?" Sergei asked. Dimitri pointed to a bedroom door. As the scientist started for it, Sasha moved to intercept him. Faux Boris raised his hand and Sasha stepped away.

The brother looked sallow. His breathing was rapid and his pulse weak. Sergei reached into his coat and injected his brother with the serum. Though Sergei's brother remained comatose, the scientist stayed at his side to observe the effects of the injection. He breathed a sigh of relief when once again two roseate blooms emerged in his brother's cheeks. The rapid breathing subsided. Sergei took Boris' pulse and found it was getting stronger. Sergei pulled the blanket up to his brother's shoulders and stepped away from the bed. The crisis had passed. Once again, Sergei had saved his brother.

"He must come back with me," Sergei demanded.

"That is not possible." The imposter noticed Sergei seemed unusually agitated, more than circumstances dictated. Years in the profession of espionage made him notice such things. He had come to understand that small, inexplicable changes in behavior usually indicated large changes in strategy.

Sergei's body suddenly straightened a bit, as if he heard something. A moment later he whispered,

"Davai."

Faux Boris heard his reply.

"I am no fool, Sergei. Dimitri, get the brother out of bed, we are leaving." Sasha and Dimitri carried Boris out into the hall. "Down that way," the imposter directed. Before heading for the stairway himself, he clubbed the scientist with his pistol. He fell to the floor. "Where should we take him?" Sasha asked. "Take him to the boat. I'll call and tell them you're coming." "It's a five hour drive," Sasha complained. "Tell Dimitri to drive under the speed limit. We don't want you getting stopped."

The three men and their captive escaped down the rear staircase.

Lev's group arrived. Seeing Sergei lying on the floor, he revived him. "Where are they?" Sergei pointed to the rear staircase. "That way I think."

A search of the escape route produced nothing; the kidnappers made good their getaway. While Dimtri and Sasha sped off with the brother, Faux Boris took his car and headed into the city. He needed to attend to some unfinished business. During the drive, he would be composing his remarks to Sergei when he met with him again. The game was still on, but the objective had not yet been reached.

"Boss, I got something. I'll be there in ten minutes. Plan to spend some time on this." McCann's voice was shaking with excitement.

"What is it?" Santoro asked.

"You're not going to believe what I have," his partner answered.

McCann burst into the office; no knocking, it's me, or anything. "Boss, I hit the mother lode.

Collins, Peters and Pearlman were engaged in trying to retrieve some secrets the Russians stole from us. It seems we and they were collaborating on some kind of research - of a biological nature. That was all my contact would tell me. You know how cooperative research goes; we hide some things from them and they do the same. Well, one of our guys came up with this breakthrough. We didn't tell them about it, but the guy blabbed it to his girlfriend during one of their pillow talk sessions. The woman just happened to be a Russian spy. The next weekend the lab was raided and his notes were taken."

Santoro was listening intently.

"We demanded they return the data. The Russians said they had no idea what we were talking about. Ergo, the collaboration was abandoned, but not before the Russians copied all of what they thought they needed. But the game wasn't over. Our guys, there were four actually, were tasked with getting the papers back, which they did. In retrieving the notes, our guys shot three Russians, two of them A-one scientists. After all these years, it seems someone has decided to even the score."

"I bet Trasker's unwillingness to give them what they wanted has opened up old sores. They don't need a repeat performance of what happened before."

"Also, I was told that certain crucial elements of our guy's work were not in the batch they stole.

The Russians would require years to figure out the rest, and there is no certainty that they ever will. All this came from one of my old buddies. It pays to have friends in key positions. I used to play basketball with the guy. We beat their school every time, but we couldn't keep him from scoring. He was too good."

"Thank him for me. He's been a great help."

"Oh, there's one thing more. I found out the name of the fourth guy."

"What's his name?"

"Isaac Jurgens; currently he's teaching at Yeshiva."

"Go and see him."

"I already have an appointment. It's tomorrow, at ten." McCann dropped a handful of documents on the desk. "Here's everything I could get; it's all yours now."

Santoro sighed, flipped open a folder and started reading.

McCann arrived early at Yeshiva; traffic had been mercifully light and there were no accident bottlenecks. A very cordial receptionist directed him to the professor's office on the third floor. While climbing the stairs, he spotted a familiar figure. It was the man he knew as Boris. He was perhaps thirty paces ahead, walking in a very determined manner. McCann followed, careful not to alert the assassin of his presence. The detective drew his weapon and held it close to his side. As the assassin strode past the professor's complaining secretary and burst into his office, McCann shouted "Halt; Police!" Surprised, Faux Boris turned, raised his pistol and pointed it at the detective while closing the door with his left hand. McCann took aim at his heart and fired first. Instead, he hit the would-be assassin in the shoulder.

At this point the door was completely shut. McCann burst through it, searching for the perpetrator. Boris ran forward, lunged at the detective and knocked him over. Bleeding steadily, he raced down the hall.

Recovering, McCann flipped open his cell and called for assistance. He hoped there would be a patrol car nearby, near enough to get to the scene quickly and nab the wounded assassin.

McCann's cursory inspection of the professor's office yielded some interesting results. Faux Boris had dropped a vial of the already significant gel; evidence, no doubt, to be spread around the scene of the intended murder. He also left behind the small caliber weapon, the one likely used on Pearlman.

Ballistics would verify that assumption. Also, there were two spots of blood, real blood this time, and unmistakably the assailant's. McCann believed it would not match the other 'planted' specimens.

A grateful professor crawled out from behind his desk, arose, and briskly strode over to McCann, his every step accentuated by a thank you followed at the end by a God bless you.

McCann holstered his weapon, closed the door and sat the educator down on the sofa. "It's over, relax. He won't be coming back. I'm Bob McCann, police. You need to answer some questions for me.

It's important that you answer truthfully, do you understand?" The professor nodded. "Collins, Peters, Pearlman and you were involved in an op to get back some important papers, is that right? I was told you did."

"Yes, and yes."

"Why are they trying to kill you now, so long after the fact?"

"You don't know?"

Something about the way Professor Jurgens asked the question sent a chill through McCann. "No, I don't; tell me."

"I can't; you wouldn't believe me if I did. I'll be taking what I know with me to the grave, if, and when, I die."

The professor's last five words puzzled the detective. "Can you tell me anything about the man who tried to kill you? Did you recognize him? Was anything familiar; his accent, the way he walked, anything?"

"He wasn't wearing his face."

"What do you mean by that?"

Professor Jurgens went on to elaborate about his hobby, costume and complexion doyen at the Rising Sun Art Center. The organization gave monthly performances of classic Japanese dances and plays. He immediately noticed that Faux Boris had done a sloppy job of blending fleshing paste along the edges of the mask he was wearing. It was done well enough to fool an amateur, but not him. "It's probably latex, cheaply made, but able to fool someone where the light is not that bright. On the stage, however, the poor preparation and blending would be quite noticeable."

"Stay here. I'll have a patrolman take you home. There'll be someone there with you until I return to interview you. Don't come back here until I determine you're out of danger." McCann looked like the cat that ate the canary. "I'll call if I need anything else." The detective dropped his card on the desk and walked out. His step was spirited.

Faux Boris had escaped. McCann knew he couldn't get far. Where might he go? The answer seemed obvious; the only refuge he knew; the estate.

Sergei Trasker and his squad drove home in silence. The mission was a failure and the scientist had suffered a blow to the head to boot. At the estate, he assessed the bump on his skull. There would be some swelling, but nothing more serious than that. After taking several aspirins and a few gulps of Vodka, Sergei felt better. Today was a failure, but there would be a next time. Faux Boris was now aware that Sergei's brother did have a serious condition and needed treatment from time to time. He would be hard pressed to refuse a visit by Sergei. The next time would be different, Sergei promised himself.

"Claudia!" Still dizzy, the scientist jumped to his feet and raced to the laboratory. He had left his new patient unattended for too long.

Claudia Morgan was resting comfortably; she seemed asleep. As Sergei surveyed the instruments that constantly evaluated her condition, his patient awoke. "Hi," she whispered.

"How are you feeling?" he questioned tenderly.

"Good, I feel good. When I think of the fall, I guess I'm lucky to be here. My only complaint is my skin is getting horribly wrinkled by all this stuff. My hands look like someone who's a hundred.

When am I going to get out of this beauty bath?"

Trasker glanced at the device near Claudia's foot. Her body was now alkaline. "Three more weeks and you'll be finished. Please be patient; I know you are anxious to get on with your life. You will, I promise". Sergei Trasker withheld the fact that Claudia had ruptured her spleen and one lobe of her liver. To regenerate them he had to grow stem cells to accomplish the task. But the procedure required the stem cell growth to be complete and her body to be alkaline. That transition had just been achieved.

Mid-morning Interstate traffic was lighter than rush hour, but still heavy. Faux Boris Trasker, alias Yuri Markov, and Colonel of the Russian Secret Police, was accustomed to being wounded. He had served in Afghanistan and Chechnya. Still, this wound, bleeding steadily, was threatening his ability to stay alert. Twice now, he had almost driven off the road. He had the good sense not to speed. Being stopped by a trooper would be catastrophic. As the northbound I-687 ramp came into view, Yuri relaxed; less than 20 kilometers now, he mused, soon I will be safe. As he approached the cutoff to the estate, Yuri swooned. Instead of turning right into the path, he continued straight on. At a gas station a half mile up the road, he turned around and headed back.

This time, he did not miss. As he pulled up to the entrance gate, he searched for his gate opener, but found he had misplaced it. His incessant honking of the horn brought several guards to the gate.

Recognizing him, one guard got into the rear seat and cocked his weapon. He placed the barrel against Yuri's head and commanded, "Davai," move ahead. Another phoned the scientist. The imposter and kidnapper had returned.

Sergei met the bloodied Yuri at the door. The scientist barked several commands that sent two of the guards scurrying. Enemy or not, Sergei could see that Yuri needed immediate medical attention. And, what the assassin had said to him earlier was patently true. He was, indeed, the only link to finding Sergei's brother. The man's pallid complexion indicated he had lost a great deal of blood. Regenerating new would take too long.

Fortunately, Sergei had a stash of plasma on hand. It was dated, but he had no choice; plasma it would be. At least that would give him time to take several samples of Yuri's blood and start growing more. As he looked into his enemy's drifting gaze, Sergei could not escape the paradox. Last night he would not have objected to his death as long as Boris was saved. Now the scientist was fighting to keep Yuri alive in order to preserve the link between himself and his brother.

One of the guards returned with the plasma. A moment later another appeared, carrying bandages, needles and various vials of antibiotics and narcotics. Within several minutes the scientist administered a drug for pain, and one to curtail infection. The plasma was next.

"We need something to carry him on," Sergei observed.

"I'll find something," one of the guards replied. In a few minutes he and a comrade returned.

Sergei seemed pleased. It was an old door. "Good."

Yuri was carried down to the laboratory and a cubicle was improvised for him. The scientist did not want his new patient to know about Claudia or witness the procedures he was using in making her well. Without any armed assault or loss of life, Yuri had managed to gain entrance to the renowned Sergei Trasker laboratory. For that matter so had Claudia Morgan.

"What was your man doing the day before yesterday? Do you know?" Grigorev did. He wondered whether Professor Potemkin would say.

"I had five meetings. James has his duties. If he had a personal errand or went to get food or collect the dry cleaning, I would know nothing about that. Why do you ask?"

"My man followed him to a building on First Avenue. Do you know who lives there?"

"No, I don't."

"That woman you took for a walk in the park; she lives there." Grigorev watched whether Potemkin would react. "Did you send him? Why did he go there?" The questions irritated the scientist.

"I don't know, I'm not his mother. Perhaps she left something here and he was returning it to her.

Women are always leaving things behind. James is good that way. That's why I have him. I'm always forgetting things, too."

"How did he know where she lived?"

"Didn't I tell you she left her card with me? I think I mentioned that fact."

Check, and mate; once again, the ever suspicious Grigorev failed to corner the professor. The aging scholar was still too fast for the Russian agent. That didn't mean that James' actions were above suspicion; simply that Grigorev had not unearthed the reason for his behavior. Perhaps the woman had indeed left something behind. The agent had to admit it was a possibility. He decided to drop the matter.

There was still time for the professor to err; he couldn't talk his way out of every scenario.

After the agent left, Potemkin summoned James. "I wish to take a walk in the park. Get my hat and coat."

"It's getting dark. Tonight is going to be a cool one, they say. Do you still want to go?"

The professor's stare burned with dissatisfaction. Yes, definitely, he wanted to take a walk. James had seen that look before. He had offended his employer. And now he would be hearing about it.

The cars already had their lights on by the time the pair entered the park. Walks were still full of strolling couples, women with baby carriages and students debating this idea or that, or talking about their favorite subject, the other gender.

"You disobeyed me, and, in doing so, you put Sergei at risk. You went ahead and contacted that woman. You didn't even tell me you were going to do it."

"Your wife sent you Boris' location. I felt she had to have that right away."

"You risked your life. Suppose Grigorev's man had intercepted you and found that out? What then?"

"I decided to take that chance."

"Did you once even consider that you risking your life also risked mine?"

James had not thought of that. Suddenly aware that his cavalier action had placed the man he admired most at risk, he became speechless. Potemkin saw that he made his point. He reached over and patted James on the forearm.

"We come from a place where only those who are heroic survive. They sometimes die, too." The rest of the walk progressed in silence. Once out of the park, Potemkin turned to his valet and said, "I am in the mood for some good Russian food. What do you say we eat out tonight?" James smiled broadly and hailed the first cab he saw.

Girgorev's apparatchik couldn't follow. What self-respecting New York City cabbie would pick up a lone, coarse-appearing man wearing an oversize topcoat and an Al Capone-style fedora, especially at night?

Potemkin and his valet returned late. Conversation about old times, especially army days, helped the evening pass quickly. James greatly admired Professor Potemkin, and with good reason. During the Russians' war in Afghanistan he conducted himself bravely, and had saved several soldiers' lives at risk to his own. For all his education and resourcefulness on and off the battlefield, Constantine Potemkin was a private person, a modest soul. More, he was the one who pulled the Russian scientific community together after the theft of the data from the Americans. Believing they had achieved a coup, the Russians found they had come up short; they hadn't gotten everything. A great deal of finger pointing ensued. It was Potemkin who rose above the fray to remind everyone that while they hadn't pilfered the entire dossier, they did have something, and that something was of significant value.

The Russian scientists settled down and went to work with Potemkin as the lead researcher.

Everyone, especially those in power, seemed pleased with themselves. Then Collins, Peters, Pearlman and Jurgens penetrated the laboratory security network and regained what had been stolen. Not only had the Americans succeeded in obtaining the original data, they had also quite by accident managed to escape with valuable records chronicling the Russian effort.

A massive manhunt ensued; the four agents were quickly apprehended, but not before they had sent the data back to the United States. The Russians demanded to know where and to whom the information was sent. There was still time to deny the Americans the victory. Russian agents operating in the United States might still be able to retrieve the paper copies. The four agents refused to say anything.

This reticence launched a most horrendous season of torture on the four. Potemkin was allowed to witness some of it. It fell to him to restore the agents to consciousness so torture could be resumed.

After four days, the agents were so close to death that the scientist could do no more. He had the near-cadavers sent to his laboratory. That Potemkin was helpless to revive them was not entirely true.

Before he escaped to the west, Trasker and colleague Potemkin were on the verge of succeeding in using 'master' stem cells from fat tissue and 'directing' them to reproduce specific cells for regeneration. Simply put, if a person needed a flesh cell repaired, they would make one; a heart cell, they would make one.

However, one key to the puzzle was missing; for some reason they could not guarantee success every time. Sometimes three of four attempts would succeed. Then several, unremarkably, would fail.

Constantine Potemkin devised a daring plan. He would restore the four agents, regenerating those organs heavily damaged through torture. His reasoning was that they were approaching death anyway, and by the time the Russian government transported them back to the American embassy with an invented story about a robbery or a brawl, they would be.

Thus, Constantine Potemkin launched the greatest experiment of his career: not only saving the lives of four enemy agents, but attempting at the same time to restore them to full health using the protocol he and his young colleague had perfected.

Potemkin told his superiors he wished to examine the remains closely to determine whether or not they contained electronic or biological implants. This, he estimated, would take approximately four months, one month for each individual. When questioned about the extraordinarily long time, Potemkin reminded everyone of the faux pas of the past, the inference of course being, that they should not wish to err once again. That silenced detractors.

The only one the professor could trust was James, his ally in war. But he was not a medical person. Still, the two, working days and many nights, managed to bring Collins, Peters, Pearlman and Jurgens back from certain death. Scars disappeared, subcutaneous bruises and injuries to vital organs vanished. Potemkin was correct in choosing the length of time required. Many cells that were grown failed and had to be regenerated.

What he could not guarantee was how long the new cells would survive. Sergei Trasker had mentioned immersing patients in an enzyme-rich alkaline solution; this to better prepare them for the injection of the new cells. His sudden departure left that hypothesis untested.

Potemkin and James had done their best. The four were alive; not completely restored, but doing remarkably well. The next step; he had to inform his superiors he had 'found nothing' and the 'cadavers' were ready for transport to the American Embassy.

Potemkin had taken the precaution of keeping the four sedated. This, to avoid any unwelcome bursts of patriotism and efforts to escape, acts he would have difficulty explaining.

Now he needed the four fully conscious to explain his plan. He revived them. As a precaution, all were restrained. "You are alive. If you want to stay alive, you will follow my instructions. Tomorrow, your 'remains' will be delivered to the American Embassy in Moscow. You will be in shrouds, but deeply sedated. I will get word to your people that you are alive. You will regain consciousness in a day or so. If the transfer takes longer than expected, and you awaken while still in the shroud. Be still, or you will die, and so will James, here, and I."

"Who are you? Why are you doing this?" Peters asked.

"Be quiet, you fool. You'll get us all killed." Potemkin whispered. "I am going to inject all of you now. Good luck." As the scientist moved from person to person, Peters raised his hand slightly and Potemkin grasped it.

"Thanks."

Several hours later a detail came into the laboratory and removed the four bodies. James glanced at the professor. The shadow of a smile crossed his face.

James shook the professor's hand. Tired from the ordeal, all the valet could think of was getting some sleep. Potemkin remained, documenting each step of his fathoming the unknown. The microchip he gave to Claudia Morgan to be delivered to Sergei contained the information about which protocols Potemkin had used to save the four spies.

Distance and time had little import on the association between protégé and mentor; they were still, and would ever remain, colleagues.

Yuri Markov awoke. This strange place was certainly not an American hospital. He recalled having reached the estate and being carried downward before losing consciousness. I must be in his laboratory, he concluded.

Being shot may have been painful and life threatening, but it did have its advantages, Yuri gloated. Here he was, in the much-touted laboratory of Sergei Trasker. Many had attempted to breach the impenetrable ring of security, but had failed. Perhaps the information was hidden here, in a drawer or a filing cabinet, or, perhaps a disk. When Markov felt well enough to get up and look around, the scientist wouldn't even suspect that he had. But the Russian found he had been restrained. A rayon belt spanned his midsection from one side of the bed to the other. It was taut. It would be impossible for him to wriggle his way free. Still, he had his fingernails. He acknowledged they were woefully inadequate for the task.

Perhaps he might be able to cut through the belt in several days. He certainly had the time. He began.

After an hour, he had succeeded in wearing away a tiny bit of the fabric. Even though progress was pathetically slow, he still kept scratching away.

At the same time, Sergei Trasker was in another part of the laboratory working with Claudia.

Having removed several different cells from her, he was engaged in providing the conditions for their regeneration. Claudia, still confined to her bed on the far side of the room, watched.

"What are we calling this thing that you are doing?" She asked.

"When I first began this work, this procedure had no name. Now, it has."

"What are you doing? Come on, tell me. As your patient, I have a right to know what you're doing."

"That's true. Give me a few more minutes to finish what I'm doing and then I'll come over and explain. Is that fair enough?"

"I'll wait."

"Can you be quiet while you're waiting?"

Claudia did not respond. It was not like her to let a remark like that pass.

Eventually, the scientist completed the protocol. He pressed a black button. The bulb next to it turned red. A soothing hum filled the room. He arose, walked across the room and sat down beside his patient. Ping, Pang, and Pong, tails wagging, sat at his feet. He bent over and petted them for a few moments. Then he turned his attention to the matter at hand.

"I'm going to tell you everything. Some of what I say may sound bizarre. Nevertheless it's true."

"I'm listening. What's that yapping?"

"My three little friends; you can meet them when you're better. As I was about to say, some stem cells are what we call master cells; they can become brain cells, kidney cells, liver cells; any kind of cell you want; the changing process is called differentiation. When this work started, stem cells were harvested only from certain areas in the body and only from certain individuals, like fetal tissue and children. When the general public found out about this, a moral uproar resulted, and it appeared that public disgust with the existing harvesting techniques spelled doom for the research. In the interim, several breakthroughs, the direct result of stem cell research, indicated that if it were allowed to continue, it might pay enormous dividends, curing and perhaps even preventing disease."

"You're giving me a headache."

"I'm just starting. After all, you wanted to know."

"Go ahead."

"Two problems existed. The first was how to tell the master cells to become the specific type of cell needed, and second, was it possible to harvest them elsewhere, somewhere not so reprehensible to the community."

"And you solved both problems?"

"No, Potemkin solved the second and I solved the first. I'm the only one on this planet who can tell stem cells which ones they must be and then produce them in quantities that meet the demand. Do you see any scars on your arm?"

"No."

The scientist produced several photos of Claudia's arm before he began reconstructing it. Its flesh had been shredded and the muscles furrowed from shoulder to wrist. He followed with photos showing the gradual new growth, not repair, of the area. "I remade your arm. I didn't allow it to heal; I made parts of it new. All of the flesh, muscle and bone on that side of your arm were made with cells I produced here in the laboratory. I took the material from your fat and induced the change."

"You took it from my fat? And what is this process called?"

"I don't know what name the medical community has for it. My technology is with stem cells and adipose material. Over time I have continued to modify my experiments as necessary. My work has experienced many iterations from the time of my first success."

"If what you have achieved is true, you are well ahead of your time. You'll be famous."

"Famous in prison, that's what. I've broken the law, United States of America law regarding the practice of medicine. If I were still in Russia I would have been allowed greater latitude. The Russian government sanctions any experiments that will elevate its national stature. Their restrictions are flexible, depending on the advantages the new discovery offers. That is why their research is kept secret. But the experiments I've engaged in are even against Russian law."

"Still, I'm grateful for what you've done. I could have become an amputee, or worse."

"I might as well tell you the rest."

"Am I going to die?"

Trasker told Claudia about the damage to her spleen and liver. It was the reason he needed the additional time.

His patient remained silent for several moments. Perhaps she was contemplating how close she had come to dying. Eventually, she looked up and whispered a very sincere "Thanks." Then she turned away; she closed her eyes.

She longed to get away, now, to dream of beautiful memories of past days, those filled with fun and the promise of the future. She called forth many exhilarating events to lift her high so that she could fly away from the realization that she had brushed death's boundary. Sleep was her only refuge. If only those little critters Ping, Pang, and Pong could stop yapping.

Sergei Trasker was annoyed with himself. Years of dodging the Russians and Becker had made him cautious, wary of any unwarranted changes in events or behaviors. Away from the beautiful woman who had such an effect on him, he started considering the reasons for her actions. Why had she risked her life to meet him? He was not that attractive. After all, they had met for only an instant. And, had he already provided her with the information she needed? The scientist chided himself for telling Claudia about his accomplishments. He had offered it because he cared for her and because he wanted to crow to someone, anyone, about his work. After all, somebody should know of his research, even if it was an industrial spy. Yes, that's who she had to be, an industrial spy.

What other conclusion fit the circumstances so well? Still, that look in her eyes, was that part of the game? Sergei wanted to think not, but years of experiencing deception and falsehoods strangled the possibility that Claudia Morgan could ever care for him. He had seen too much of the dark side of human nature. I'll make her well and release her, he thought, I haven't told her enough to make a difference. To have the entire picture, she would need my notes. But that one in the other bed, he would want to get them, too.

The scientist went to Yuri's enclosure. He surprised the man abrading the belt with his nail.

Feigning indifference to what he had seen, Sergei took his patient's pulse, rolled up his eyelid and observed the eye. He evaluated the Russian's complexion. "I'm going to give you a sedative. It will give you some comfort from the pain." Moments later, Yuri fell into a state of conscious sedation.

"Can you hear me?" Sergei whispered.

"Yes," Yuri answered.

"Where have you taken my brother?"

"We're taking him to our base in Canada near Lake Manicouagan."

"How will you get him across the border?"

"Sodus Point, there's a boat there."

"How soon will this be?"

"They will get under way as soon as the car gets there."

"How long will it take to get there?"

"Six hours."

Sergei experienced defeat. Soon his brother would be out of reach, in another country, and he was helpless to stop it. Only a miracle could prevent what was about to happen. None was in sight.

"Hello, Lev? Come down to the laboratory and bring someone with you. Ring the bell and I will let you in. We are going to move one of our patients to an upstairs bedroom." The scientist placed his face next to Yuri's and whispered, "You can scrape through your belt upstairs, you bastard."

After having the imposter removed, Sergei Trasker looked in on Claudia. She was asleep.

Stepping up to her bed, he examined, and then tightened the restraints. Because of her condition, she needed to stay in the laboratory. He made himself a promise that soon he needed to have a heart-to-heart talk with her about her true identity and whether or not she had feelings for him. Had he been a fool to hope that she might?

Driving along I-87 from Albany toward Canada at night was an experience, especially where it undulated through the valleys adjacent the peaks of the Adirondack Mountains. Dimitri, Yuri's second in command, had prudently followed the advice of his superior and driven below the speed limit of 65 miles an hour. Having driven through rural New York State once before, he was aware that wild animals roamed the region, some during the day and many, at night. Given the circumstances, a crash would prove catastrophic. How would he and Sasha explain the presence of the comatose Boris?

"How much longer," an impatient Sasha asked.

"About three hours. We'll stop in a little while and get something to eat. I'm hungry; a cup of coffee would be good, too."

Satisfied with Dimitri's answer, Sasha settled back in the rear seat. A quick glance to his right told him Boris was still asleep, and, by the looks of it, would remain so for some time.

Just then, a deer jumped over the guide rail several hundred feet in front of the car. Dimitri slammed on the brakes. The screaming tires frightened the animal and caused it to bolt across the road and into the woods. Dimitri pulled the car onto the shoulder and turned the engine off.

"Are you all right?" Sasha asked.

"Yes, I'm fine. I think my next job is going to be lion tamer. It's not as hard on the nerves." Soon the three were on their way again. They left the Interstate and found a brightly lit diner, its parking lot full of cars and trucks. That was always a good sign; truckers don't normally patronize a place that serves bad food.

"Is he going to be all right in here?" Sasha questioned.

"He'll sleep until morning, but who knows? We'll check him every twenty minutes, just to be safe. It is better to be cautious." Sasha agreed.

The people in the diner were spirited. Dimitri and Sasha were caught up in their mood and quickly forgot about their charge. The food was tasty and the coffee robust and comforting. No one could have blamed the pair for setting aside their duties for a short while. Just hours ago, they had avoided capture, or worse. The decision to drive north with Boris was made on the spot, so the pair had to leave their belongings and personal items behind.

"Boris!" Dimitri exclaimed, suddenly aware of the length of time they had spent in in the diner,

"We've been here three quarters of an hour. Go and check on him."

Sasha left immediately. He was back in what seemed an instant. "He's gone."

The pair raced out of the diner into the parking lot. A regular stop for tractors and their loads, the area was filled with semis parked every which way. The pair split up and began their search. It wasn't long before Sasha shouted "Here, here!" Boris lay in a heap on the ground. The pair carried him back to the car. "Go get some more coffee," Dimitri commanded, "I'll stay with him." An unexpected and short return to consciousness had allowed Boris the opportunity to escape, but the injection Sergei had given him was still potent. Sasha returned carrying a brown bag, vapor steaming from its opening. "I got us some Danish, too."

The three sped off.

"What's going on? The entire police force can't find one wounded shooter? I never heard of such a thing." Of course Santoro had, and, all too often. He snapped shut his cell with more authority than usual.

It was decision time. Santoro knew Faux Boris would most likely head back to the estate. But what should the detective's next move be; command a full scale assault on the property? That would take ten, perhaps twenty, fully armed police. And from the looks of it, there would be more places to hide than police available to search them. Such an operation would take days. How many hiding places might there also be in the woods?

The Senior Investigator discarded that approach and decided instead to pay a visit to the scientist.

Who knows, he might be ready to talk, he thought, having a brother being held for ransom with the imposter on the run, wounded and hiding out somewhere might change his perspective.

"We're going to the estate." McCann seemed pleased with Santoro's decision. Perhaps he had come to the same conclusion.

Grigorev was receiving his weekly update from Yuri Markov. "You have been wounded?

Where are you? He's taking care of you? I'm surprised he didn't let you die. After all, you are holding his brother as ransom. You were in his laboratory? Oh, he didn't trust you there. Now you are in an upstairs bedroom? You think he's treating someone else? Do you have any idea who?" Concerned about the seriousness of Yuri's wound but pleased he had survived, Grigorev focused on the identity of the 'other patient' in the scientist's laboratory.

Who might it be; what was the reason they were being treated by the scientist? The Russian gave it a great deal of thought, but could not find any reason for anyone he knew to need the scientist's expertise. Suddenly, one surfaced. "I know. It's the protocol; that's why he has this patient under his care and not in a hospital. He's reconstructing someone, a procedure no hospital could perform or would ever allow."

Markov's superior gave him an order: "You get out of there as soon as you can and go into hiding. Never mind about the data, I'll take care of that. It's important the police don't find you."

Having established the whereabouts of his minion, Grigorev focused on the professor. "That old fool, it's time I pried some answers out of him."

Storming out of his apartment, he was intent on achieving the goal which up to this point had eluded him. If threatening Boris' life hadn't produced results with Sergei, perhaps threatening the life of his former colleague Potemkin would.

Upstate New York terrain near the shore of Lake Ontario is flat. Low growing flora and fauna are abundant because the climate, while severe during the winter months due to the proximity of the lake and its biting winds, is still conducive to plant life during the other three seasons. The howling winds from the north and west blasting across the Great Lakes take their toll on inhabitants, many remaining indoors for the greater part of winter's day, longing for the arrival of the warming breezes of spring.

Early fall weather posed no problem to the three occupants in Dimitri's vehicle. The roads were clear and the sun was just rising over the eastern horizon. Having driven the last half of the night, Sasha was still in good spirits though starting to get a bit stiff. He fantasized about consuming a plate of bacon and eggs and downing a huge, steaming cup of coffee. Thirty kilometers to go, he guessed.

He suspected that he might have missed the turn that would bring them to the south shore of Lake Ontario. He didn't mention his concern to Dimitri. If all was well and he hadn't, a boat would be waiting to take them to Canada, their new destination. Since it appeared they would be arriving early in the morning, they would have to wait until dark to board. That meant there would be plenty of time for a good rest and some food. Sasha settled in and made a mental note to drive more carefully.

The Russians had a sophisticated surveillance network in Canada since the Second World War.

That should not have been a surprise to anyone, since many nations routinely spied on one another, extracting valuable information from host governments and thereby ensuring their own survival. In this regard, the Russians had, in 1970, smuggled in, piece by piece, an operational 'pocket' submarine for use in the Great Lakes. With the recent turn to war on terrorism and the intensified scrutiny of border crossing vehicles, trains, and boats, the usual methods of sneaking people into the country had to be replaced with more sophisticated methods. The Russians acquired a sight-seeing steamboat company, one that plied the lake between Canada and the United States. The sub had its electronics brought up to date. Tethers along the hull of the steamboat served to comfortably nestle it below the water line and thus made undetectable by sonar. This was to be the transport vehicle for the three occupants of the car. The real Boris Trasker would be on his way to Canada in less than a day.

But Dimitri was about to find out that Sasha had erred, and greatly. Instead of taking the Thruway west and then proceeding north to Sodus Point, Sasha had inadvertently switched to the Northway. This happened because Interstate 87 ceases to be the Thruway route number at Albany. Going farther west the Thruway is designated as Interstate 90. Staying on Interstate 87 would mean leaving the Thruway and driving directly north toward Canada and Montreal via the Northway.

Approaching the Canadian border, Dimitri stopped at a gas station and bought a map. To his horror, he found they were many miles east of Sodus Point, a small village on the south shore of Lake Ontario and the rendezvous point. Now he had to drive parallel to the Saint Lawrence River southwesterly until he reached Lake Ontario; then west along its shore. Dimitri dared not inform Markov of his mistake.

He would devise a suitable excuse later. His faux pas could be rectified by driving an estimated three, perhaps four hours or more along local roads. No harm done, Dimitri told himself.

"Get out of my house," Sergei Trasker shouted to Yuri Markov. "I am not going to get arrested for harboring a criminal."

"Now you don't like me?" Markov fired back. "What about your brother? Don't you want to see him again?"

"You can speak to me over the phone. I can't afford to get arrested."

"You are worried about that other patient, the one in your laboratory. I can't identify who it is yet, but I will find out."

Markov hit a nerve. "Lev, Lev," the scientist shouted, "Get this scum out of my sight. Drive him to wherever he has to go in his car. Have someone follow and bring you back." The guard and a subordinate lifted the wounded man out of bed and escorted him out of the room. Minutes later, Trasker heard the roar of the sports car fading as it sped away.

"The discussion," the scientist muttered, "it's time for a talk."

"Hello," smiled Claudia Morgan, "my, you look grumpy; what's the matter?"

"Are you a spy? Why did you come here? Was it to see me, or did you have something else in mind, perhaps stealing my notes?"

Claudia frowned. She was uncomfortable at Sergei's implication. "I work for Triple I, an industrial espionage company. My assignment was to relieve you of your secrets. For that, I would get $2,000,000. My firm, Triple I, would get twenty. Becker Pharmaceutical was behind the entire operation."

Sergei Trasker was stunned. He placed his cupped hands over his eyes. "What a fool I've been."

"But something happened; things changed. The more I found out about you and your work, the more I wanted to meet you. And when I did. . ."

"You fell in love with me. Do you really expect me to believe that? And now, here you are in my laboratory. Men have tried through coercion and deception to get where you are, and they have failed.

You've won the two million dollar prize. All you need are my notes. I should pull out all these tubes and send you away, but I'm not like that. I'll cure you. After that, after that. . ." Trasker left the room.

Investigators Santoro and McCann arrived at the estate. They were escorted to the main house.

A somber Sergei Trasker greeted them. His recent encounter with Claudia Morgan still had him reeling.

"What can I do for you," the scientist asked in a tone of voice that was flat, lifeless.

"Boris Trasker, or, at least the man we know as Boris Trasker, just tried to murder someone else.

Is he here? I remind you that harboring a fugitive is a crime," Santoro stated.

"He was here. I bandaged his wound and sent him away. I didn't know about his attempt. I just saw that he needed medical attention."

"Do you know the name of the person he tried to murder?

"No, I don't. He never mentioned anything about that."

Santoro decided to advance a confidence and perhaps receive one in return. He wanted to know just how much Sergei Trasker knew about the entire affair. "Jurgens, Isaac Jurgens; he and three others were engaged in some espionage decades ago. Did you know anything about that?"

"Constantine knew of them. He had saved the lives of the four. It had to do with the experiments we were conducting."

"Who's Constantine?"

"Constantine Potemkin, a former colleague; he's here in New York for a conference. I'm not sure where he's staying, but I'm certain you will be able to find him."

"Why haven't you visited him?" Trasker's reply started with a smile. "And get kidnapped by the Russians the way my brother did? I would be back in Moscow by week's end. No, we dare not meet, both for his safety and mine." The scientist then alluded to the nature of the research he and Potemkin were conducting; its benefits, risks, and the strong possibility of achieving a telling scientific breakthrough.

"Doctor Trasker, isn't it time we joined forces? They've got your brother, we want the imposter, and you want to be rid of them. What do you say? There may be another victim, we're not sure yet."

"Who would that be?"

"That Claudia Morgan woman; we've searched and searched and can't find out where she is.

Even McCann here, the precinct bloodhound, can't find her."

"She's in my laboratory. I'm treating her for some very severe injuries."

Santoro was surprised but relieved. "Well, at least she's alive, thank God for that. She's the one who put us onto this phony brother, you know. She laid it all out for us. At first I wouldn't buy it, but little by little it all fell into place. She put herself at great personal risk to find all that out. You may want to thank her."

Santoro stepped close to the scientist and half-whispered, "Let's collaborate. Let's get these guys."

"You want your brother back? We can help," McCann chimed in.

"They're taking Boris to Sodus Point, on Lake Ontario. From there, he'll be transported to a hideout on a lake in Canada, a place called Lake Manicouagan. If that happens, it will be impossible to rescue him."

Santoro pulled out his cell. "Hello, this is Chief Investigator Frank Santoro. I'd like to speak to Commander Grant Richardson. Yes, he knows me. We're old friends." The operator connected him.

"This is Frank Santoro, Grant. Yes, it has been a long time. I need your help, and pronto. We have a situation. Can you mobilize a S.O.R.T. force and get to Sodus Point, ASAP? It's a small town on Lake Ontario. We have a person who has been abducted and we believe the perpetrators are taking him there in an effort to smuggle him into Canada. Yes, I would suggest full array. Okay, do that; nose around and get back to me." The detective closed his cell. "We'll have troopers there before your brother and his captors arrive."

"Who is this man?"

"Grant Richardson heads up the New York State Trooper Special Operations Response Team.

They'll rescue your brother."

The scientist exhaled as if he had been secreting a great ball of air in his lungs and could finally release it.

"Thank you," he said softly. The scientist summoned one of his men. "Please get us some coffee and something to eat. It's going to be a long night."

Grigorev rang the doorbell and James opened the door. "Where is he?" Grigorev asked. "In the study," the valet answered. James was the first to enter the room. As Potemkin looked up, James shot him a glance. Potemkin caught its message; 'Trouble.'

"You are a traitor. I know you've been sending messages to Sergei. It took me some time to find out how, but now I know. It was through that woman, Claudia Morgan. Walking through the park, and then James entering her apartment building; all very clever, but not clever enough. You're going back to Russia. You will never again see anything outside its borders as long as you live." Grigorev scrutinized Potemkin. Had he made an impression?

"And you, Grigorev, are a donkey's ass, a much greater one than I thought possible. Me, a traitor? No one would believe such a preposterous allegation. If you had half a brain you would have already seen that I am here for the same reason you are, only my weapons are honey and old memories of collaboration, not muscle, and guns, and torture."

Grigorev was surprised by the rejoinder. Was this a ploy? "You wouldn't betray your friend."

"I have been trying to accomplish what Sergei Trasker has for years; ten, before we joined forces and five after he left. Those five wonderful years we were together we made enormous strides. But being on the brink of what he was about to discover, he realized that no one government should exclusively possess such knowledge.

He became a man concerned about the world. Can you imagine that? All that indoctrination, all those lectures about the Soviet dream, they failed. The man still had a conscience. After he left, I was sure I could duplicate what he had achieved. I would be the hero and history would remember Constantine Potemkin, not Sergei Trasker."

"And what happened?"

"I could not. Trial after trial, I could not." Potemkin stared at Grigorev. "I want to see him more than you can ever imagine. Now, get out!"

Irritated and informed, a silent Grigorev took his leave.

The hours dragged on as Dimitri picked his way through the web of traffic lights, stop signs and yields that slowed his journey. More and more irritated with every mile travelled, he became less and less cautious. He wanted the trip to end. More irritating was the blunder; Sasha should have stayed on the Thruway at Albany, and not chosen the Northway. He considered beating his partner's head against the dashboard but his only recourse was to occasionally slap himself in the head. Doing that made him a little dizzy.

After passing through the last traffic light in some nameless hamlet, a stretch of road absent any stop signs lay before him. He decided to increase his speed; to hell with the speed limit. The faster he drove, the better Dimitri felt. Perhaps he could shave some time off the trip. No one was around. Who cared how fast he was going? Faster and faster he drove; the greater the velocity the better. With Sasha, the matter wasn't as clear cut. Putting his hand on Dimitri's shoulder he whispered "Aren't we going too fast? Shouldn't we slow down?"

Dimitri ignored his cohort's good advice. After all, wasn't it Sasha's fault they were having this 'trudnoct'; difficulty?

Flashing lights appeared some distance behind them. Dimitri took out his 9MM pistol and laid it on the seat beside him. "No, no, don't do that." Sasha cautioned. "Be quiet," Dimitri responded, "Perhaps I can bargain with him. You know how these Americans are, they like to negotiate." All Sasha could do was sink back into the shadows and hope for the best. Thank God Boris was still unconscious.

A short burst of the siren indicated that Dimitri should pull over onto the shoulder. As the trooper approached, Dimitri reached over and grasped his pistol. "No, no," Sasha whispered. "Shut up!" Dimitri snarled.

"License and registration, please; do you know how fast you were going?" the trooper asked.

"77, but my speedometer is a little off. What's the speed limit here?"

"It's 40; there's a sign half a mile back. You couldn't have missed it. It was right under a street light."

"Can I pay my fine now, to you?"

"No, I can't do that."

"Too bad," Dimitri raised his pistol, shot the trooper twice, and sped away.

"Why did you do that?" Sasha screamed. Now, they'll be after us."

"After who; no one saw us. We'll be all right."

Troop Commander Richardson was on the phone informing his friend Frank Santoro of the situation. Sodus Point had a lighthouse in the vicinity, Sodus Light. The beacon assisted those seeking safe passage, warning them away from several maritime hazards. Inadvertently, it also aided American and Canadian smugglers. Homeland Security, the FBI and the immigration folks were all aware of Sodus Point. There would be no difficulty amassing enough firepower for the operation. Santoro hung up, obviously satisfied with the situation.

"They're getting ready. All they need to know is when the guests will be coming."

"How are they going to make sure my brother is not harmed?"

"You told me there were two, didn't you?"

"Yes, there are two."

"Two won't be a problem. Snipers with night vision can shoot the wings off a mosquito at fifty yards. Didn't you mention you gave him something by injection?"

"Yes, I did."

"Would it have any effect on his ability to say, walk, or respond normally?"

"Boris wouldn't be able to do anything by himself for twelve hours, perhaps longer."

"They'll be able to distinguish between those who can walk and the one who can't."

Santoro's words calmed the scientist. "What now, do we just wait?"

"There's nothing else we can do. Maybe we'll get a break and learn where they are, but I don't look for much help in that category. If anything like that pops up, it will be sheer luck."

"Would you excuse me, I want to go down and see how my patient is doing." The scientist seemed in better spirits.

"Can we go, too?" McCann asked.

"I don't allow anyone in the laboratory."

A few minutes later the scientist was standing beside Claudia Morgan.

"Hi there; feeling a little better?" Claudia Morgan was trying to rebuild bridges.

"I want to apologize. I never realized the risk you were taking. . ."

"Don't say another word. It wasn't right for me to deceive you like that. In the beginning I'll admit it was the money. Now, I'm not sure where my allegiance lies. But I promise I won't betray you. You saved my life."

"Betrayal seems to be in vogue these days. Take my colleague Potemkin, for example; why is he here? He never went to many conferences before; he thought they were foolishness. Others are also trying to get at me for their own reasons." The scientist wagged his head in disgust. "I'm afraid to trust anyone; I can't trust anyone. Even you were after me."

Sergei Trasker left Claudia Morgan to mull over what he had said. He had other things on his mind. The 'soup de jour' was saving Boris.

Electronic surveillance revealed that one dwelling near Sodus Point was experiencing heightened activity in cell phone transmission and reception, all of it between its occupants and someone in Canada.

After pinpointing the dwelling, the police took positions around it. Infrared scanning indicated there were four people inside.

Commander Richardson was in charge of all aspects of the operation. While he hadn't been apprised of all of the reasons for Santoro's concern, he knew intuitively that it had to be significant.

Otherwise, his long-time friend would not have bothered to call.

The commander also directed that any communication from Santoro be given priority, an unusual procedure under the circumstances.

"Has anything happened yet?" Santoro asked nervously. Richardson answered "No, nothing; we're watching the house. There are four people inside; that's all we know right now."

"Thanks for the update. Listen, Grant, I want to fill you in on what's going on. Can you spare the time?"

"Go ahead," Richardson replied. Santoro then proceeded to explain what had happened and how important it was to free Boris Trasker from his captors. He emphasized several times that the victim had a medical condition and no harm should come to him if that were at all possible.

Grant Richardson's response was "We'll do our best." To Santoro, that meant the commander was anticipating a firefight. Experience had taught him that gun battles had a way of getting out of hand.

"What did he say?" A concerned Sergei Trasker asked.

"He'll do his best."

Trooper John Clarke regained consciousness shortly after being shot. Feeling his chest wound bleeding profusely, he reached into his pocket, retrieved a handkerchief and applied pressure. He knew his car-cam had recorded the license plate of the car. Now he had to get back to his vehicle and make the call for help. Stumbling, falling, and then crawling, Clarke managed to raise himself up to the front seat, and grasp the microphone. With great difficulty and life ebbing from him, he uttered the words Situation 31, and then collapsed on the front seat. His troop car had GPS.

Several other troop cars arrived on the scene simultaneously. For Clarke, they were too late.

Running the car cam provided the information necessary to issue an APB, an All-Points Bulletin. It also provided a visual record of the murder. Clarke had not even drawn his weapon. It was a clear case of murder in cold blood.

News of the event reached Grant Richardson in minutes. The nature of the crime and the location of the vehicle, along the route to Sodus Point, caused the commander to contact Santoro. Both agreed that the car's occupants might be the men they were looking for. The vehicle was still about an hour from Sodus Point. Richardson ordered the APB cancelled, at the same time alerting his men encircling the house in question. He also notified those units patrolling the route approaching to avoid apprehending the speeding vehicle, but only report its location and direction. Santoro informed Trasker of the situation and asked whether or not he had anything to offer. He did not.

The vehicle bearing Dimitri, Sasha, and Boris was now travelling near the massive Lake Ontario.

Being near a body of water that great on a moonless night produces some interesting effects. Looking in the direction of the lake, one sees only pitch black. Still, there is a sense of being uncomfortably close to the domain of a great and unfathomable force. The night being calm, the water makes no sound and yet it is there, billions and billions of gallons of it, and miles, untold miles, of undulating surface.

Sasha senses all this. Dull-witted Dimitri does not. He is filled with frustration, and not a little anger. What flashes through his consciousness is how he will explain to Yuri all that occurred since he left Westchester. There is the matter of the trooper; how will he tell Yuri about that? Dimitri makes the decision not to tell him. He likes his job and intends to keep it.

"Sasha, don't tell Yuri about the trooper. I will tell him."

"Shall I tell him about Boris escaping?"

"He didn't escape. We still have him, don't we?"

"I suppose so," Sasha weakly agrees.

"We'll be there soon. Then, we will have completed our mission."

"Look, a trooper car, there, behind that sign!" Sasha shouted, "You're speeding; are we going to have to shoot another one?"

This time, the troop car does not take chase. Instead, they radio the command center. Richardson relays the information to Santoro. "They're ten minutes away."

Richardson leaves the command post and takes up a position near the house. Minutes drag by.

The tension among the troopers is palpable.

"Lights," one announces, "Headlights, over there; they're coming"

Yuri Markov was home in bed. He calculated that by now, Dimitri and Sasha were well on their way to Canada. He still had the upper hand; he still had Boris. When he felt better and his shoulder stopped hurting, he would return to Yeshiva and finish off Jurgens. That could wait. What could not, was obtaining the information Sergei protected. There had to be another way to apply pressure. If it wasn't Boris, did Sergei have another Achilles' heel?

Yuri decided to phone the scientist.

Sergei answered.

"Pack your bags, Sergei, and keep them packed. Every time you want to see or treat your brother, it will be in Canada. They say it's a beautiful country."

The scientist's response was numbing. "Dimitri killed a New York State Trooper. They know where he is; approaching Sodus Point. Fifty policemen are waiting for him; check, and mate, you scum!"

Sergei waited for a reaction.

"How could that be?" Asked a concerned Yuri.

"Don't send stupid men on important missions. You, the smart one, hired dolts to do your work.

As long as you were there to keep them out of trouble, everything was fine. But left alone, who knew what they were going to do?"

"You are right, it is my fault." Yuri's candor surprised Sergei.

"I must stop talking. In a few moments they are going to capture your stupid squad and rescue my brother. I want to hear every word."

Ted Wagner had not heard from Claudia for some time; it was not like her to remain out of touch for so long. For a man who always appeared so dispassionate and businesslike, Ted did have feelings.

And right now they were engaged in his concern for his favorite colleague. A spark of love may have been hidden somewhere within that concern, but it would never have come to fruition; Ted's lifeblood was dominating, not sharing.

Wagner's cell vibrated. "Hello, Wagner here." It was Triple I CEO Janus Karper. "How may I be of service, sir?"

"Ted, Becker called a few moments ago. They are getting anxious about our ability to get the goods, if you know what I mean. They've given us a month. If we deliver by then, they will double our fee; that's four million for Claudia and 20 for Triple I."

"That's tremendous."

"Ted, if we, you I mean, fail, it would be a disaster. Other bosses might threaten an employee with dismissal, but you know I would never do that. Some might tell their employee they would never get another job as a security professional for as long as they lived. You know I would never do that, Ted. A few might even go so far as to threaten that employee with bodily harm; after all, twenty million is quite a lot of money. You know I would never do that, isn't that right, Ted?"

"Yes, of course, sir."

"I'm going to pencil you in for an appointment twenty eight days from now during which time you will deliver said goods. I'm sure that will be all right, won't it, Ted?"

"Yes sir that will be fine. I might even have to move up the date, that is, if you have no objections."

"Is there good news?"

"Claudia is in the laboratory. I don't know how she will accomplish it, but when the time is right, I expect she'll be coming out with the goods."

"Why, that's wonderful, Ted. I knew I could count on you. Well, I must go now. Let's keep the surprise under wraps for now. I'm going to enjoy seeing the faces at Becker when I drop the goods in their lap. I knew you were the right man for the job. And that Claudia Morgan woman, she is something, isn't she?"

"Yes sir, she certainly is."

"By the way, if this works out, an envelope containing one hundred thousand may be coming your way; a sort of thank you from a grateful employer."

"Thank you, sir." Karper hung up.

Threaten me, maybe kill me, then reward me, the shaken Wagner mused, what kind of man are you?

Irony of ironies, Ted Wagner had lied to his boss, but in point of fact, mouthed the absolute truth.

Claudia Morgan was indeed in Sergei Trasker's laboratory. Whether or not she would steal the 'goods' was another matter. But for now, Ted Wagner believed he had saved his job, and, perhaps his life.

The frightened man was thinking at fever pitch; I have to find Claudia. Where do I start looking?

The money, the thousands I advanced her, she must have spent it somewhere. Perhaps she wrote a check; yes, that's it. I'll call the bank and find out who the recipient was. That's where I'll start. When this is all over, Janus Karper, I'll still be your number one man.

Sodus Point

The car containing Dimitri, Sasha and Boris rolled to a stop. The only sounds were from the tires passing over the small stones in the driveway. A door opened and someone stepped out into the darkness.

"Dimitri?" he called. "Yes, it's me," was the reply. Both men advanced, embraced and went into the house. Sasha remained in the car with Boris. It was good that he did. Motionless and quiet, he began to see others moving through the trees and brush toward the house. The silhouettes were unmistakable; they were police. He resisted the urge to bolt out of the car and run to the house.

Opening the car door cautiously, (fortunately for Sasha, the car's dome light was off) he made his way toward the house, careful to remain in the shadows. The blast of light when he opened the door and went in was the only indication he had left the car.

"Police, they're all around us. I saw them creeping toward the house," He announced.

"Are they very close? Dimitri asked. Sasha nodded. "Why haven't they attacked? Perhaps they already know we have Boris. Are they awaiting the arrival of the boat? Whatever the reason, they're not closing in, so I think we should be safe for now. I just spoke to our Canadian friends; they say they'll be here in minutes. We'll walk to the boat, Sasha; you, me, and Boris. We'll do this very calmly. The rest of you will stay here and hold them off."

"But they will kill us before we get to the boat," Sasha argued.

"Not as long as we have Boris as a shield," Dimitri answered.

Minutes later they heard the sound of an approaching launch. Dimitri opened the door slowly and stepped out. Not yet accustomed to the dark, he couldn't see whether anyone was near. Sasha followed. Both men went to the car to get Boris. The two helped him navigate the path that led to the dock. The others shut the door and remained inside, armed and ready to lay down a blanket of fire to cover the trio's departure.

Richardson, already informed the route would be by water, directed several of his men to take up positions along the gangway to the dock. Two snipers with night vision scopes were assigned 'the tall one' and 'the short, skinny one,' Dimitri and Sasha respectively, as targets. Identifying Boris Trasker was not a problem; he was the one being assisted.

As the craft pulled up to the dock, two men jumped out and fastened the boat to the mooring.

They were oblivious to the police situation. As they jogged along the dock and then the gangway, Dimitri waved them back. Not understanding his meaning, they returned his wave and proceeded toward the trio.

"Get back, the police are everywhere," Dimitri said in a stage whisper loud enough to be heard in Boston.

Richardson gave the signal and his forces began their advance. "Halt, Police" was repeated several times by a number of officers. The boat crew drew their weapons. Gunfire from the boat and the gangway was frequent but ineffective. The flashes from the weapons gave away the locations of the shooters; a firestorm of police bullets headed in that direction. When the volley ceased, there was no reply.

That left the two felons and Boris on the gangway. To return to the house would mean certain capture. The way Dimitri saw it, there was only one choice, and that was to make for the boat. Placing his arm around Boris' waist, Dimitri drew his pistol and ambled down the gangway. Sasha, drawing his, brought up the rear.

A rifle shot erupted and destroyed the stillness that had reestablished itself after the original gun battle. Sasha dropped his weapon and slowly melted downward to the planks on the gangway. His comrade turned and saw the large hole in the back of his friend's head. Shaken but undeterred, Dimitri forged ahead. A second shot, this time coming from a greater distance, entered his chest. He died a few moments later. Shots however, once fired, go where they may. Changing direction after ricocheting, the now errant missile entered Boris' body, seriously wounding him.

As the troopers arrested the four in the house, taken without a shot, Grant Richardson called Frank Santoro. "We got them Frank, we got them all."

"And how's the brother. Is he okay?" The pause in conversation led the him to think the worst. "Oh, no, don't tell me. . ."

Richardson cut him off with "The guy is wounded. We're flying him to the hospital." The Troop Commander then explained in detail what had happened. "I hear the hospital 'copter now; talk to you later."

An anxious brother asked the detective what he had heard. "Is Boris all right?"

"He was shot. He took a slug in the chest. They say it was a ricochet. He's on the way to the hospital by helicopter." Santoro's countenance grew dark. "A ricocheted slug is bigger than the original; it probably mushroomed. That makes a bigger hole."

"He can't go to the hospital. They can't operate on him. He'll die."

"What's that?" Santoro was puzzled.

"Have them stop the bleeding and do what they must to keep him alive. I'm the only one who can treat him. Have him sent here; and, as soon as possible."

Santoro contacted Richardson and relayed the message.

"So you're the one who launched my Claudia," Ted Wagner said to the crane owner. "I hope you have good insurance because this is going to cost you a pile of cash."

Rick Slocum, owner of Slocum's Crane Services, didn't seem that anxious. "I get my share of nutty requests. As long as I perform them without breaking any laws, I'm home safe."

"I was downtown and tried to find your permit. I suppose they lost it. What do you think?"

"So I did what I did without a permit. Are you going to report me? You weren't even there."

Wagner went to plan B. "Exactly what did she want you to do?"

"I was to raise my boom to give her a launching platform for her hang glider. It was a hundred feet if I remember right. She took off just fine, into a real stiff gust of wind. I didn't expect it to work, but it did."

"Was anyone with her; someone who was supervising the affair?"

"Yeah, Todd was his name, Jimmy Todd. He was the one who set up the whole thing."

"Do you know how I can reach him?"

"Sure, I have his phone number in the office. Wait, I'll get it for you." Slocum went to his office.

He returned holding a scrap of paper in his hand. "Here it is. Hey, you're not really going to take me to court, are you?"

Ted Wagner smirked. "I'm thinking about it, that's all."

The speeding gurney slammed open the doors to the hospital operating theater. Boris Trasker should have been bleeding heavily because of the bullet's location, but, incredibly, was not. His clotting capability seemed remarkable, even to those directly attending. In gunshot cases to the upper chest or shoulder, blood loss is a major concern. In this instance, it was not. Vital signs, a blood sample, temperature and respiration had already been taken by attending EMTs.

An attending nurse read off the data: "BP 123 over 68, temp 98.6, blood oxygen level 98." The doctor, surprised at the readings, glanced at the nurse.

"And what is the patient's blood type?"

"We don't have any information on that, yet."

"What about clotting? Is there any indication of random clotting anywhere? What about areas not around the wound?"

"I can't find any."

"Let's begin; tell them to hurry with the blood type. He may need more blood; see to it." One of the nurses left to get the information and check on the availability of the patient's type.

The surgeon made the initial incision. "This man's body is not under stress. After being shot like that, there's no physical trauma. It's amazing."

The attending nurse reached over to swab the incision. Hardly any blood was excreted. There were perhaps twelve drops. Localized clotting had quickly closed the wound. She shot a glance at the doctor, who returned hers with one of equal puzzlement.

As the procedure progressed, the bullet removed and the opening closed, it was apparent to all who were observing that they were witnessing something they had never seen before. Boris Trasker's body had the ability to very nearly repair itself by conserving the flow of blood no matter the location or nature of the wound. "I wonder, given enough time, whether you could have healed yourself, too?" The doctor whispered to his unconscious patient.

"Doctor Steward. . ." The nurse had returned with the information about the blood type. "They can't determine the patient's blood type." She took a deep breath. "And there's a trace of amniotic fluid."

"Let me see that." The surgeon snatched the report from her hand and read it. "Impossible," he exclaimed and stalked out of the operating theater, intent on finding out for himself just what elements this incredible patient's blood contained.

Without any warning, a very obviously empowered alien group of individuals entered the surgical area.

"We're here for the gunshot wound patient," the leader announced.

"He's about to go into surgery and can't be moved," the nurse answered.

"Where is he?" the leader demanded.

"Through those doors. I told you he can't be moved," she shouted after them. Boris Trasker was wheeled out of the hospital. A large, twin-rotor helicopter was waiting.

Back from the laboratory the attending surgeon rushed over to the nurse. "What's happening here?"

The leader of the group stepped forward. He reached inside his jacket, pulled out a wallet and flashed a badge. "We're taking your patient; we have authorization. Do you have any questions?"

"I'm Doctor Steward, the attending surgeon. He can't be moved. He's about to undergo a very serious surgical procedure."

"We have it that he can be moved without any danger at all. Internal bleeding is not a problem for him." The doctor stared back at the leader.

"Who are you?"

"He'll be all right, doctor. We'll take good care of him."

Dr. Steward turned to the nurse. "What happened; how did they get in here? Why didn't you call me?"

"They just came in and took him." The sound of the helicopter revving up drowned out any further discussion.

"Someone is going to hear about this," the surgeon promised. To make the puzzle of the new patient even more confusing, the laboratory confirmed that they could not type the patient's blood. An orderly approached.

"Someone wants to speak with you, Doctor Steward." The surgeon headed for his office. A tall, thin man in a dark blue suit was already outside, waiting. The two entered the office. The man closed the door.

Whoever he was, 'blue suit' spoke with authority. In a flat, dull tone he addressed the surgeon.

"There was no gunshot wound patient. There was no operation to remove the bullet. Do you understand?"

"Yes, I do," the doctor replied. "Why are you doing this? I'm the attending surgeon and he is my patient."

"I thought we agreed nothing happened this evening."

"Don't be absurd, of course something happened this evening." The doctor shook his finger at the stranger. "Someone's going to hear about this."

The stranger took out his cell. "Lance, can you and Brett come in? Yes, I'm in his office." Soon, two very large athletic men, also in blue suits, came into the office.

"Choices, doctor; they are yours to make. If you insist on pursuing this matter, then Lance and Brett, here, will take you into custody and you will be incarcerated. If you remain silent, you can remain here. Which do you prefer?"

Steward's shoulders dropped; he was beaten. "Alright, have it your way. I'll comply."

"Thank you," the stranger replied. "Let's go," he ordered. The three left the office.

The helicopter aloft now, Dr. Thomas, the doctor in charge, contacted Commander Richardson.

"You said this was a special case and to call for further instructions when we had the patient in hand.

What's up?" the doctor asked.

Richardson replied, "I'm patching you through. The man you will be speaking to is the patient's brother and his physician. I don't know what this is all about, but I've been told you're to follow his instructions."

Not a little miffed, the doctor, Bruce Thomas, a qualified surgeon in his own right, barked back,

"I didn't need a surgeon with a mother complex."

"Here he is," Richardson announced, "His name is Sergei Trasker."

"I know that name, everyone knows that name. What can I do for you, doctor?"

"Do not give my brother any saline solution, it will kill him," Trasker commanded.

Thomas looked over at the patient. A male nurse was just inserting a needle, preparing to administer the drip.

"No," shouted Thomas, as he reached out and snatched the needle from the man. "This one's special; no saline." "Yes, sir," the nurse answered as he settled back in his seat. Thomas returned to the phone. "Anything else we need to do?" "He must receive furosemide and sodium bicarbonate; we have to induce alkaline diuresis. Monitor his potassium. None of this will hurt him if he is hydrated. Keep him sedated. I want him asleep when he gets here."

Doctor Thomas assembled his cadre and started the regimen as instructed. "I don't know what's happening, but if Sergei Trasker is involved, it has to be ground-breaking."

James opened the door and stepped outside the Potemkin suite to get the morning papers.

Grigorev and two burly associates were waiting for him. "Good morning James," Grigorev whispered,

"Take him."

Potemkin was sipping his coffee in the parlor, waiting for his valet to bring him the paper. After what seemed an appropriate interval, the professor called out. There was no answer. Making his way to the front door, he opened it and spied the undisturbed newspaper. Scuff marks along the white marble floor leading to the elevator told the story. "Grigorev," Potemkin muttered.

"Your brother is on the way," Santoro observed. The scientist had already surmised that might have been the case. The shooting was over and the perpetrators had been captured. All that remained was now occurring.

Commander Richardson had apprised them over half an hour ago. Repeating good news; what could it hurt? That was Santoro's angle.

Ping, Pang, and Pong surrounded the scientist's chair. They seemed asleep.

"Nice dogs; can I pet them?" Santoro questioned.

"Of course," Trasker replied. "Pet," he commanded, and pointed at his guest. The three awoke, approached, and started rubbing their muzzles against his trousers. "Hey, they're really friendly," Santoro observed.

"When you've had enough, just say 'sleep'." The scientist sank back into his seat.

The entire day and previous night's events had been daunting. First, the attempt to free Boris, then the escape, and then Yuri Markov's admission that Boris was being taken to Canada. On and on it went, event after event. It all seemed too much to comprehend. Santoro glanced over at the scientist. He had fallen asleep. Shooting a glance over to Bob McCann, the policeman smiled.

His partner replied with his own. "We did good today, didn't we?"

Santoro shot back. "Damned straight. Now, all we have to do is nab that faux Boris or Yuri Markov, or whatever the hell he calls himself. I want him, Bob. He's murdered some good people. He's going to pay for that. Santoro glanced at his partner. Without saying anything further, they had already decided that whatever the circumstances, there would be a firefight and Yuri would be killed. It would result in a savings; no big lawyer bills.

Hours passed. Santoro wondered what was keeping them. Even with the large twin-rotor machine, it was about two hundred miles; that would account for some of the delay. They may have had to stop for additional fuel. They may have had difficulty getting clearance to fly through the heavily congested Westchester-Long Island grid. They may have had to maintain a holding pattern because other planes were stacked up waiting for clearance to land at Kennedy or LaGuardia. There were dozens of reasons for the delay in their arrival.

Suddenly, Sergei Trasker sat upright. He was fully awake. "Claudia, I must move her upstairs. Boris will be coming soon. I will need space for him." Before Santoro could say anything, the scientist was up and on the way to his laboratory. The detective lost sight of him as he entered the doorway at the end of the hall.

McCann, startled out of a deep sleep, awoke looking confused. "What just happened?"

"You got me," Santoro replied.

"You have served Potemkin well, James. I'm told you even saved his life. I don't want to hurt you; you're a war hero and I know you love the motherland. Just tell me what I need to know and you can go back to your boss."

James stared at his captor. Grigorev knew that look well; it mirrored the same defiance the Russians showed through their bravery through both word and deed during the Second World War.

"I expected no less. I respect your faithfulness, James, so we will resort to a less violent method."

Grigorev left the room. Soon, a person in a white lab coat entered. He had a syringe in one hand and a vial of something in the other. Gently, he injected the valet.

Ted Wagner, for all his undesirable traits, had one distinct quality that eclipsed the rest; he was extremely aggressive. Riding up and down between the Putnam County line and the city of White Plains more than he cared to recall, he was sure something would break in his favor. Not quite certain what it would be, he tenaciously clung to that belief.

It was mid-morning. Tooling along at 55 and daydreaming just a bit, Ted Wagner was wondering what his next move would be if he failed in his protracted surveillance. Without warning, a truck emerged from what appeared to be a clump of bushes, fully occupying Wagner's travel lane. Swerving hard left he managed to avoid a collision. Fortunately there was no one coming the other way. A half mile down the road he stopped at a gas station. Cars need gas. While the attendant was busy pumping, it gave him the time to think about his near mishap. Somewhere in his stream of consciousness, a connection occurred.

Was the truck leaving the Trasker estate?

Traveling slowly along the shoulder of the road, he was able to find the well-hidden driveway. He turned into it. Proceeding cautiously, he looked for the hazards he felt surely existed along such a primitive route. To his surprise, there were none. The truck had left a clear path of flattened grass to follow, so when a left turn was indicated, Wagner followed. A short time later he found himself in front of a formidable iron gate. Moments later, an armed guard's weapon was lightly tapping on his window.

Wagner rolled it down.

"You are lost, yes?"

"I'm Ted Wagner. I'm looking for Claudia Morgan."

Wagner became alarmed at the guard's non-verbal response. He snapped back the bolt of his automatic weapon and pointed it at Wagner as he called the main house. "Yes, he is here. We will wait."

The guard directed Wagner to step out of the car. A golf cart with two guards appeared in the distance. Wagner joined them off they sped to the main house.

Meanwhile, Sergei Trasker had been thinking about that day at the police station, the day he first met Claudia Morgan. Someone accompanied her to the police station. He assumed correctly that Wagner must have been her escort. She would not have been there unless Chief Investigator Santoro needed her to identify faux Boris. The civil service employee ruse was weak, but, given the circumstances, it was appropriate. Conversing with Claudia over the past weeks cleared up many lingering questions, one of them her reason for being at the station.

Two guards escorted Wagner into the room where Trasker was cavorting with his three canine companions, Ping, Pang, and Pong. The scientist acknowledged Wagner and the two guards retreated several paces.

"Who are you?"

"Ted Wagner, I'm Claudia Morgan's supervisor."

"Please sit down. NEW," Trasker commanded; the three terriers approached Wagner and familiarized themselves with his scent. They returned to Trasker's side. "I'm told you want to know where Claudia Morgan is. Are you a Becker or Triple I person? Before you answer, let me tell you I know everything. Claudia explained it all to me so don't waste your time telling stories."

Trasker's statement was not entirely true. He needed more information and he decided he might get it if he tried fishing.

"I'm from Triple I. You must already suspect I'm also working for Becker. They want your work, any way they can get it."

"They've been after me for some time now. It surprised and disappointed me that Claudia worked for Triple I, vis-à-vis, also for Becker."

"Two million is two million. Recently I received a call from my boss. Now it's four million. That's Claudia's share. Where is she? May I speak with her?"

"She's upstairs, recuperating. I'll have someone show you where she is. But, before you go," One of the guards stepped forward and very thoroughly frisked Wagner.

"Not taking any chances, are you?"

"Becker has not been able to penetrate this estate yet. You won't either. Searching you is just a precaution, you understand. Slav, here, will remain in the room while the two of you talk. Do not attempt to enter any other part of the building. A word of advice; don't do anything foolish. He is very good with his Kalashnikov."

Wagner stared at the scientist and then Slav. His statement was not intended as a joke. "Before you go, Mr. Wagner, what is the name of the Triple I boss who contacted you?"

"Janus Karper. I hope you never meet him."

A shadow of a smile tiptoed across Sergei Trasker's face.

The guard escorted the visitor up the staircase.

Trasker turned to his three terriers, their tails wagging. "Pet," he commanded; Ping, Pang and Pong raced to find their place on the sofa next to their master, each vying to be the first to receive an affectionate stroking. Theirs was not an emotional need.

Constantine Potemkin placed his coat and hat in the closet. The exhilarating walk in the park did not diminish his concern for his dear friend James. The scientist acknowledged he had little power here, in the United States. In Russia, a phone call to the proper person would have produced swift results. As the professor approached the parlor, he smelled cigarette smoke; Turkish cigarette smoke, the kind Grigorev used.

The Russian agent was sitting in an arm chair. James lay unconscious on the divan. Potemkin started to say something but Grigorev raised his hand and cut him off.

"He's all right; just recovering from a little truth serum, that's all. I haven't harmed a hair on his head. After all, he is one of us, isn't he?"

Potemkin flushed red with rage. He went over to the bureau and took a pistol from the top drawer.

"The magazine is here." Grigorev took it from his pocket and waved the clip at the professor.

"Get out, get out."

"Alright, alright, I'm leaving. I just want you to know James told me about Claudia Morgan. Now that I know her name and that she is the link between you and Sergei, I'll dig a little deeper and see who she really is and who she's working for. When James awakens, thank him for me, will you?"

Potemkin threw the pistol at the agent as he passed through the entrance door. The door was nearly shut as the projectile hit. The pistol fell to the floor.

The professor turned his attention to his friend. James was just regaining consciousness. "Can I get you anything ? Do you hurt anywhere? I know Grigorev sometimes lies."

"I'll be fine in a little while. There was no torture, just truth serum. He said I was a war hero. That's why he wouldn't do those things to me. Besides, he got what he wanted rather easily, didn't he?"

Potemkin, relieved that his friend had not been harmed, sighed, "Yes, he did."

"Are you okay, Claudia?" There was a hint of genuine concern in Wagner's voice.

"I'll be fine, thanks to my guardian angel downstairs."

Now her boss turned to other matters; he had a job to protect and a possible assassination to prevent.

"Did you find where he kept his notes? Were you able to get any of them? Do you think you can get them at all?" There was a pleading, pathetic tone to his inquiries.

"No, no, and, no. I'm out of this one, Ted. I can't do this anymore. Sergei Trasker is an honest, dedicated scientist; he saved my life. I won't betray him."

"I just got a call from Janus. He's set a date for delivery."

"Or he'll fire you - or worse. Is that why you're here? You don't care about me, do you? It's just you that matters, isn't it?"

"I do care about you, but that's not the issue. If I don't deliver, I'm toast. Karper alluded to that, you know. He even mentioned getting rid of me - permanently; like, forever."

"He threatened to kill you?"

A very frightened Wagner nodded.

"That's terrible; my god!"

"The ante's been raised to four million for you and twenty for Triple I; that's a lot of money.

Janus Karper isn't going to let little me stand in his way. He's going to get those documents to Becker, even if he has to invade this place."

"Things certainly have changed, haven't they?"

"If you won't try, then I will. I'm going to shake this guard. I'll find the lab and get what I need."

"Don't try it. You'll never succeed; this place has too many guards and too many alarms. Ted, they'll kill you."

"I'm dead either way. I'm going to gamble on this. I have no choice." Wagner turned to the guard and signaled he wished to leave. As the door clicked shut, Claudia was alone, alone with her concern that this might have been the last time she would see her boss.

As the guard preceded the visitor down the long staircase, Wagner pushed hard, sending the armed escort tumbling over and over down the steps, finally landing unconscious at the landing.

The visitor jumped over guard's body and ran down the hall, slipping into one of the many rooms along its course. His was a pyrrhic victory. True enough, he had gotten rid of his overseer, but which way should he head now? Observing the bunker as he approached the main house, he concluded the lab had to be below ground. Wagner started opening and closing doors, searching for one that had stairs leading downward.

Four of Sergei Trasker's guards dotted a grassy knoll on the estate. They were searching the skies for the approaching helicopter carrying Sergei's brother. They could hear the bap-bap-bap of its rotors but could not as yet see the machine.

"Tahm; there," one of the guards pointed. The huge machine arrived overhead and started its descent.

The four raced away from the grassy center. Moments later, the helicopter landed, bouncing once on the turf, as if performing a hip-hop.

Touchdown energized both those inside and outside the craft. The guards started up the all-terrain vehicle modified with an ad-hoc stretcher and slowly approached. Inside, the attending physician and his team prepared Boris for transport. Working together, both groups accomplished the transfer without incident. Doctor Thomas insisted on accompanying his patient to the main house. Reluctantly, Lev relented and let him ride along. The helicopter kept its engine running. The crew would remain with the machine and await Thomas' return.

Sergei was waiting at the front door. Lev and some guards manned the stretcher and headed for the lab with the scientist leading the way and Doctor Thomas trailing behind. At the door to the lab, the scientist punched the proper sequence of letters into the keypad. Lev knew where to take Boris, so he led the way.

Thomas attempted to follow, but Sergei placed his arm across the man's chest. "Not for you," the scientist commanded.

"He's my patient," Thomas objected.

"Not anymore," Trasker parried.

"I'm going in there and make sure he's properly taken care of," Thomas insisted as he pushed forward. Just then, Lev appeared at the top of the stairs. His huge frame filled the doorway Thomas was attempting to enter. On the way up, he had heard the exchange. "Come, doctor, I'll escort you back to your men. Thank you for bringing Boris." Slipping his muscular arm under the doctor's, Lev 'escorted' Thomas out of the building and back to the helicopter.

"Regards to your friends at Becker," Sergei Trasker shouted after him. The scientist had deduced the reason for the good doctor's inordinate concern for Boris once he was being taken to the laboratory.

Returning to the room where Santoro and McCann were, Sergei Trasker's countenance had changed dramatically. His brother was back and Sergei could restore him. Clearly he was a man on a mission.

Seeing their presence was no longer required, Santoro and McCann decided to take their leave.

"There's nothing more we can do here. We'll be going. Good luck with your brother." Santoro said.

The scientist shook Santoro's hand, then McCann's. "I can't thank you enough for what you've done."

"Get back to your brother," McCann suggested.

It wasn't long after Santoro and McCann got in the car and left the estate that they began talking about the bizarre sequence of events surrounding the murder investigation. Apparently both detectives had independently been analyzing every aspect, trying to make sense of the entire matter. They failed.

Santoro started speaking while in the middle of a train of thought. It didn't surprise him that McCann's thoughts were confluent and he was able to follow without dropping a stitch. "We'll know what this is really about when we get a sense of just what kind of discovery this guy has made. That will clear up a lot of things. For Markov to go through the motion of trying to set up Boris again, especially after the man has already been in prison, speaks to just how important his work must be."

"That's right. And, if they've gone to this much trouble already, it's odds on they'll be trying again."

"Our problem is we don't know who all the players are. We agree that Markov, acting as Boris is the murderer of all three victims, Collins, Peters, and Silverman. We can walk away from Sergei Trasker. In the department's view, we've identified the killer and when we get him, we'll be done with this case. Or, will we?" Santoro turned and looked at McCann with that I know-what-you're-thinking glance.

"The two that were shot at Sodus point; one or both of them might have been disguised as the other Boris. Markov needed at least one other mannequin to pull off his three Boris ruses."

"That makes sense," Santoro agreed.

"We've got to figure out a way to stay on this case. It's not just the murders; we know more now.

Come on, Frank, when have we ever left someone exposed like that? We've always figured out a way to stay involved, most times according to the book." McCann couldn't help but smile when he uttered the last phrase.

"Markov may be on the run or hiding if he suspects we're on to him. I don't think he'll be a player, at least for the time being. It's Becker Pharmaceutical I'm worried about. From what Wagner said, they're not very nice people. They've got the cash and the legal clout to get to Trasker and then defend whatever happens in court until the cows come home."

"And, who's behind Becker?"

"You know, I never gave that a thought; maybe the Russians, or, maybe Big Brother? Could our own people be behind it all, layered back a few levels? It's possible." The talking ceased; hard thinking resumed. Both had come to the same conclusions.

Santoro's cell rang. "Yes, chief, right away. We're in Westchester right now. We'll probably get there too late to meet with you today. The traffic here is horrendous."

McCann stared at Santoro. There were no more than ten vehicles in sight.

Santoro continued his conversation. "Yes sir, tomorrow at ten."

"What?" McCann asked.

"It seems one of Becker's top execs has taken an interest in the Boris Trasker kidnapping. Sergei worked for them years ago, didn't he? The chief said this guy Moroka just wanted to help a former employee if he could. The chief also said he might prove to be a 'positive force' in the investigation."

McCann winced a bit when Santoro uttered the words 'positive force.'

"The chief isn't up to date, then? He doesn't know about the rescue?"

"No, and I'm not going to tell him, at least not right now. Let the troopers tell him. And, if they assume I told him, they might not either. If our luck holds, he won't know for a while, so he won't be able to bring any of the corporate big wigs up to date."

"Right, and the less this new guy Moroka knows, the less of a threat he'll be to Trasker."

"We hope," McCann added.

So far, Ted Wagner's luck had been phenomenal. The guard he pushed down the stairs was just regaining consciousness. Not knowing where the laboratory was, he was guided to it by the parade that was carrying Boris Trasker. Attention was focused on Boris and then Doctor Thomas. The distraction caused the door to the lab to remain open a crack. Wagner managed to slip through as the guards and Sergei watched Lev grasp and lead Dr. Thomas down the hall. Now, all Wagner needed to do was hide and be quiet until everyone left. Then he could search the laboratory and get the notes. He might be satisfying Karper's demands sooner than expected.

The scientist and his chief guard returned to the lab and began to prep Boris for treatment. The procedure would take hours. Ping,

Pang and Pong, always at the scientist's side, were making nuisances of themselves. He commanded them to 'sit.'

Wagner watched with amazement at how swiftly and skillfully the two men functioned. Not a medical person himself, still, he could appreciate their confluence and coordination. Hardly a word passed between them.

In the same position for some time, Wagner needed to move his leg; it was beginning to cramp.

Ping raised his head. He yapped once. It was an alarm yap. In an instant Pang and Pong were also on alert. Made aware of a possible threat, the presence of an intruder, the scientist still continued his work. Had Ping's warning been correct?

Lev's cell rang; he stepped away from patient Boris and took the call. After receiving the information, he approached his boss and whispered into his ear.

Indeed, Ping's alert had been correct.

"Here," Trasker commanded; the three Yorkshire terrier robots stood in front of their master.

"New; find." The three ran off, searching everywhere, looking for 'new,' the person they had met recently.

Pang was the fortunate one. Yapping authoritatively, the dog announced that he had found his prey.

"Okay, okay, puppy, I'm coming out."

Lev pulled Wagner out from under a table stacked with medical equipment.

"I instructed you concerning the limits of your access in my home. Is that correct?" The scientist was upset.

"Yes, but Claudia told me she wouldn't betray you, so I had to act for myself. My boss threatened me. He's going to hurt me if I don't get the information he wants; it's nothing personal."

"And the guard you pushed down the stairs; is his broken arm nothing personal?"

"I'm sorry about that."

Lev stepped forward and punched Wagner in the nose. Even before he landed on the floor, blood was flowing from it.

"Please escort Mister Wagner to his car."

For the second time this evening, Lev was escorting a persona non grata from the estate.

"Don't you have a band aid or something? I'm bleeding."

"You're a gentleman. You must have a handkerchief - use it," the scientist replied.

Sergei Trasker turned his attention to his brother. Lev would be returning. There was much to do.

Boris Trasker's metabolism was not yet completely alkaline. The treatment during the helicopter transport helped, but more needed to be done. His condition remained critical. He had to undergo a similar regimen as Claudia had. While his captors did not mistreat him, they did not address his unique medical needs. Only brother Sergei knew of Boris' true condition, or so he thought. He was the only one who could treat him.

Lev returned. "His handkerchief wasn't enough. I gave him a towel from the bathroom," a smiling Lev quipped.

"Boris will require immersion. Let's get to work." Sergei examined and diagnosed Boris' vital signs. For the moment, his regeneration had to be on hold.

During their last conversation Janus Karper had detected the unsteadiness in Ted Wagner's voice and come to the conclusion he was lying. Not one to wait around for something to happen, the Triple I executive went to work developing his own plan. Dirk Spanner was an old acquaintance from bygone days, when Karper decided to plumb the depths of government service for the opportunities it might provide. Ten years passed. Karper, frustrated, resigned. Spanner, for reasons of his own, did likewise. He went to work for an industrial espionage firm. Karper started his own, and in less than ten years built it into the colossus that everyone knew today as Triple I.

Perhaps it was pride, or something else he cared not to reveal, but Spanner never approached his former acquaintance for a job, even after Triple I absorbed his parent company's clients, thus forcing them out of business. Dirk was not a saint, but he clung tenaciously to his own code of ethics as any honorable person might.

"Dirk, finally, I'm finally able to reach you. It's good to hear your voice. It's Janus, Janus Karper."

How are things? Oh, out of work? Is that your greatest trouble? Listen, I just happen to be looking for someone, and guess what? I thought of you. How about that? You'll have a job, and I get to help a friend.

Why don't you come down and we'll see whether I can pay you enough to come and work for me. Is tomorrow at ten all right? Good; I'll see you then."

The Triple I executive was pleased with himself. Now, no matter what that dolt Wagner does or doesn't accomplish, he mused, I'll have a viable plan B in place.

He could feel Sergei Trasker's documents in his possession; that's how confident he was about his decision to hire Spanner.

The Fountain of Youth

Claudia Morgan had recovered. As she surveyed her body in the mirror, she marveled that she found no scars or any other indication of the injuries she had sustained. Everywhere her skin seemed to be at full blush, as if she were young again. The woman was beginning to perceive just how far Sergei Trasker had advanced the science of healing. If he can heal this miraculously now, then what else might he be capable of? Might he have the ability to recreate a human being? Has Sergei Trasker, the kidnapped youth turned genius from Riga developed techniques that might make living young forever an achievable goal?

Such thoughts, and others, cascaded through Claudia's consciousness as she toweled off and gazed at her wonderful body. She appeared twenty. The view excited her.

Someone knocked on the door. Donning a robe, she responded.

"Come i-in," she intoned seductively.

Sergei Trasker entered. Upon seeing his patient and how well she seemed, he gasped. "You're looking wonderful, Claudia. I think you'll be able to go home soon. Are you feeling dizzy? Do you have any pain?"

Always the doctor, Claudia mused. "I'm fine, just fine. The scale says I've lost ten pounds, and, when I look in the mirror I find I'm ten years younger. Just how did you do that - I mean the ten years?

And, to boot, I can't find a scar on my body, not a one." Claudia approached Sergei. "Do you do black magic?" Almost nose to nose now, Sergei's heavy breathing was evident, as was Claudia's.

The scientist retreated two paces. "I have to help my brother."

"He's here?"

"Yes, the troopers rescued him and brought him here."

"Shouldn't they have brought him to the nearest hospital?"

"Boris is . . . special; only I can treat him."

"Special, how; how is he special?" Claudia tugged at Sergei's sleeve, as if trying to pull the answer out of him - or get him at least to respond.

Uncomfortable at the turn the conversation had taken, he pleaded, "I'll tell you everything, but not now. I have to go. Please let go."

The lines of anxiety carved on Sergei's face impressed Claudia. She released her grip.

Grigorev was recovering from a disastrous gambit at Sodus Point. Those waiting offshore told him there was a firefight. The launch did not return. That was all the information they could provide.

From those bits of information he surmised Dimitri, Sasha, and those in the house were either dead or in custody. The launch that was to transport Boris to the mini-sub must have been seized. The people manning it who came ashore most likely resisted and, like Dimitri and Sasha, suffered the same fate. The underwater vessel and its crew, waiting in the dark farther out in the lake, escaped without incident.

What now, the Russian pondered. Potemkin was also after Sergei; there wasn't any doubt about that. Collaboration with the old professor was out of the question; certainly not after James' kidnapping.

One gambit remained; kidnapping Claudia Morgan. Perhaps she might prove a more valuable commodity than Boris, especially if Sergei had feelings for her. "Where are my cigarettes," Grigorev shouted, as if someone were in the room to hear him. "I need a smoke." Settling into a chair, the Russian began planning his next move. He would kidnap Claudia Morgan. This time, he promised himself, there would be no *faux pas*.

Still suffering from Lev's jab, a determined Ted Wagner appeared unexpectedly at Janus Karper's office. It was ten o'clock, the same ten o'clock on the same day that Dirk Spanner was to meet with the Triple I executive.

Both men, not acquainted, sat across from each other, wondering what the other was doing there.

Janus Karper finally stepped out of his office ready to greet Spanner, certainly not Wagner. His smile at seeing Spanner and his surprise at seeing Wagner told the entire story; one was expected, the other, not.

Still, the executive disguised his feelings as best he could, inviting Spanner in, and instructing Wagner to wait until he was finished with the stranger.

"It's good to see you," Karper purred as he shook Spanner's hand and patted him on the back.

"Here, have a seat, this one. It's closer to my desk."

Spanner had misgivings about the executive's cordial behavior. This was not the Janus Karper he remembered. The one he had known was not as cordial; he would have destroyed anyone who stood in his way.

"How's the family? Is Lisa well?"

"Cut to the chase, Janus; what do you need?"

"I've always liked that about you; you never mince words." Karper observed. "I have a mission, not quite legal, but very profitable. Do you want me to go on? It would be very costly if you were to tell anyone about it."

"Dollars; tell me about the dollars."

"If you succeed, two million; if you fail, a million to Lisa and the family."

"So it's a suicide mission? I get three million and two for Lisa and the kids if I don't get back."

"I agree to your terms."

"That was fast. What's this all about?"

"There's an estate in Westchester; a scientist lives there. I want the documents that detail his research. They're very valuable and some people I know will pay a great deal to get them. The scientist in question, has a number of guards on the estate. . ." Spanner raised his hand; the executive stopped talking.

"Four million, I want four million. If the chance for survival is as slim as I think it is, I want more money."

"Alright, four million," Karper replied.

Triple I's new mercenary sat silently during the rest of the presentation. After the executive finished, Spanner remained unresponsive for several moments. This annoyed his boss.

"Have you forgotten how to speak?"

"I'll need six men; I'll pick them myself. You will be paying. Handle that as you please. I'll need forty thousand for hardware, body armor, and some other special equipment to neutralize any electronic devices. If I need more cash, I'll call. I need two hundred thousand up front for Lisa and the kids in case I'm away any longer than planned and before you make good on the deal. No one but you and I will know what this is about. The six I hire will be going in blind, to extract 'important papers.' Does that suit you?"

"Yes it does. Oh, there's one thing more. I have an appointment with those interested parties in two weeks for an update on our progress. I'd love to hand them the papers at that time. Can you move that soon?"

"Depending on how quickly I can recruit my team and survey the premises, ten days sounds doable."

"Miss Tierney, please bring in a check in the amount of two hundred forty thousand dollars, made out to Mister Dirk Spanner; S-P-A-N-N-E-R." Karper released the button on the intercom. "The check will be here in a few minutes. Anything else you want to talk about?"

"I'll be writing down our agreement and leaving it with Lisa, to be opened in case, well, you know what. Don't try to screw me the way you did Vanderbilt at GAO."

"The General Accounting Office; you haven't forgotten."

"No, I haven't. Be honorable this time, just for a change."

The secretary entered the room. "Here you are, sir." Tierney handed Karper the envelope and left.

The executive examined the check, signed it, placed it back in the envelope and handed it to Spanner who seemed pleased with the entire transaction.

"Good hunting, see you in ten days; less, I hope."

Wagner was still waiting outside. Suddenly, there was an audible click, the door swung open and Spanner walked out, envelope in hand. The gazes of the two met, but nothing was said.

Wagner watched Spanner as he walked down the hall and into the elevator.

"Now it's your turn," the executive said.

The Triple I agent entered the office and sat down. Wagner was uneasy. "I've come to give you a report on our progress. I was in Trasker's laboratory."

Karper leaned forward in his chair. "You have the goods?"

"No, they caught me before I could make a thorough search. They beat me up and threw me out."

"Bravo, Wagner, that's what I like to hear; total devotion to duty no matter the cost."

"I did my best. There's little chance I could gain entry a second time. They're on to me now."

He lowered his gaze. "You're not going to kill me now, are you?"

Karper laughed. "I'm not going to kill you, Ted, although I must admit it did cross my mind. I've made other arrangements to obtain what I need."

"Do you mean that Claudia and I are out of the running?"

"Oh, no, I don't mean that at all. Let's just say you two have competition. Whoever gets the goods wins the prize. You understand, don't you? I need what I need, and soon. My clients are not patient people. They won't allow me to fail."

Ted Wagner detected a flash of fear in the CEO's eyes. The self-confident gaze was gone and a hint of terror had taken its place. "I'll do my best. Claudia is still inside the estate. For how much longer, I don't know. Perhaps she can get the documents."

"It certainly would solve the problem. As I told you, I have engaged others. I'm not counting on just Triple I anymore."

Wagner strutted out of Janus Karper's office feeling fulfilled. It was satisfying to see someone else's feet being put to the fire, especially the person he just left.

Claudia Morgan had recuperated so marvelously she was able to join Sergei Trasker for an evening meal. Several more days and she would be ready to go home. Lev had done some shopping in town and returned with a few new garments for the woman, namely an aquamarine jump suit, three pairs of slacks, and two blouses in different colors. Surprisingly, the man had good taste. Claudia approved of his selections.

It was not without regret the scientist confronted the reality of Claudia's leaving. He had finally admitted to himself that he cared for her. In addition, he was aware that the gaming of Becker, Grigorev, Markov, and Potemkin was not yet over. Trasker envisioned a scenario where she might take Boris' place as the 'prize' to be redeemed. Still there was nothing he could do; Claudia was well and he could not detain her any longer. He persisted in his struggle to eke out a satisfactory alternative.

"Do you always eat this extravagantly?" Claudia Morgan asked.

"I eat this way only when 'Queen Frederika' is present, and, of course, other very special guests."

The scientist turned to Claudia and smiled broadly.

"Is it over? Now that you have your brother back, will they stop trying?"

"Your friend Wagner tried; he even managed to get into the laboratory. We threw him out."

"No!"

"It's true. Did he tell you of his intentions when he spoke with you?"

"He said something cryptic; Janus Karper was going to kill him if he didn't succeed. He felt he had nothing to lose whether it was being killed by him or one of your men."

"And you didn't tell me?"

"I didn't think he was going to do it immediately. I didn't know."

Claudia's volley caused the scientist pause. "The mignon and scalloped potatoes; don't the haricots vert compliment them? Oh, and the dessert, I think you'll enjoy that."

"Once again peace reigns at the Trasker table. The meal is lovely, Sergei. You must have gone to a great deal of trouble. I can't let this moment pass without thanking you again for saving my life; thank you, thank you, thank you." Morgan could not have been more sincere as she uttered the last six words.

Sergei Trasker lowered his head and stared into his plate of food. He remained in that position for several seconds. Then, as if in reply to a message sent from the gods, he whispered, "Thank you Fibonacci."

Claudia Morgan immediately recognized the name. "What does Leonardo *filius* Bonacci of Pisa have to do with all of this?"

"Actually, without Fibonacci, I could not have restored your body tone to the state it is today. I shall tell you all about it one day, but not right now." The scientist raised his hand and motioned. The server brought in a small cake, its sugared top shaped like a hang glider. One wing was broken.

Claudia Morgan laughed. "Oh, it's wonderful; I just love it."

The piece accomplished its intended objective. Each person consumed half the cake; he the broken wing and she, the one still intact.

She would be leaving soon, that was undeniable. Further, having been associated with him, she might be at risk. How might that be avoided?

"Morning, chief; what's up?" Frank Santoro, standing before his superior in his office, tried to sound as casual as possible. From the tone of the chief's voice on the phone, it looked as if Bob and he were in for it.

"Where's Bob?"

"He's outside."

"Get him in here. What I have to say goes for both of you." Chief Davis' face was turning red.

Santoro ushered in McCann. The glance he gave his partner indicated that trouble was just ahead.

The chief motioned them to sit. Fingering the intercom, he said "No calls, Nancy; I'll be unavailable for about half an hour, maybe as long as an hour."

Half an hour, Santoro thought, what's this all about?

"The Superintendent of State Police called me yesterday and wanted to know how the person wounded in the drug sting operation was doing. I told him I would get back to him as soon as I checked with our top drug investigators Santoro and McCann. When did you two transfer from homicide to drug enforcement? After all, I'm only the Chief of Special Operations, you know, the guy who sits behind a desk shuffling all those papers. By the way, who gave you the authority to set up a sting operation of any kind? Staten Island is short a couple of traffic cops. Do I have to threaten to send you two there before I get some answers? Start talking; it had better be good."

Santoro reached over to the intercom and pressed the talk button. "Nancy, update; the chief won't be available until noon. Thank you." Santoro and McCann proceeded to lay out the entire situation for the chief. They also made a case for staying in the background but remaining on the case to protect Sergei, Boris, and Claudia while the department pursued Markov. If the Russians got the scientist, the adverse effect to the United States could be significant. Without having any knowledge of his 'discovery' or its implications, that's what the pair believed and that's what they told their superior.

Some of the Chief's people were known to exaggerate; others, not to tell the truth. But Santoro and McCann weren't like that. They prided themselves on their accuracy and truthfulness. For them to be alarmed indicated something truly significant was occurring or about to occur. These two were his finest; they deserved his support. Davis glanced at his watch.

It was one-thirty and Santoro and McCann were still talking, hoping to convince the chief to let them stay in the mix. The chief raised his hand. Both men stopped.

"Before I became chief, we three used to catch lunch at McGinnity's; remember? You two look played out. Come on, I'll buy you lunch. But I'm still pissed about you not telling me all about this up front. That *will not* happen again, right?" Both men nodded. As the three passed by the reception desk, Chief Davis told his secretary "Tomorrow, save all my calls for tomorrow." Davis' decision was the right one; the food and drink at the pub further reduced tension and loosened tongues further. The chief learned more than he could have in the adversarial atmosphere in his office.

"This isn't about the murder of three men," concluded the chief, "That's plain now. Stay on the case and do anything necessary to remain on top of the situation. If you need support, call me on my cell.

If you need more backup than our department can provide, I've got some friends at the federal level.

Don't worry about the troopers screaming about not going through the usual protocol. I'll take care of that. Richardson might even get a commendation when this is all over." Santoro and McCann relaxed.

"You're the best. I've always believed that. There's no reason to change my mind now. You've just stumbled into a bigger game, that's all. Stick with it," Davis pointed his finger at the two. "And don't get hurt."

Fame is a ruthless mistress, and many are they who wish to possess her. Constantine Potemkin was one of these. In this foreign land, he was at the disadvantage. At home, he could have called a dozen people to help him pinpoint the whereabouts of Sergei Trasker. His only allies here were his valet James and regrettably, Grigorev.

Other casual acquaintances, such as embassy personnel and guards were of no use. Anything he might have chosen to tell them would immediately be reported to superiors. James, totally faithful, was ill equipped for the current needs of the professor. Like it or not, Potemkin had to rely on Grigorev's crude ways to facilitate what he needed most; to see his former colleague. The professor's star was in retrograde; his health was failing. Still, he was determined to make his mark in the scientific world before succumbing to the inevitable.

It is precisely at this point and under these circumstances that terrible decisions are made. Time and events collaborating against him, Constantine Potemkin reached a heightened and unimaginable level of desperation. He did not wish to leave this world unheralded. He was brilliant. He felt he deserved a place in the annals of scientific achievement. Given more time he most likely would have discovered what Sergei Trasker had. But time, cruel time, had dictated the circumstances that controlled his destiny.

His path was clear. He needed to contact colleague Sergei by whatever means were at his disposal and secure his place in history, even if it meant usurping the scientist's discovery.

He had become a predator.

After their initial interlude, Sergei and Claudia met for dinner five more times, each event being more pleasant than the last. Facing the industrial spy was a brilliant scientist and intended target of corporate espionage. He, in turn, faced a professional corporate thief. On its face it was the most ludicrous of events. The inconsistency tugged at Sergei Trasker. Claudia Morgan might well have entertained the same thoughts herself.

And what blunted that reality? The pair was maneuvering through the maze of impressions that occur when people are falling in love. Not willing to admit it yet, they were deeply engaged in finding the common ground between them. The most formidable chess master would have paled in disbelief when he observed the gambits playing out at the dining table.

"So when are you going to tell me about your discovery?"

"Four million for you, twenty for Triple I, that's what Wagner said you and the firm were getting.

Do you think anything could be worth twenty four million dollars?"

"Don't you have the picture yet? I'm on your side. Once the money was my primary objective;

I'm not ashamed of that. Then I met you and found out what was going on; Boris, prison, and those murders. Do you think I would sell you out now? Not in a million years."

"You'll be going home soon, perhaps tomorrow or the day after. I spoke to Lev and he is going to send one of his men to watch over you. It's just a precaution, you understand."

"Why would they come after me? I don't know anything." Claudia smiled. "I get it: doctor saves damsel, doctor secretly falls in love with damsel, doctor will do anything to keep damsel from being harmed. Is that it?"

The scientist squirmed at the question. He remained unresponsive.

A somewhat surprised Claudia Morgan asked again. "Do you love me? You do, don't you; yes, you do!"

"I'll miss you greatly, Claudia." A flustered Sergei Trasker threw down his napkin and walked out of the room.

Lev and another man entered. "Madam, this is Timon. He will be with you all the time. Anything you need, just ask. I will have someone get your things ready early tomorrow. We will leave whenever you wish."

"And Sergei, will he come to say goodbye?"

"Boris is gravely ill. His mind is occupied with that. You will not see him again."

James opened the door and Grigorev stepped inside Potemkin's borrowed suite. For an instant there was a nonverbal exchange between the two. How could James be friendly to the man who kidnapped him? This was not the time to settle old scores. James showed the Russian into the room where the professor was waiting.

"Please, sit," the professor invited. "I'm having some tea. Would you care for some?"

Grigorev was on his guard. The unusual cordiality, especially in light of what had just happened, confused him. What was the reason for the professor's remarkable about face?

"I need your help. I have told the embassy I wish to stay one more month. After that, I will be returning to the motherland. But I cannot leave without seeing Sergei. I desperately need his notes to complete my research." Potemkin took a cube of sugar, placed it in his mouth and sipped some tea. "Will you help me?"

"What I am hearing? Professor Potemkin asking for my help? I'm going to have a heart attack.

You treated me so despicably the last few times I was here, even before I kidnapped James. I serve the same motherland as you. You have no right to treat me like that." Grigorev was angry. It subsided. He sighed.

"All right, I'll help. It seems we both want the same thing; cooperating may bring the success we couldn't achieve operating independently."

Now it was the professor's turn. "Thank you. How can we accomplish this? I'm sure you have thought about it a great deal."

"There are several plans I've been considering. Unfortunately, my last attempt failed. I lost some good men as did our Canadian brethren. The men I sent to do the job were not that capable. That will not happen again. I will choose my people more carefully."

"Why don't you tell me what you know and I will do the same. Perhaps by pooling what we know we can find a solution to our dilemma."

Grigorev was anxious to begin the exchange.

Lev drove Timon and Claudia Morgan back to her condominium and helped them with the bags.

Morgan had the few changes of clothing Lev had purchased and some personal items, nothing else.

Timon on the other hand, carried a small bag with his clothing while Lev carried a heavy bag containing the guard's weapons and ammunition. Claudia thought to comment, but decided it might be better if she didn't.

Soon everything was in place. Timon would be sleeping on the couch. Lev insisted Claudia sleep with a pistol under her pillow. He gave the woman a two-minute seminar on how to grasp the weapon, release the safety, point it and fire. Claudia was a good student. Satisfied he had done all he could, the chief guard left.

"Can I make you some tea?" Claudia asked.

"Thank you," Timon replied.

Soon, the TV was on and the two settled in for a quiet evening. Her guard watched the shows while she retreated to her office. She had written down much of what she had heard while at the estate.

One word, Fibonacci, gnawed at her. How does the Italian come into the picture? Recalling her school days and statistics class, she began reciting the mathematician's ratio: 1,2,3,5,8,13,21; the forward number being the sum of the two preceding. When she got to four number values, she stopped. Claudia couldn't imagine or even invent any relationship between the Italian mathematician's ratio and Trasker's breakthrough.

Her thoughts turned to the gel. Amniotic fluid; what was that all about? She was at a loss to form even the most elementary concept about it. Having experienced enough excitement for one day, she bathed and went to bed.

Dirk Spanner opened a new account at the Federal Savings Bank and deposited the check Janus Karper had given him. The teller cautioned that it would have to clear before any withdrawals could be made and that it might take as long as four business days.

"See to it that the money's available in two. I have a lot going on." Spanner ordered.

The seven Spanner had chosen for the operation served with him in the military. He knew them all personally and had taken pains to keep in touch, occasionally organizing a trip to Yankee Stadium, or Belmont Race Track. To a man they all were dissatisfied with civilian life. On more than one occasion the topic of conversation turned to discussing 'the big one,' the ultimate op that would make them all rich.

The soil had been fertile for a long time; now Spanner had the seed. Only one of the men, Philip Remsen, lived outside the Greater New York Area. He lived in Manchester, Vermont. Spending almost an entire evening, Spanner was able to contact all of them and arrange to meet in front of the Metropolitan Museum of Art cafeteria. Remsen, away on business in the northern part of Vermont said he might be late, but that he definitely would be there.

Two days later, all seven had arrived. Reunited, they went to lunch, consuming cafeteria fare in one of the many small eateries in the Borough of Manhattan. They reminisced about old times. When the meal was over, Spanner suggested the group go for a walk in Central Park. It seemed like a good idea; the day was sunny with a mild breeze blowing from the south. The mood was festive.

"Let's stop here." Spanner sat down on a bench. The group formed a circle and drew near. "This is the big one, guys. I can't tell you all the details, but if we can do this, each of you will get at least a couple of hundred grand; more, if I can get it." Everyone seemed excited by the proposal. "If you're still interested, I've got a more private place we can talk." Anticipating the need, Spanner had already rented a suite at a three star hotel.

Once inside, Spanner retrieved the brown leather briefcase he had left in the closet. Dialing the combination, he pressed the release and opened it. He thumbed through several sheets and retrieved the ones he needed.

He gave the first one to Remsen, a former Black Hawk helicopter pilot. Remsen was to obtain a light plane for reconnaissance and afterward a helicopter for the mission.

Sheet number two was for Ronnie Johnson, a former sergeant and weapons expert. It was his job to obtain the necessary firepower for the mission. Spanner emphasized the group might have to use tear gas or stun grenades.

Master Sergeant Carlo Batelli was a demolitions expert. Spanner showed him a plan of the estate and then left it for him to select the appropriate explosives if there were any obstacles that he felt needed to be breached.

Specialist Sean McCarra was the electronics guru. He envisioned needing night vision goggles, and strobe lights. McCarra suggested several infra-red devices. He also suggested they carry electronics to disrupt motion detection devices. Spanner concurred.

Angel Romero and Herbie Karl were the transportation specialists. Spanner had not yet decided whether it would be safer to fly in by helicopter or mount an assault by vehicle. Until that decision was made, he directed the two to look for three used Hummers in good condition.

Sam Kosky was the communications man. He would receive and relay all messages between the players from this point forward. It was up to him to provide everyone with cell phones and code words to disguise the topic being discussed. Because of terrorism, authorities most likely were monitoring all calls.

"Rem, let me know when you get your hands on a light plane. We need to do some recon. I want to evaluate the target as soon as possible."

"Give me a couple of days."
"You've got one."

Sergei Trasker stood silently at his brother's side. It was not going well. The monitor screens that surrounded the bed reinforcing his findings. Despite all that Sergei had done for him, Boris' health was not improving. It was a warning. If Boris did not get better, when would he start to get worse? The scientist racked his brain, digging deep into his past experience and medical knowledge. Perhaps a different protocol might turn the tide. Had he neglected something in the treatment? Had a wrong quantity of a drug been administered? He and Lev had worked feverishly to prepare everything for Boris' regeneration. Had they somehow erred? The thought that annoyed him most was the possibility that the combination of bacteria and compounds were reacting in an unprecedented manner and birthing an unknown organism. He had a strong suspicion but refused to acknowledge its existence.

As if the present entanglement was not enough, he was also tormented by the possibility that Claudia Morgan might be abducted by Grigorev and become the next person needing to be rescued. True, he had assigned Timon as her protector, but was that enough? The scientist's discomfort was becoming palpable.

"Sergei." Boris called out to his brother. The scientist leaned over and whispered into his brother's ear. "You're going to be fine," he said, "in a few weeks, we'll be playing cards again."

Boris smiled weakly, and then fell back to sleep. Trasker wept. Did he suspect?

Janus Karper was a sleeper, one of those agents sent by the Russians to the United States as a young man to infiltrate American society. Trasker met him in Riga while they were still young men. Both were on the fast track to success, Sergei went to Kiev and then Moscow to continue his studies, while Janus went to Tashkent to receive his final training before heading to the United States. Sergei never did learn his comrade's real name.

Karper's initial thrust was to graduate from an American college. He received his four year degree from Duke University, and likewise his Master's in Political Science. Striking out into the business world, Karper eventually gained employment in the federal government. It was a dead end. He was unable to gain access to top secret documents.

A security-for-hire firm seemed to be the answer. What better way to gain access to information than be hired to protect the very same documents others wished to pilfer? Industrial espionage became the legitimate sister to the theft of government information. Triple I was the ogre Karper created to accomplish those objectives.

Both Markov and Grigorev were under his command without knowing it. All directives were delivered by courier or other clandestine non-electronic means. Because of this reticence to use any wireless device, Karper succeeded in obscuring his identity to his minions, as well as eavesdropping enemies. But now, because of Markov's bungling, he had no choice but to become more involved and risk exposure. Karper decided to begin using a cell phone; not his own, but a throw away. He had his secretary secure him several, each from a different store.

Time was slipping by. Potemkin needed to know how far Trasker's research had advanced and be able to use that knowledge to continue his work at home. He couldn't remain in the United States forever.

The nut had to be cracked, no matter the risk. Karper would have to shed his cloak of invisibility and become personally involved. He was uncomfortable about that.

Sergei Trasker had taken great pains in selecting the personnel he hired to guard the estate and its treasures. Timon was no exception. He was skilled in weaponry and took great pride in his ability to size up a situation and make the appropriate preparations to ensure success. Scrutinizing Claudia Morgan's condo, he identified the likely points of entry and then, the most unlikely. He concentrated on the latter.

Those were the ones he would choose if he wished to invade the premises. The guard had also included a number of flash and stun grenades in his bag of paraphernalia. Trip wires and attachment hardware were a given. Of course he was heavily armed, packing adequate ammunition. He wore cutting-knife-ware as reserve.

Each night, well after Claudia Morgan had retired, Timon set trip wires and flash grenades near the front door, windows, balcony, service door, and even the refuse dumbwaiter. Rising early, he would remove them before his charge awakened. The one exception to this protocol was the device placed at the window in Claudia's bedroom. There, he rigged a special non-explosive surprise for the unsuspecting intruder. It was aimed directly at the window and triggered by a tripwire set across its opening. Claudia was instructed not to go near the window under any circumstances. The guard slept on the sofa and she in the bedroom. The door between the two rooms remained open.

"Any news on Markov?" Santoro asked McCann. "The city is a big place. He could be anywhere.

Now that we've flushed him, he'll be super cautious, not like some amateur. He's good, Frank, really good. I don't like him, but I have to respect the way he operates. We'll have to be a little lucky to bag him."

"I know. We've got resources. But then, so does he. The only thing we know about him is that he's committed to getting Trasker spill what he knows. Now that Boris is out of play, whom else might he use as currency?" Santoro looked at McCann. They both came to the same conclusion. "The girl, what about the girl?" Santoro was the first to voice their thoughts. "Claudia Morgan - that's right - and he likes her. But does he like her that much," McCann questioned.

"It's worth a shot. Let's go see her. Maybe it's nothing, or maybe we're on to something. Where is she now?"

"She's probably home, or on the way; that's my guess."

"Rats, with this traffic, we won't be there until dark, or even later."

"Want to use the siren?"

"And tell the whole world we're rushing into lower east Manhattan to chase a hunch? Not on your life," Santoro barked back.

"If that's the case, why don't we get a bite and let the traffic die down. I could use some Pastrami."

"On rye with deli mustard; that's the first good idea you had today."

McCann led the way. "I always get raw onions," he added.

"I have two men. You can't come. Stay here, in your apartment." Grigorev knew Potemkin wanted to participate in what was about to occur. The professor assumed they were going to abduct Sergei. The Russian spy instead was planning to abduct Claudia Morgan.

"As you wish." Potemkin shot a glance at James. A slight nod indicated he understood. The Russian left.

"What do you want to do?" James asked. "We could follow them, but if they find out we are, how would they react?"

"If they are successful in getting Sergei, it might be the last chance I'll get to see him. You know how that one lies."

"I thought you two agreed to cooperate with each other."

"Like Lenin cooperated with Trotsky?"

"I'll get the car."

"Too late, they'll be gone by the time you get to the garage. Wait, I'll call him. I'll say I have something important to tell him. That will give you time to get the car out of the garage and into the street. After I talk with him, I'll walk downstairs and wish him good hunting."

James slung his jacket over his shoulder and bolted out of the room.

"Grigorev, I have something important to tell you. You haven't left yet, have you? Good; come up, it will only take a few minutes. No, it can't wait. Didn't we agree to cooperate? I thought I heard you say we would. Good; I'll see you soon."

"Sergei," Boris whispered, waking him from a deep sleep. Even the uncomfortable chair he sat in could not deflect his need for rest. Try as he might, he could not find the reason Boris was not responding to the scientist's miraculous treatment as he had in the past. That nagging alternative kept surfacing.

"How are you, brother?" The question was academic. The patient's color and skin condition announced that all was not well.

"This is the third time, Sergei, the third. You gave me life twice before."

"I will, again."

Boris rolled slowly to the right, then left. "You know, the first time I was happy you saved me.

But the second, I was a little sad you did not leave me as I was. I think this time, maybe you should let me go. What do you think?"

Tears welled up in the scientist's eyes. "I will not let you go, Boris. No I won't. I won't."

Ping! A bell indicating a test being performed on one of the machines sounded. Sergei Trasker arose, went over to it and read the paper printout. He returned to his brother's bedside. Paper in hand, he read its results to Boris.

"What does that mean?"

"The gel is not creating the expected changes in your stem cells. It means I might not be able to cure you using the methods I know. Boris, you're going to die unless I can find. . ."

"Do you believe in God?"

"No."

"I didn't either until that second time, when you saved me again. I didn't want to come back. I was happy where I was. I was going to chastise you for what you did, but I couldn't. You loved me so much. But now, I'm telling you; even if you find a way, let me be; let me be, please."

The scientist gently stroked his brother's forehead, and then placed a kiss where his hand had been. "I understand," he answered, his voice cracking.

"We're being followed; ever since we left Potemkin's building," The driver mentioned.

"It's the professor and his valet," Grigorev explained. "They think we are going to get Sergei. If they want to follow us, let them. What harm can it do? Just go slow enough for them to be able to stay up."

"Yes, sir," the driver answered.

"That Potemkin, he's a valuable man, you know. I wish we had more like him."

Grigorev's car slowed a bit, as did the car behind them.

The Russian's plan was simple and straightforward; abscond with Claudia and hold her ransom.

This time there would be no medical issue or ploy to weaken his hold. He would put it plainly to Sergei:

It's the research or the girl. If you refuse, she will spend the rest of her life somewhere in Russia tamping down blacktop pavement or breaking stones. And it will be your fault. Well, what will it be? Grigorev rehearsed his ultimatum time and time again until he knew it by heart.

For him it was a form of entertainment. At last he would trump Sergei. Victory would be sweet.

Dirk Spanner's phone vibrated. "Oh, it's you. Yes, Janus, it's all going according to plan. We'll be going in soon. Please don't call again. This is the fourth time this week and its only Tuesday. Look, I've got a lot of things to do and you're only getting in the way. Call me after the weekend."

"I'm told your boy didn't go to school today; it was the flu or something else that made him stay home. That's so sad. Children need their education."

"Karper, if you touch one hair on my children's head or hurt my wife. . ."

"Lisa, isn't that her name? She missed her appointment with the hairdresser. It seems her car wouldn't start. Automobiles, they can be so unreliable sometimes, don't you think?"

"You bastard!"

"I told you when you took this assignment that it was important to me. While you're out there doing what I want, Dirk, remember Vanderbilt at GAO and what happened to his family."

"When I get done with this, I'm going to kill you!"

"No you won't. And do you know why? I know where your Achilles' heel is; it's your family.

Hurry along, little worm, the clock is running."

The pressure exerted by Karper forced Spanner to panic and cut short his preparation. It would have been better to wait until he and his men knew exactly how many guards were patrolling the estate and what their routines were. But now, with 'bastard' threatening his family, the leader made a to-hell- with-it decision and moved up the timetable. To hell with the guards, his men would neutralize them wherever they were. To hell with everything, the job had to be done, and, regardless of the toll it took on his people, he would get it done. I'll deal with that scum later, he promised himself.

Spanner decided to overfly the estate one last time. It would be his fourth. Because of the abbreviated timeline, it would be today at midday, generally not a good time due to the changing of guards, and the vehicular movement observed on previous, higher altitude observations.

This time Spanner decided to go by helicopter. It would be slower, and that would give him more time to observe those on the ground and the terrain around the main house. He also wanted to get a closer look at the pillbox structure. He assumed that was the laboratory.

But pilot Remsen told Spanner reconnoitering in a helicopter wouldn't be a good idea. It was much louder than a light plane, announcing its nearing long before it came into sight.

Spanner ignored his friend's advice.

"Krilyah," one of the guards shouted on his cell phone. The word meant 'wings.' Lev, in the main house at the time the alarm was given, stepped over to the window and scanned the sky for the intruder.

The helicopter, flying low and slow, was obviously surveying the estate. Lev decided to get a closer look.

Tilting the high-power telescope in the living room toward the inquisitive bird, he spotted the passenger using binoculars.

All of the guards had taken cover according to previous instructions. Spanner was unsuccessful in obtaining a significant part of the information he needed for a successful raid.

Now Lev was on alert. He contacted Sergei, who was just leaving his laboratory. "We might be having guests, perhaps as soon as tonight. What do you suggest?"

"Let them come; do not engage them. Make sure they find the passageway leading to the laboratory." The long corridor was a trap. Once the invaders were inside, sensors automatically locked the bulletproof doors at each end. The occupants were then gassed and rendered unconscious.

"Should I make the signs large?"

"Don't be too obvious or they will suspect something."

"Is there anything else?"

"Come down as soon as you can, I have an idea." Sergei went back into the lab and resumed his search for the answer that would save his brother.

Spanner and Remsen called the group together that afternoon. "We're going tonight. Meet here at eleven. I'll have more for you then."

Remsen was concerned. "Shouldn't we wait a few days? They must have seen us hovering and circling around. Why not wait a week? By then, they may have dropped their guard."

"We're going in. It's about the cash. I want it as soon as I can get it."

For all the training and expertise Dirk Spanner possessed, his decision to press forward with the house invasion so soon after the flight overrode every instinct he had worked so diligently to develop. A thousand little voices plagued his consciousness. Each one in its own way was saying don't do this, it's too soon, you don't have enough information. Many other iterations had the same theme; you're making the wrong decision. Spanner ignored them all. Whether he was driven by the fear that Janus Karper would make good on his threat and hurt his family or feeling that the sooner he completed the mission and bid goodbye to his sociopathic boss the better, one can only guess. But whatever the reason, Dirk Spanner was a driven man. Even Remsen's very obvious good advice did not cause the revision in his thinking it should have. The rest of the group noticed the change in the leader but no one challenged him. It was the money. So what if the risk was a little higher? They could handle it, couldn't they?

Claudia Morgan was sound asleep. She never heard the glass cutter making the circular pattern on her bedroom window. After popping out the disc, the assailant placed it on the concrete ledge where he was perched. He removed his belaying line. Holding the window sash with one hand, he reached in with the other to unlock the window. Too late he felt the snap of the trip wire. The projectile Timon rigged came blasting through the window, sending the would-be assailant and window parts to the sidewalk far below.

Claudia's guard heard the ruckus and quietly rolled over onto the floor. He looked under it, searching for feet coming from the balcony window. There were two. The intruder turned and started toward the bedroom. Timon downed him with two short bursts from his Kalashnikov. Claudia screamed.

He raced into the bedroom and whispered "We are leaving." It took the woman less than a minute to don a blouse, slacks and shoe herself. "That way," He whispered as he pointed to the service door.

The pair slipped out.

Grigorev, the one who had belayed the 'window man' into position, heard the commotion. He couldn't determine what was happening from his present position, so he decided to take the stairs and descend to Claudia Morgan's floor.

James and Potemkin were waiting outside in their car, expecting Grigorev and his minions to emerge with the Morgan woman. James had concluded that they were headed for her condo about halfway through the trip. The professor was disappointed it was not Sergei, but he was mature enough to know there was more than one road that led to Rome.

Another vehicle pulled up in front of the building and two men stepped out. Neither the professor nor his valet recognized them.

James and Potemkin leaned over, making it appear their car was empty.

"The 911 came from here? This is where that Morgan woman lives, Let's get up there," Santoro commanded.

McCann nodded. Both men raced through the lobby and took the elevator.

Grigorev had descended to the Morgan floor. Cautiously, he opened the stairway door and entered the small landing. The door leading to the condo was closed. Extracting a set of tools from his pocket he picked the lock and entered. The apartment was empty except for his dead comrade lying on the living room floor. The shattered window in the bedroom told the entire story of what had happened to man number two.

The Russian agent looked out of the window to the sidewalk below. A crowd had already formed.

He heard the sirens of approaching police. It was time to go. He would take the elevator. As he moved toward its doors, they opened to reveal Santoro and McCann.

"Stop, police!" Santoro shouted as both officers drew their pistols. Grigorev drew his first, and fired. Santoro felt a severe thud and then a mounting ache in his shoulder. As his partner sank to the elevator floor, McCann fired five rounds at the shooter. Grigorev fell forward with three bullets in his heart, the fourth below, the fifth above. McCann ran over, kicked the gun away and checked the Russian's condition. Then he returned to his partner.

"Frank, Frank!" McCann shouted, "Where is it?"

"Here, my shoulder; I think he missed the artery."

McCann removed a handkerchief from his pocket, shoved it under Santoro's coat and commanded "Hold this down-tight." Santoro nodded.

McCann requested an ambulance for a 'police officer down', then dialed the coroner's office and indicated there was a corpse to be processed. To his surprise, he found out they were already at the scene processing a 'jumper' at the same address. McCann made Santoro comfortable and then headed for the Morgan condo. Intruder number one was still on the living room floor. McCann checked for a pulse.

There was none. He entered the bedroom and surveyed the window. This guy was no jumper, he thought, he was invited to leave. McCann too, glanced out the window to the scene below. They must have come to get her, he mused. Did they succeed?

He followed the ambulance carrying Santoro to the hospital. It turned out the wound, though serious, was not life threatening. After the ambulance left, Professor Potemkin and James decided to go home. With all the tumult, they deduced Grigorev could not have succeeded. Minutes before, James had made his way through the crowd and recognized the body on the sidewalk as one of Grigorev's men.

Mission failed, mission over, he whispered to himself.

With his thumb on the safety of his automatic weapon, Timon sat in the back seat scanning the road. Claudia guided her car at high speed but carefully up FDR Drive. The object was to get to the estate as soon as possible, and with as little fanfare as possible. Several minutes passed and the guard relaxed.

"No one following. Just the same, I watch." The woman owed her safety to the soft-spoken man in the back seat. There was no time for it now, but she told herself she would thank him properly when they got to where they were going. She wondered how many others in the past had benefited from his protection.

"Whose men do you think they were?"

"I never see them before; could be anybody. All kind of people after Sergei's secret; Russians, Americans, hooligans, maybe even Chinese, who knows?"

Claudia knew that word, hooligan. To the Russians, it was a distasteful description of those who went around 'making trouble.' She thought the guard might be describing an independent, non- governmental group in business for their own personal profit. She had never considered that. If they were after Sergei's secrets, what did they want with her; to hold her as ransom the way they did Boris, the brother? But why choose her? She recalled the question she put to Sergei. He cares about me, she thought.

Claudia stepped on the accelerator.

"How's it going?" McCann asked. His boss looked tired; his face was drawn.

Santoro spotted the concern in his partner's face. "Getting shot when you're as old as we are is different. We need more time to heal. I'll be fine. What happened? Did they get the Morgan woman?"

"I'm not sure. I found another one shot to death in the living room. There was no blood or sign of any scuffle in the bedroom. Whoever was with her set up one hell of a booby trap. That guy trying to get through the window didn't have a chance. Two dead plus the one I killed could mean. . ."

"Someone was guarding her. Now who would care for her enough to assign protection?"

"If she and Lancelot did get away, they're probably heading for the estate. Should we try to cut them off?"

"They're probably safer there than anyplace else I can think of. For now, let them be."

"I'll do the background check on the dead guys." McCann reached out and grasped Santoro's hand. "Hey, get better, will you? I have no one to go with me for Pastrami."

"I'm on a regular diet, you know. You couldn't. . ." Santoro winked.

"Is tomorrow okay?"

Folly

Ted Wagner had his bout with being impulsive a number of years ago. Generally speaking, he had gotten the better of it. But how can a person restrain himself when $4,000,000 is involved? If Claudia had suddenly found religion and wouldn't steal the goods, then why shouldn't he do the job and get the four million? So what if there were guards? So what if there was an eight foot high fence surrounding the place? He could do it, he knew he could.

Ted Wagner began to take inventory. Speaking out loud made everything more plausible. "I'll need a rope, say, 16 feet long. I already have black clothes; they'll do. I have plenty of gloves. Night vision goggles might be a good investment; I'll buy a pair. And, I'll need one more thing. . ."

Wagner opened the top drawer of his armoire and moved aside a few sweaters. The Colt Marksman .22 caliber pistol was still there. Some time ago he had pilfered it while stealing documents from a CEO of a chemical company. Wagner saw it as his trophy for a mission successfully completed.

He even went out and purchased extra clips and bullets.

Late that evening he placed everything he needed for the mission on the bed. It's all here, he mused. Admiring himself in the mirror he liked what he saw; a person dressed in black who resembled a Ninja warrior. Wagner collected his equipment. He placed the pistol in the right pocket of his jacket. The extra clips went in the left. Just in case, he told himself, something unexpected came up.

He was feeling lucky. He was already in the process of choosing how large a yacht he might like.

The mind game helped assuage the panic he was experiencing.

Sergei Trasker ran outside as soon as he heard the car coming up the drive. The guard had called while in transit and explained what had happened. As soon as the door swung open and Claudia stepped out of her car, she found herself in his arms. This time she returned his embrace.

"Thank heavens you're safe. I would have never forgiven myself. . ."

"Your Timon is a very brave man. If it weren't for him, you may have had to deal with another. kidnapping. This is the second time you saved my life." Her tone expressed a sense of connectedness.

Events were changing expectations and drawing the two closer and closer together.

The scientist was embarrassed by her gratitude. "Good work, Timon," the scientist praised, "Please get Lev; we'll be in the laboratory"

The guard nodded, acknowledging the compliment, and left.

"We may be getting visitors tonight. I'll take you down to the laboratory," Sergei announced, "you'll be safe there." The scientist paused, as if giving a matter some thought. "It's time." Before she could respond Sergei firmly grasped Claudia's arm.

As they walked through the house, the Great Dane approached. Trasker pointed his finger at the beast and said, "Basil, guard!" The dog ran ahead of the pair and stationed himself at the entrance to the laboratory. "He knows all the guards, and, you. Anyone else trying to enter will have to confront him."

Claudia glanced at Basil. He was a huge muscular beast and if ever a Great Dane could exhibit determination, Basil was the one. She pitied the person who challenged him.

Claudia accompanied Sergei to Boris. She gasped a when she saw the brother. He had the appearance of a balloon losing its air. His life force seemed to be leaving him. The scientist, seeing the reaction, glanced at her. His unspoken message was clear. She summoned up a smile and quickly said,

"Hello, I'm Claudia Morgan. I understand you're Boris, Sergei's brother; hi." Boris' returning smile was weak but showed effort. Beautiful Claudia was having the intended effect; a positive response.

"I was in that contraption just before you came. It worked wonders for me. I'm sure it will do the same for you."

Boris, silent, turned away. This time there was no smile.

"We must go now; Boris needs his rest," The scientist exclaimed. Claudia glanced his way and saw Sergei doing a poor job of holding back tears. "Yes, let's go," she agreed.

The pair went to Sergei's desk, located in the more remote reaches of the lab. The dogs Ping, Pang, and Pong were there, sitting stone-still. "Energize," the scientist commanded. Suddenly, the dogs became animated. Tails wagging, the three engaged in short bursts of running and cavorting for several minutes. "Sit," Sergei ordered. The three stopped wherever they were and sat. Speechless, and perhaps a bit terrified, Claudia Morgan stared at the man beside her.

"Think of an army, no, ten armies, and having that kind of control over them. Now do you see why they want what I have? And I have more, much more."

"But they're only dogs. Can you do that with humans?"

"Correction; what you see is one dog. The other two are as the first, and I am their midwife."

"You mean you cloned them?"

The scientist turned to one of the Yorkshire Terriers and said, "Pang, jump." The dog flipped.

"Pang, jump twice." The dog flipped twice, sat, waiting for the next command.

"Alright, that's great, but they're just robots. What's the good of that?"

"They are robots who can never die. When they are wounded, they can be restored. All I need is a scrap of their DNA. That was how Potemkin. . ." The scientist stopped short.

Claudia sensed the dismay. She touched his arm and asked "How Potemkin what?"

"How Potemkin restored me."

"Restored you?"

"I'm not like you."

"What happened back there; what happened in Russia?""

"They wanted to know how far my research had progressed. I wouldn't tell them, so they tortured me, in ways you cannot imagine. I developed an infection, and, being as weak as I was, it spread. And, no matter what they did, I kept growing worse. Potemkin asked them to let him try to save me. Of course, he and I had learned quite a bit about the techniques I used on you, but I kept the key elements to myself. He restored me without actually knowing all of the details. He turned the knobs, made the injections and pressed the buttons. I knew what was happening, and what the compounds were. That is why he needs to see me now. He wants those answers. I have advanced my research immeasurably since that time. He has no idea what I have achieved." Trasker frowned. "And, perhaps more than I dared imagine."

"Is that when you decided to leave?"

"Yes, I couldn't see them having access to that kind of information. In fact, I wonder if there is anyone I can trust." Sergei Trasker stared at Claudia.

"The pharmaceuticals offered Triple I $40,000,000. What you have is worth ten thousand times more than that. Whoever controls this technology will, in time, control everything."

"Isn't that frightening?"

Claudia did not respond.

Ted Wagner glanced at his watch. It was after midnight; time to go. Night vision goggles made finding the way to the fence surrounding the estate easy. He decided that climbing the fence, getting past the guards and into the house were problems to be confronted as he encountered them. His was the most daring of all raids; mounting an assault without a plan. Inordinate greed makes fools of us all, and he, for all his savvy and cunning, was no exception. A more rational person would have seen the futility of what he was attempting, but the Triple I manager disregarded every instinct that was warning him to abort his quixotic misadventure.

Already in a heightened state of security, the guards had no trouble spotting the intruder and his movements. His behavior indicated that he was unskilled, a novice. Lev, in the main house, watched the man clad in black bumble across the large lawn, and wondered why he had attempted this intrusion alone.

Only assassins and petty thieves were known to work alone. Was he here to murder his master? The thought brought Lev to his feet. Taking his weapon with him, he hurried to the second floor balcony and concealed himself behind the balustrade. Turn on the spotlights, he texted.

Suddenly, the exterior of the estate was awash with light. Not only did it reveal Wagner, but it exposed Spanner's approaching helicopter, suddenly shooting in from the wall of darkness surrounding the estate.

"What the hell is he doing down there?" Spanner said. "Don't know," replied Remsen, "but this is no place for us." Remsen banked the craft around and headed for home. "Abort, mission abort,"

Spanner screamed through the radio. The men in the approaching hummers heard the message in time and reacted as ordered.

Confused and frightened by the lights and then the helicopter, Wagner took out his pistol and began firing at the helicopter. When blackness once again engulfed the departing craft, he turned his attention to those on the ground. His was a pyrrhic decision, to fight, without cover, against men armed with automatic weapons, well-concealed, and far better shots than he.

Lev put his sniper rifle's crosshairs on the intruder and fired. Wagner collapsed.

"When are you going to get out of that bed?" McCann chided. "Come on, get up."

"The doc says I can go home tomorrow, no lifting, no pulling and no hanging around with shady characters."

"I was going to tell you something, wise guy, but now I'm not going to."

"Tell me; I wouldn't be able to sleep if I knew you knew something I didn't."

"Someone tried to get into Trasker's home last night. They shot him. He's still in surgery."

"Is he going to make it?"

"I think so. You'll never guess who it was."

"Okay, who was it?"

"It was that Wagner guy. He got in over the fence. He was dressed in black and get this, he was armed."

"No."

"He had a .22 caliber pistol. Can you just imagine him holding off all those guards with that peashooter? Oh, and there's something else."

"What else?"

"When the lights went on, there was a black helicopter hovering overhead. They don't know whose it was, but it was there, all the same."

"Do you think it was backup for Wagner?"

"No, I don't think he's into that kind of planning. I'd say he was operating by the seat of his pants. It looks as if he might have been the first girl at the prom. He ruined the dance for the second."

"Someone else was going in? Who could that be?"

"I don't know. You said we didn't know all the players. It looks like you were right."

"Help me get up. I'm getting out of here."

"The doc said tomorrow."

"I'm not going to miss one more second of this. Besides, I'm getting sick from all the flowers.

Help me get my arm through this sling. There, I'm ready to go. Nurse, nurse, I'm leaving."

"I thought you said you were going tonight. What happened?" Janus Karper angrily asked.

"Someone beat us to it. When we got there, the place was all lit up. I saw one guy. I don't know how many more there were."

"Did they get in? Do you have any idea who they were?"

"From what I could see, they were discovered long before they got to the house. Trasker's men probably rounded up the rest. We'll have to lay low for a while. They'll be on high alert. We won't stand a chance now," Spanner observed.

"But I promised my client I would meet with them soon. I can't postpone that meeting. I would look like a fool. They'll find someone else."

"Look, Janus, I can do this. Just give me a chance. Let's wait a few days and let things calm down. Give me 48 hours. I'll try then."

"Don't fail me, Dirk. I won't tolerate it."

"Call me in three days. I'll have something for you. Count on it." Spanner hung up. He was sweating.

"Are you going to press charges?" Ted Wagner looked distraught. His wound was not life-threatening.

Lev had decided to spare him, though not for any reason of benevolence. He wanted Wagner alive. Dead men can't be questioned. Sitting up in bed and staring at Santoro and McCann, he was out of options. He noticed the policeman's wound. "What happened to your arm?"

"A honey bee stung me. I had a reaction," Santoro replied. McCann shot a glance at his partner.

Santoro's lips curled a bit in the reply.

"Who was in this with you? Who were the men in the helicopter? Come on, speak up."

"No one was with me. I was alone. I was surprised as anyone to see the damned thing come out of the dark. Believe me, I was alone."

"Where'd you get the pistol? You don't have a permit for it. Where'd you get it?"

"I borrowed it."

"Who lent it to you?"

"Alright, alright, I stole it when I was robbing some papers from a competitor."

"Did you really think that toy would be of any help to you against the firepower of Trasker's guards? Were you crazy? They could have cut you up into dog meat. Are you that stupid?"

"Karper said he'd kill me if I didn't get Trasker's papers. What was I to do? I had to try to get them."

Santoro took pity on the idiot and softened his tone. "Who the hell is this Karper guy?"

"Janus Karper, he's the chief executive of Triple I, the company I work for."

"Do you know of anyone else he hired to invade the estate?"

"No, I don't. Wait; there was someone else I saw. He was just leaving his office as I entered.

Karper seemed nervous, as if he didn't want me to see him. But I don't know who he is. I never saw him before."

"Bob, get a shield to stay here in the hall. I think we have to protect this bird. After he gets here, you and I are going to see Trasker. He might need our help."

McCann nodded. "I'll also call the chief and bring him up to date."

"That's a good idea. You never know, we might end up needing a S.O.R.T. in addition to a swat team."

"This isn't a multiple murder case, it's a war."

"You got that right," Santoro agreed.

The police officer got out of the elevator and headed toward the room. McCann briefed him.

The two detectives went on their way.

"You heard me; I want at least one team ready, on 24 hour call. No, keep at least one team in the house. When will something happen? I don't know, but, when it does, it will be big. Take my word for it.

Have your A team ready. We'll need the best we've got. That's all I've got for now, I'll keep you posted."

Chief Davis had given Bob Reilly, the SWAT team commander all the information he could entrust to him. The Chief had decided to handle the situation with local forces. McCann had phoned him and filled him in on the aborted one-man invasion of the Trasker estate. The added reference to the mysterious helicopter altered the playing field. Until the new would-be invaders were identified, the chief decided to keep all involved personnel on high alert.

Davis requested McCann and Santoro come to the office. In the meantime, he alerted Reilly to be battle ready at a moment's notice. He also commissioned a twin rotor helicopter to leave LaGuardia and be stationed at SWAT headquarters' helo pad. He hadn't informed his two lead investigators of these decisions, but he would; they were on the way. Eventually the door to the chief's office swung open and the two entered.

"What's up," Santoro asked as he and McCann sat down.

"It seems this little game has raised some eyebrows in high places. The triple deaths at Morgan's condo caused a few people in the State Department to take notice. I just spent an hour convincing some *grande fromage* that we were on top of things and that we could handle whatever came up. They were not happy, but they backed off. I've got Bob Reilly and SWAT on high alert for an indefinite period of time."

"Even if they were deployed, they could never get to the estate in time to be of any use."

"I have a twin rotor ready and waiting to take us wherever we want to go."

"Not bad, chief, not bad," McCann commented.

"Now, what do you think of the 'copter that showed up last night over the estate?"

"That was an eagle-eye for directing an assault. From the way Wagner described it, it was too small to carry more than four people at the most, and fully armed, maybe - maybe three. I think the main force was coming by car, or truck, probably three, maybe four," Santoro reasoned.

"What do you think about posting surveillance?"

"That's a good idea. Two patrol cars, one down the road say, three miles away, and one say, at a mile. That would be super."

"What would they be looking for?"

"They'd be trying to spot a caravan of two or more heavy trucks, pickups, or vans. The assault would most likely come late, maybe even pre-dawn. And, they'll be lined up like ducks in a row."

"Why do you say that," Chief Davis asked.

"It's the military way; once you get that stuff in your blood, it shows up in all kinds of ways. It's just like the British marching to battle row on row in those bright red coats. Stupid, but it was the way they did things then. I'd bet you twenty they come up the road one behind the other, with no one else in between."

Chief Davis sighed. "So what happens now?"

"We'll go to the estate tomorrow to see Trasker. I'm sure his men are armed and ready, especially after that numbskull tried to take them on single-handedly. But he did do them a favor; he thwarted a real assault that might have been in the making."

"I'll make the call and get those two cars in position."

"There's no rush. They know Trasker's people are on alert. They'll want to wait until the guards stand down. I'm guessing it will be three, maybe four days. After that, they'll try again."

"I'm sorry, really sorry, Claudia. I didn't know what I was doing. Janus made me crazy."

"Ted, did you really think he was planning to kill you?" Claudia asked sarcastically. "He wouldn't do that."

"You're lucky Lev didn't finish you off. He's a crack shot," Sergei Trasker explained.

"My shoulder is a mess. After I get better, I'm scheduled to have reconstructive surgery. They tell me it will be painful."

Wagner turned to Claudia. "You didn't see Janus when he mentioned getting rid of me. All he could think of was the money. People have killed other people for much less than that."

"You have a point," she replied.

"Once, I heard of a drunk who murdered his friend, another drunk, for a bottle of vodka. Either would certainly have murdered an entire village for the kind of money we're talking about." Sergei stepped closer to Ted Wagner. "Tell me about the helicopter."

"It was small. I saw two faces, the pilot and a passenger, reflected in the light. I don't think it could have held any more. As soon as the lights went on, it revved up, turned sharply, and sped back into the blackness. That's all I know."

"And, it wasn't hired by you?" pressed the scientist.

"No, no; I wanted to do this alone. I know it sounds crazy, but I felt I could do it. I knew where the laboratory was, and, if I could just slip by the guards. . ."

"And have Lev shoot you through the eye. You know, I believe you are mad." The scientist left the room.

"You brought this on yourself," Claudia Morgan observed.

Wagner lowered his head and closed his eyes.

"Hello, Sergei." It was Professor Potemkin. He was standing just inside the outer doors of the hospital.

The scientist froze. For an instant, the scene took on the appearance of figures in a wax museum; no one was moving. Finally, Sergei extended his hand, as did the professor. "Hello, old friend, it's good to see you." The scientist drew back. "Have you come to take me back to Russia?" Potemkin noticed two men behind him. Lev and Timon were moving closer, ready to take 'appropriate action,' if required.

"I want to know what you never told me," Potemkin demanded, "I want to take my proper place in history as one of the scientists who discovered the most profound secret known to mankind. You know I deserve that."

"And who will protect mankind after you and I are gone? What guarantee is there that it will not be misused?"

"That is for those who come after us to decide. Right now, it is our prize to share, to enjoy; what comes afterward is no concern of mine."

"You are coming with me. Lev, escort the professor to the car. Where is James? He can't be far off. Oh, there he is. Timon, bring him along. Don't worry, he won't resist. We are all old friends."

The two Guards and James commandeered a taxi while Potemkin, Morgan, and Trasker rode back in the estate vehicle.

The conundrum that faced Sergei Trasker was this: how much should he trust Constantine Potemkin? Certainly he could use the professor's help in the event he decided to try some untested procedure on Boris. But Potemkin was a colleague. Allowing him into the laboratory would provide him with the chance to see the equipment the scientist was using. He might even deduce how it was being used. Sergei Trasker wrestled with that question all the way home. Meanwhile, the professor and Claudia Morgan, sitting together in the back seat, managed to carry on a spirited conversation on a variety of subjects. It pleased the professor that the person he was engaging had such a robust background. Why, she even knew where Ossetia was.

"Here we are," Sergei Trasker commented.

"You have done well for yourself," the professor observed, "this building is even larger than our Commissar's home. Your Russian education has served you well."

"You mean my indenture." Trasker stared at Potemkin. The professor did not respond. "Claudia. show my good friend into the great room. I have to do something." The scientist rushed down to the laboratory.

At first blush Boris' condition seemed unchanged. But upon closer inspection, the scientist discovered something he could never have anticipated. After a more focused examination, his original suspicion was confirmed.

Glancing at the placard he had placed over his desk, he read it again. He had returned many times to this very place to read the excerpt for inspiration.

It has not escaped our notice that the specific pairing we have postulated immediately suggests a **possible copying mechanism** *for the genetic material.*

The authors were J. D. Watson and F. H. C. Crick. The excerpt was from their paper titled *Molecular Structure of Nucleic Acids*, published April 25, 1953, page 737 in Nature magazine. The scientists, along with their colleague M. Wilkins received the 1962 Nobel prize in Physiology or Medicine for their discovery of the molecular structure of DNA.

Trasker had added the bold type to what he felt were the significant words. At this, his latest reading, the statement seemed prophetic. He covered his eyes with his hands and exclaimed, "What have I done?"

An hour passed and Sergei Trasker had not returned from the lab. Claudia Morgan called Lev.

He was standing in the hall, just beyond the doorway. "Stay with the professor, will you? I'm going to see where Sergei is."

Claudia went directly to the laboratory. She surmised the worst had occurred; that Boris had died. It turned out that something akin to the reverse was true. Boris seemed to be improving. His face had taken on a roseate tint and he seemed calm, if comatose. Continuing her search, she found the scientist sitting at his desk, gazing into space. "Sergei, are you all right?" The woman repeated the question several times more before he responded.

"Where did you leave Potemkin?"

"Lev is with him. I came down to see whether you were all right. I thought the reason for the delay might have been that Boris. . ."

"Boris is fine; unfortunately too fine." Claudia couldn't discern whether the remark was sarcastic or fatalistic. It disturbed her.

"Let's not keep the good professor waiting any longer. Come, we'll see what he has to say."

Constantine Potemkin had been assessing his situation from every perspective. If his former colleague wouldn't cooperate, perhaps it was time to use force to obtain the necessary information. The professor was still unaware of Grigorev's death. He knew his minions had perished, but assumed their leader had not.

Potemkin knew Sergei Trasker didn't hold all the cards. The professor's ongoing research had uncovered several unintended consequences of their collaboration. In order to keep them secret it was he who ordered the deaths of Collins and the other three. Only two others received Trasker and Potemkin's restoration; Boris and Sergei after his torture in Moscow. The professor wondered whether Sergei, too, had discovered the same anomaly in his brother. Unknown to the professor he had, just moments ago.

When Sergei and Claudia returned, Lev resumed his position in the corridor.

"How was the conference?" The scientist asked.

"We all know so little, but when we speak to our colleagues, we try to convince them we know more than they do. In that way, all conferences are the same."

"But you came because you wanted to see me."

"I see your insight has not diminished. Yes, I came to the United States because of you."

Potemkin leaned forward. "It's time we joined forces again. There are some things I need to tell you about our work; effects we never dreamed might occur."

"I know all about them."

"Boris?"

"Yes."

Claudia Morgan might well have been an end table. She could not participate in the conversation because she had absolutely no idea what the two were talking about. About to burst from curiosity, she demanded "Would one of you please tell me what this is all about?" What she experienced instead was an icy glance from each. "Well! I'll see you later." The 24 gun frigate Morgan set full sail and tacked out of the room.

"Do you have any idea how this happened?" Potemkin asked.

"My research has advanced a great deal since I left Russia. Perhaps you don't know about my employment at Becker Pharmaceutical. Even though I spent some time there, I kept the true nature of my work hidden. The day they came to confiscate everything, I barely escaped."

"Becker works for the United States *and* the Soviet Union. I know everything about your time there. All I'm missing is the documentation of what you have achieved. That is why I have come and I am not leaving without it. It was I who ordered them to seize your papers."

"And the men who were murdered; was that you, too?"

"Dead men tell no tales. I couldn't risk anyone finding out about the unintended consequences of our work."

"You were so certain it would happen to them?"

"No, I wasn't, but I could not gamble."

"Those men are dead because of you? You saved their lives, and then you took it away; why?"

"I told, you, I could not risk discovery."

"You could have had them kidnapped; you could have made them disappear."

"I could not risk discovery."

"I brought you here because I thought you might help me with my work. I see now that was a mistake. You are not the person I once knew. You should go."

"I was always this way; you simply glossed over what offended you."

"Get out." The scientist nodded to Lev, who had already entered the room. "He will drive you and James home."

Over his shoulder Potemkin stated his case again, "I will get what I need, Sergei, you know I will."

Lev nudged the professor and they left. James had been detained and guarded in another room.

He joined the professor.

"Who was that, in that car," McCann asked.

"This place is getting to be like a train station. For such a secluded location it sure has a lot of traffic," Santoro responded.

As they pulled up to the gate, the guard recognized the pair and let them in without delay.

"That's a new one. We're getting VIP treatment," McCann noticed.

"Right; look in the rear view mirror. Do you see that vehicle with those two armed men behind us? I'd say they trust us a little more, but very little."

Sergei Trasker met the two at the front door. "I see you had guests," Santoro mentioned.

"Yes, that was Professor Potemkin and his valet James. He's also after my work. How's your shoulder?"

"It'll be good as new by Christmas, which one, I'm not sure." The remark drew a smile from the scientist.

"Can we go inside?" Santoro asked. He began to speak as soon as the front door closed.

"The way I see it, you're going to be assaulted by a force of some size and skilled in weaponry. I can't say how large, but it will be large enough to take on your personnel. I'm guessing this will occur within three weeks. Bob, here, and I have gone over this and we both feel the chances are good for an earlier rather than a later attempt."

"Lev and I came to the same conclusion. What do you suggest?"

"Chief Davis has a SWAT team at the ready. He also has positioned patrol cars at key intersections, ready to alert us when the group draws near. Do you know an Isaac Jurgens? He's a professor at Yeshiva."

"Is he one of the. . ." Santoro cut Trasker off. ". . . men who robbed the Russians? Yes, he is."

Santoro replied.

"Is he still alive?"

"Yes, he is," Santoro answered.

"He's on Potemkin's list. He's going to be murdered. You must protect him."

Santoro called Chief Davis. Davis ordered SWAT Team personnel to Jurgen's home.

The scientist seemed pleased. "There has been enough killing."

An hour passed. Santoro's cell vibrated. "Hello; yes Chief, I understand. They'll keep looking?

Good, yes, I'll tell Trasker."

"Jurgens; is he dead?" The scientist asked.

"He's missing. His wife says he didn't come home from university last night and he hasn't called."

Professor Potemkin sat stone still in his chair. Even James puttering about did not draw any reaction from the academic. He had gotten his wish; he met with Sergei Trasker. But the results he had hoped for, joining forces and collaborating again, weren't materializing. He had travelled so far and harbored such high hopes. And now, abject failure seemed to be his reward. The one ace he had, the chimera that was about to manifest itself in the last of the four men he had saved, was already known to his colleague. Now, there was nothing to bargain with. Grigorev mentioned in one of their conversations that Markov had killed three of them. Had he the fourth? Why hadn't Grigorev contacted Potemkin to update him? He was always making a pest of himself, why not now? Grigorev was dead, that was the reason, the professor concluded. There was no other answer. The police must have caught him escaping or, in the act, and shot him. Yes, that was it.

Regardless, the professor decided he would put his own plan in motion. He dispatched James to the embassy to find the names and addresses of the four men. James would visit the homes of each and determine whether the fourth was still alive. Perhaps there was, indeed, another ace in the deck.

Still, Potemkin would have to call off the dogs. How would he go about withdrawing the kill order? He didn't even know how to contact the assassin. Most embassy personnel knew nothing about covert operations. Which official did? The professor couldn't send James there asking 'Are you the director of covert operations' of everyone. Still, saving the life of the fourth man, if he was still alive, would give the professor an advantage. Potemkin had to try.

Janus Karper was agitated. What was wrong with Spanner? Why hadn't he made the assault?

Time was running out. The intercom buzzed. Karper pressed the incoming button. "It's Albert Moroka from Becker Pharmaceutical," his secretary said.

"Hello, Mister Moroka. It's good to - oh, you want to see me? Of course, that would be fine. The goods, we can talk about that when we meet. The telephones here are terrible; you can never tell who is listening. Tomorrow sounds fine; then two o'clock it shall be." Karper wiped the sweat from his brow with his handkerchief.

He had never spoken to Albert Moroka; any communication was always through an intermediary.

The fact that he called was in itself an event worthy of note. He understood; the Becker executive fully intended to complete the transaction no matter the cost or consequences. And he, Karper, was the pivotal player; the success or failure of the operation rested with him.

What would he say to Moroka when they met? He began to craft his reply. A little voice inside kept repeating, 'it's no use, it's no use,' but he overrode his panic. He remained confident. The CEO had been in similar situations before. His cunning and deception had saved him then, and he was sure they would now. After all, he had two highly skilled operatives attempting to obtain the same information.

Success was just a matter of time. One of them would succeed. He was sure of it. The question now was, how much more time would Moroka grant him?

Boris Trasker was improving. The reason for this change in condition was all too clear; an unimaginable consequence of his brother's treatment protocol. Brother Sergei had responded to the situation by barricading himself in his laboratory in an attempt to discover the reason for the anomaly.

Hour after hour he labored, refusing to eat, drink, or rest.

Exceptions to rules are problematic. They raise questions and, at times, challenge current lines of reasoning. And, always, there surfaces that nagging challenge; which is the rule and which is the exception? The first area the scientist reviewed was the makeup and potentialities of amniotic fluid. The research community had settled questions about the liquid, its constantly changing composition and function during gestation decades ago. Now, with Sergei Trasker's ability to extract stem cells from adipose, fatty tissue, and now the Boris challenge, several established concepts appeared in question. As his brother's condition demonstrated, a sea-change in paradigm was at hand.

The scientist brushed aside his concern about Boris, developing situation and focused on the unexpected chain of events that set it in motion. Once more he delved deeply into the data of the human genome the medical community had recently developed. As those who had created the atomic bomb also came to realize, they had opened an unintended door whose consequences they had not envisioned. Sergei Trasker was on a similar path.

Eventually, the scientist's physical needs overcame his intellectual desire to press on. As he closed his eyes, his thoughts drifted back to the time when he and mentor Potemkin shared their professional lives, hopes, and dreams.

It seemed to everyone concerned that master assassin Markov had vanished from the face of the earth. The police and their informants were unable to find him. His picture had been distributed to every law enforcement unit in New York City and adjoining counties. Foot police were on alert and patrol cars, moving along at a snail's pace, peered into as many faces of the walking public as they could. Such a massive manhunt should have reaped results. It did not. The adversary was too clever.

Whenever the Russian left his lair, he clothed himself as if homeless. He frequented soup kitchens and occasionally slept in city shelters. He had always harbored a secret penchant for the muses.

That was the reason he carried the faux Boris ruse off so expertly. Once again, his satchel filled with cosmetics, rouges, wigs, and the like were serving him well.

Anticipating such a scenario, Markov had selected and furnished a number of hideaways in different parts of the city. It was a part of his modus operandi as an assassin. Many of his prey were famous or influential people. It would follow then that once the targets were successfully eliminated the authorities would do everything in their power to apprehend him. He would hide in one sector while the police searched another. Once they moved on, he would return to the lair in that sector while they searched elsewhere. He had played this predator and prey game many times, always managing to elude them.

One of his lairs was in one of the below-street level storage rooms at Carnegie Hall. While hundreds of uniformed officers were searching everywhere, Colonel Markov was enjoying the venue being performed above on the Hall's acoustically magnificent stage.

Still, even the best strategies have their weaknesses. Carnegie Hall's docket advertised a scheduled performance of a world renowned Russian baritone. Markov felt this gifted singer not only had to be heard, but seen. No matter the risk, he decided to attend the performance.

Memories

Moscow's winter snows had begun. From this point forward, the city would receive this white sprinkling until the warming winds of spring chased the moisture-laden clouds away. To some, the never ending white tatted shawl would become Mother Moscow's defense against the dull, gray canopy that marked the cold, harsh winter.

Professor Constantine Potemkin surveyed his assistant asleep at the desk. There was much to observe. Ripped away from his Latvian homeland against his will, the victim seemed to have not only survived, but made the best of his unwelcome incarceration. His remarkable adjustment trumpeted how solidly he had been reared.

The aging professor had taken the young scientist under his wing at the request of the Soviet, the request itself a rare occurrence. The ruling body must have seen extraordinary promise in the young man, since it was well known that Professor Potemkin did not tolerate young assistants very well. Reports from the university must have been stellar.

"Wake up, my Latvian genius, the Central Committee did not send you here to sleep away the day. It was to learn, and someday realize the potential they believe you have."

Sergei Trasker awoke, and, with a start, stood up. "I'm sorry Professor Potemkin, I didn't intend to fall asleep. . ."

"Of course not, but don't you think working day and night might be a bit too much? What are you trying to accomplish?"

The young scientist did not answer. "I've fallen behind on the evaluations you wanted. I must get them done. They say you have a terrible temper." Trasker smiled as he slipped through the door to the adjoining room.

This last remark, which might have been interpreted by some as disrespectful, was just another indication of the mutual respect mentor and assistant had for each other. Sergei admired the dedication and unflinching devotion to detail the mature scientist exhibited, while his mentor saw in the young associate many of his own qualities. Each wished he was the other when they both, in fact, were.

Potemkin had played this game of cat and mouse for over four years with his young associate.

The obedient and skillful novice, had exceeded every demand the professor placed before him. Still, in those rare blocks of time when his superior had no need of him, his charge carried on his own research in secret, even returning to the lab late in the evening to continue his work.

Potemkin, impatient, decided it was time to end the stalemate. First, because he was tired of the cat and mouse game, and, second, his charge's growing apprehension indicated to the professor he might be getting close to some sort of discovery.

At week's end, Potemkin invited his young colleague to dinner. "We've done well this week.

Let's go out and have a good time."

"I feel the same way. But who, tell me, would ever dare invite his mentor to dinner?"

"You see, I have already solved the problem."

The food was delicious and the vodka smooth, a necessity in good Russian restaurants. Potemkin thought the time might be right to ask about his charge's individual quest. "Sergei, what are you doing?

I'm asking about the personal project you've been hiding from me."

"I expected the question weeks ago, but you have exhibited an astonishing restraint. If I were you I would have hounded me to death." The professor laughed loudly at his response.

"So, you think I should have hounded you?" Potemkin became serious. "Tell me, Sergei."

"First, allow me to tell you a story. My grandmother, God rest her soul, told me about Adam and Eve, and how God made Eve from Adam's rib. I was fascinated, and asked her to tell it to me again and again, even after I started school. One time, after she had finished the story, she leaned over and pressed her forehead against mine. 'Since you have been such a good boy, I'm going to tell a secret,' she whispered, 'Do you know why God could make Eve out of Adam's rib?' I shook my head. 'Because Adam was already like God, he was both a man and a woman. God couldn't allow him to stay like that down here.' I must have looked astonished because my grandmother made me promise not to tell anyone else about the secret."

"Well, that's a new way to stir the pot," Potemkin commented.

"For me, the story was significant. How many times have others told that story and never thought of that possibility?" The young man lowered his voice. "Sir, I have done something miraculous. I have extracted stem cells; master stem cells."

"You couldn't have."

"From adipose tissue."

"From body fat; that's not possible."

"A thousand years ago, someone sitting in your chair might have said, 'Vodka from potatoes; that's not possible.' But, it is." Sergei Trasker raised his half-full glass to his lips and emptied it.

"How can you be sure? You've not performed any controlled experiments."

"Oh, but I have, and many."

"How was it that I didn't know?"

"You limit yourself to three rooms of the laboratory. The others are for your subordinates to roam around and do your bidding or, when not directed, do as they please. Someone could have built a battleship in one of them and you wouldn't have known until the cannons were fired."

What Sergei had said was true. Like an Admiral who always remained on the bridge, the professor relied on others to see that everything was going well elsewhere. The only reply he could voice was a listless grunt.

The night wore on. There was a great deal of small talk, inconsequential observations of minor events, opinions concerning this or that, complaints about certain foods, the avoirdupois of overstuffed colleagues, and, finally, the long, shapely, muscular legs of one of the secretaries.

But the lips were not expressing what the minds were thinking. Potemkin's was racing, reviewing the many applications of his protégé's discovery and the fame and notoriety it would bring him on the world stage; perhaps a Nobel Prize.

Potemkin reached across the table and took hold of Trasker's hand. "I think it's time to collaborate and bring great honor to our scientific community. I can't wait to tell the Central Committee of our discovery."

"Wait, please; all the tests are not completed. I would not like to tell the world something was so when it wasn't."

"We'll work together and bring our work to fruition as soon as possible."

Potemkin's use of the word 'our' angered the young scientist. What the hell did his mentor have to do with his private research? It was at that moment Sergei Trasker decided to leave Russia.

Intermission was approaching. Markov was more than satisfied; he was elated. So far, the baritone's performance had been impeccable. Attending had been well worth the risk. As the crowd emptied out into the lobby, Markov and a small group headed down the street to the Russian Tea Room for a drink. Not a bit concerned about being confronted in this venue, he had left his pistol in the car. A half hour, two pate' tarts and four Vodkas later, Markov reentered the great hall to hear the remainder of the concert. The second half was even more magnificent than the first; a tour de force. The Russian spy was delighted. It had been a long time since he had enjoyed himself this completely. Here, there was nothing to fear; he could let his guard down.

After the concert, he sauntered back to his car humming some of the familiar melodies he had just heard. He was headed downtown to a Russian restaurant.

A taxicab door opened and a man got in. "Follow that car," the man ordered. It was Professor Jurgens.

The meeting Janus Karper dreaded was at hand. The secretary opened the door and he entered.

Moroka was standing behind his desk gazing out of the window.

"Good morning, sir," He offered.

The executive raised his hand. "Silence; I'm watching a hawk wring a sparrow's neck. How is your neck, Janus?"

"We're making great progress, sir."

"Can you put anything on my desk today?"

"No, sir, I can't."

"What about tomorrow?"

"I'll have something by next week, sir."

"That doesn't sound very definitive."

The CEO chose not to respond.

"Twenty bidders will be sitting in my office at the end of this month. Don't, I repeat, don't make me call them to cancel their flights." Moroka pointed at the door. "That is the way out."

"It's been a week, and there's been no assault on the estate. Do you think they've gotten cold feet?" Chief Davis was hoping for some reinforcement from Santoro and McCann.

"I'm looking for any time now. They've waited long enough for things to die down. I'd expect something very soon. I'd call around and buck up the troops. Tell them it's going to happen very soon.

That way they'll be on their guard." Santoro glanced outside. It was one of those moonless nights.

"That's a good idea. I'll give them a buzz. This working around the clock is for the birds. Even my staff is beginning to complain."

"Is there anything on your murder suspect? Do you have any leads?"

"He's a professional. He knows how to disappear. He's clever, but we're persistent. Eventually he'll make a mistake and we'll get him." Santoro rubbed his shoulder. "I've got something for him."

"Then I'll call in the dragnet? It doesn't seem to be doing any good," Davis observed.

"Leave a few men around Jurgen's home, and maybe one at Yeshiva. After this is over I'd leave a man or two near the Trasker estate. Those are the only places he might be interested in. Running across him on the street or in the city is a low percentage possibility."

The office door swung open and Davis' secretary's head popped out from behind the open door.

"Chief; take the hot line." As quickly as she had appeared, just as quickly she vanished.

"Chief Davis, yes, they're on the way? Did you contact Reilly? Oh, you called him first. He'll be in place by the time they arrive? Good; keep me posted." Davis glanced at Santoro. "You called it."

They're on the way." Santoro and McCann headed for the door. Chief Davis followed.

"Where are you going?"

"I wouldn't miss this for anything. A high profile case, and we've got the upper hand. It's the stuff front page headlines are made of."

Santoro smiled, looked Chief Davis straight in the eye and said, "Goddamn politician." Davis responded with a grin.

During those dark days in Moscow, who could young Sergei Trasker trust; no one. Faithfully following an innocuous regimen day after day for several years, the young scientist had extinguished any suspicion he might try to escape. The Russians stopped shadowing his moves. His curfew was lifted. He could move about freely. He had even become acquainted with a young woman, without doubt an agent provided by the government to monitor his moves surreptitiously.

Escaping Moscow was relatively easy, but once accomplished, the rest of the journey to freedom remained a hit or miss proposition. He had few acquaintances outside of work. All the people he knew were government personnel.

Sometimes extreme anxiety drives the memory to perform far more efficiently than it would under ordinary circumstances. The primal dictum to survive takes precedence over everything else.

Sergei suddenly recalled another bit of advice his grandmother gave him. "Always pray; God, his angels, the cherubim and seraphim will guide you." Of all the alternatives he was considering, praying seemed the most illogical. The grandson had not prayed in years. Why should he start now? What hypocrisy, he thought; pray when it benefits you, for what you want. Would it open the door to freedom? Freedom, the thought filled Sergei's soul. He found his hat and coat and headed for a Russian Orthodox Church. It was Sunday, late morning. Would he arrive in time? He quickened his pace along the snowy street. He slipped and fell. Was it an omen? Convinced he was on a fool's errand, he nevertheless continued making his way through the snowy streets. The spark of belief that his grandmother instilled in him was still there. He would try.

Dirk Spanner's headphones were too tight, but he didn't loosen them because he was afraid the noise from the rotors might interfere with his ability to hear what his men on the ground were saying. The three hummers were closing in on the target. From his vantage point high above the Trasker estate he couldn't see them yet, but from their last transmission he knew they were near. Besides Phil Remsen the pilot, communications expert Sean McCarra was aboard, in the back seat. Spanner valued McCarra and his expertise as the team's most valuable asset.

"Raise us another five hundred, will you? I want to see where they are." Pilot Remsen nodded.

The helicopter began to rise. Spanner scanned the area through his night vision binoculars.

"Got them; there they are, three pair of headlights equally spaced, in military formation. It's them." What Spanner did not notice was the number of other vehicles positioned under the trees close to the estate's entrance. Besides State Troopers, Reilly's SWAT team was also part of the force waiting for Spanner's team.

"Take us back down," Spanner ordered. The pilot maneuvered the helicopter to its original altitude. Spanner glanced across the estate grounds. "It seems awful quiet down there. We've been here for a while and I haven't seen one guard walking a post or cross the lawn in front of the house." In an instant, everything became clear. "Phil, take us up again; I want to see how close our people are now."

The three vehicles had just turned off the main road and were making their way up the grassy lane.

Spanner spotted several flashes of reflected light just ahead of them. Suddenly aware of the ambush, he shouted into the microphone "Abort, abort; this is eagle eye, I say again, abort."

Suddenly the forest below was ablaze with spotlights. The vehicles were surrounded; the men inside them outnumbered and outgunned. A megaphone transmitted the order to surrender. Spanner watched in silence as his team discarded their weapons and stepped out of the vehicles. At about the same time a group of men, Spanner guessed they were Trasker's, jumped into their ATVs and sped from the manor house to the front gate.

It's time, Spanner whispered to himself. "Phil, get this thing away from the light. Head around to the back of that building over there and see if you can find a dark spot to put us down. We've got ourselves the perfect diversion."

Moscow had many churches. Virtually all were built after Napoleon's entry into that city in 1812.

The retreating Russians had set fire to it. Without the provisions he expected to find there, the Emperor had little choice but to turn westward and head for home. Young Sergei Trasker was aware of a different kind of destruction. The Orthodox Church in Russia was no longer free; its spiritual substance had been extinguished by governmental intrusion. Many of the clergy owed their positions to the government. The bearded, black-robed prelates were in effect no more than ecclesiastic clerks, government employees.

Sergei's task was to find one of the few priests, the faithful, who still resisted and might help him escape.

Thoughts such as these were racing through his consciousness as he trudged through the snow.

Sergei walked past the large cathedrals and many of the mid-sized ones. He well understood the politics required to be a prelate in one of these. On one of the side streets he spotted a church one might, for all its shoddiness, describe as measly. The liturgy had just concluded and the parishioners were making their way out, old ladies who could barely walk, men of advanced age, both groups being assisted by several youth, too few to have any telling effect on the need.

And, at the open church door, stood one who seemed to be the most ancient and decrepit priest the young scientist had ever seen. Sergei Trasker's heart leapt. No government apparatchik would ever desire this post. He started climbing but then hesitated. Losing his nerve, he turned to go. Someone tugged at his sleeve. An old man pointed at Sergei, and then at the priest. "He wants to see you," the man said. As Sergei looked up, he noticed the prelate beckoning to him. Sergei resumed his ascent.

"Do you have a watch?" the priest asked. Sergei held up his arm to show that he did. "It must be broken. You are late for liturgy," the old cleric grinned. His gold-plated left incisor twinkled in the morning sun. "Come inside. I have tea after the service. I always have to drink alone. Today you can change that."

No one had spoken to Sergei Trasker that warmly in decades.

The shaded oval was near perfect for Spanner's assault; a phalanx of mighty oaks stood between Trasker's main house and the clearing.

It was just wide enough to provide the space for the helicopter to land. Remsen stayed at the controls and kept the helicopter idling while Spanner and McCarra moved forward toward the main house.

The huge building held only a few inhabitants. Kitchen staff and grounds personnel were elsewhere. That left Sergei, Claudia, and Lev. But, at the last moment, Lev decided to go and see how everything was going with the capture of the alleged intruders. That left Basil the Great Dane as the lone protector of the scientist and Claudia who were in the Great Room. The huge beast stationed himself at the entrance. Suddenly the Great Dane went to the window. "What?" Trasker whispered. Basil growled in response. "Come, we must go to the laboratory," he urged. Claudia Morgan grasped his hand and the pair started to leave.

"Defend," the scientist commanded. Basil went out into the hallway and retreated to a position where he could see both the front entrance and the French doors that connected the Great Room to the terrace.

The inside pocket of the scientist's jacket still contained a vial of those pesky 'blahas,' the flea- like nano-devices.

Spanner and McCarra's approach had been uneventful. The activity near the front gate had engaged everyone's attention. Gaining entrance through the French doors, the pair began to methodically search every room without having any idea what they might find. Spanner and Remsen had observed the pillbox configuration on one of their flights and deduced that it was the laboratory, or at least the place someone might have chosen to hide something valuable. In the house now, their only objective was to find the door leading to it. The pair split up, hoping in that way to speed up the search.

Suddenly, McCarra screamed. Spanner rushed to the room where he was. Basil had come up from behind and caught part of the man's head and neck in his huge mouth. There was a crunching sound.

McCarra fell to the floor. As the Great Dane turned to attack Spanner, a burst from his automatic weapon ripped through the huge beast. Death was instantaneous. Basil and McCarra lay in a heap on an Oriental rug.

In the laboratory below Sergei and Claudia heard the gunfire. Sergei needed to contact Lev, but how? He had left his phone upstairs. The scientist went over to the fuse box and pulled the master switch.

Immediate and total darkness followed. He repeated the process a number of times. Near the gate, Lev and his men turned to observe the display. In an instant the lead guard read Sergei's SOS and started running toward the main house. His crew followed. Spanner was no fool; he knew the signaling would summon the guards back from the front gate.

With a parting glance at McCarra, he raced toward the French doors. Lev came in the front door as Spanner made his exit.

The helicopter was aloft and almost out of sight when the head guard arrived at the clearing.

Sergei, Lev thought, and raced back to see where the scientist and Claudia Morgan were. Pounding on the laboratory door and shouting as loud as he could that it was he, Lev, he succeeded in convincing his boss to open the door.

"Are they gone?" Trasker asked. Lev nodded they were. The three walked up the stairs and back into the main house. The head guard moved ahead of Claudia and Sergei and closed the door to one room.

The scientist seemed puzzled. "Don't go into there until I've had the men clean it up," Lev suggested.

"Basil?" Sergei asked. "Yes," answered Lev. "And someone else?" "Yes," Lev replied.

The young scientist's indenture in Russia's capital city was once again about to become uncomfortable. Sergei had allowed Professor Potemkin to witness what he had accomplished; but he was careful not to explain every detail of how he achieved such a towering discovery. The young genius wanted to leave Russia, but he resolved to delay his departure until he concluded his next series of tests.

The decision resulted in a tightrope walk, performing the tests while at the same time keeping his mentor at bay, and from time to time offering him scraps of information and reams of paper containing innocuous data.

He understood he couldn't keep the ruse up forever. The charade did, however, go on for nearly three months. Sergei began to notice a change in Potemkin's mood. He should have taken it as a warning, but immersed in his own research, he ignored it.

One morning, Sergei spied his mentor speaking to two soldiers. After the conversation, he glanced at Sergei and nodded his head, as if to indicate 'that's him.' The two advanced, took hold of the young man and dragged him away.

There are many ways to torture a person and Sergei Trasker was exposed to the most severe and sophisticated of the array, the object being to obtain the necessary information but spare the individual.

The more the young scientist resisted, the greater became his pain. The Central Committee wanted what the young man knew and how they got it did not matter. Potemkin, on the other hand, shared the same goal, but did not wish to put Sergei's life in jeopardy. An infection set in, and it seemed the young genius' life would be coming to an end. Potemkin, at risk to his own reputation, offered to restore his charge. The Central Committee deferred to the professor.

Guided by his patient, the old scientist, using the first iteration of Sergei's gel-immersion technique, performed the necessary functions to energize Sergei and restore those parts of his body that had been scarred and deformed by torture. As soon as he was well enough, Sergei made himself a promise he would visit Father Joseph and make good his escape. He also told Potemkin that if he survived, he would explain every detail of his research to his mentor. The torture stopped. The professor felt victorious; international fame was at hand. Sergei Trasker duped him.

"Do you trust me yet?" The old priest asked young Sergei. "Moscow is a place where there are many people, but few one can trust. We have known each other for some time now. Have you come to trust me yet?"

The young genius nodded. "Yes," he answered. So much hinged on what he would decide in the next few moments. He wanted to be free. His moral compass told him he could trust Father Joseph, but what if he was mistaken? What would happen then; back for more torture, prison, isolation, perhaps execution? Sergei started to shake. He couldn't control the tremors. Father Joseph noticed.

"One of my dearest friends fell out of favor with the government. They decided to do away with him. I heard his confession. He was shaking, the same way you are. He was going to die." Father Joseph placed his hand on Sergei's head. "But you, my son, are going to live and become a free man. I, Father Joseph, guarantee it."

The priest's promise drew a smile from Sergei. Here was this old relic of a prelate, sitting in the midst of millions of communists, guaranteeing safe passage to someone he had met only thirteen months before. From his worn, discolored shoes to the crop of his black, burlap headpiece, the guarantor was consummately poor. Still, there was something in the way he said the word guarantee; it had a certain ring to it. Sergei composed himself. "I need to leave Russia. I want to go; I must go or I will rot. Help me, Father. I have no one else."

"Tomorrow night; come tomorrow night with your things. I want you to meet my friend. You will like him."

Freedom, the thought of it was like having too much wine; it made a person giddy. Sergei wondered how long it would take to leave Russian soil. Would he journey north, or west, certainly not east; perhaps southeast travelling might be best.

The next morning, Constantine Potemkin found his young rooster humming to himself as he went about his duties at the laboratory.

"You seem in a good mood today. Have you found a woman?"

"Perhaps," Sergei responded.

"What is her name?"

"In due time; I'll tell you when I've found out whether she's true to me or not."

The rest of the day and early evening found the two scientists observing, commenting and collaborating on Sergei's new discovery. When Professor Potemkin relented due to exhaustion, he paid his colleague the highest compliment. "If this isn't worthy of the Nobel Prize, I don't know what is. Now I must go home. I need to rest. We'll continue this tomorrow."

"Until then," the young scientist agreed. As soon as Potemkin left, Sergei Trasker sprang into action. He transferred those notes not yet stored on electronic media onto several discs. He taped the dozen he had already copied to his body. He had trouble finding places for the last three, but finally, it was done. Now he was prepared to meet Father Joseph. Sergei looked at his watch; midnight was half an hour away.

"I thought you might not be coming," Father Joseph exclaimed, "You should not be late for important appointments."

"Am I too late? I couldn't get away any sooner; it was not possible."

There was a sound. The young scientist turned to it and saw a man whose form filled the entire doorway. Sergei was speechless.

"This is my friend Ilarion. He will take care of you from now on. Follow his instructions and he will see to it that you gain your freedom."

The giant human being smiled, stepped forward and shook Sergei's hand. Ilarion bowed before Father Joseph and the old priest blessed him.

"Yours is a holy work, my son. Every time you escort someone to freedom, you risk your own life. May God protect you." The giant arose and turned to go, motioning to Sergei to follow.

Out on the street, Sergei had trouble keeping up with his protector. "Can't you slow down?" He gasped.

"Be quiet and move swiftly. The quicker we get out of the city, the better. Don't talk any more.

Someone might recognize you by your voice. Breathe deeply and save your strength. We have a long walk ahead of us."

Although public transportation paralleled the way they were going, Ilarion refused to take any.

Sergei finally came to the conclusion that it might not be a good idea to take a public conveyance. He started to feel better about his guide. The man knew what he was doing; he had a plan. After a time they approached a secluded part of the 'Reka Moskva,' Moscow River. The sky was overcast and it was well past midnight. The moon was not helping.

There is no blackness like the blackness one encounters near a body of water when there are no lights nearby. Ilarion seemed to know his way along the bank, darkness or not. During the several times when Sergei stumbled, his guide looked back in disgust and wagged his head. What does he want from me, Sergei thought, I'm not a boatman.

Sergei heard the sound of wood tapping against something hard and it wasn't far off. Ilarion stopped and waited for his charge to catch up. "I don't care what happens to you. Fall if you like, on the ground, in the water, or in a hole, but remain quiet. Your freedom, and mine, depends on it. Sergei started to say something, but Ilarion put his finger on Sergei's lips.

The two clambered aboard the row boat and listened. They heard nothing. Ilarion placed the oars into the oarlocks and began rowing, slowly. The burlap between oar and oarlock silenced the sound of the movement. The slowness diminished any splashing to nothing.

Sergei was on his way.

Almost

Markov was always careful; always. But on this night he had indulged himself and thrown caution to the winds. Considering his present circumstances it was the wrong time to do so. Nevertheless, the Russian baritone had performed magnificently. The orchestra was phenomenal and the social interaction stimulating. This would be a night to remember. Being the subject of a city-wide manhunt and having successfully eluded everyone only served to heighten his pleasure at attending Carnegie. Why, he could write a story about it; a burlesque.

Outside the famous concert hall, someone behind him stepped on a kernel of gravel. Markov froze. He reached under his jacket. It was at this moment he recalled having left his pistol in the car. "If its money you want, I have some. Here, take it."

"Jurgens, CIA; Do you remember anyone with a name like that?"

"I should have killed you when I had the chance."

"Wasn't it too bad the police got there before you could?"

"Are you going to kill me?"

"You're going to stand trial and go to jail. Please give me one reason, any, to shoot you."

"Don't worry, I won't. I want to live, just like you."

"Then why did you. . ." Markov bolted and knocked his captor down. Fleeing was the order of the day. By the time the former CIA man got to his feet, the Russian was out of sight.

"It's not over," Jurgens growled.

Boris Trasker was improving, remarkably so. The brothers now understood what was happening.

Unorthodox as it was, it was to be the precursor to an ultimate phase in the evolution of mankind. There was not a person on the planet who could have imagined such a monumental change in paradigm. Sergei was elated that Boris was not dying. Claudia was frustrated that she was being kept in the dark about what was transpiring. Lev was intermittently happy, frustrated, annoyed, and confused. The only thing lacking in this circus was a dancing bear. Still, a dark cloud had been lifted from the brothers. Spanner's assault had been thwarted as had the attempt to kidnap Claudia. Grigorev was dead. All that remained was finding Markov. Sergei felt certain another assault would not be attempted. For the first time in many years, the future looked brighter.

"Who's on the phone; it's Professor Jurgens? What does he want?" Detective Santoro was irritated. He had more important things to do than indulge a college professor. He would probably be asking whether the assassin was apprehended, and, if not, how were we progressing; yada, yada, yada.

"He saw Markov; almost took him down. He spotted the guy at Carnegie, at a concert. Can you beat that for balls? I think you should talk to him. He's dropped the professor stuff. These days he's one pissed off former CIA agent," McCann said.

"Okay, I'll see him. Where is he?"

"He's on the way in; he should be here in twenty minutes he says. He called from his cell."

Santoro wiped his fingers across his chin. It was a habit he employed when he became apprehensive. Might the professor provide the police with the lead that would bag Markov? That would be super, like winning the lottery, only better. Santoro entertained some thoughts about getting even with the scum who murdered Peters. The methods he was considering were not sanctioned by the Geneva Convention.

Without knocking, McCann burst into the office. "He's here." Professor Jurgens stepped forward and took a seat. "I had him and I let him get away. I wasn't sharp enough; not up to my old self; too much educator and not enough agent."

"Hey, don't beat yourself up. You got a bead on him. All our forces haven't been able to even get near him. Were you armed?"

"You know the city doesn't allow that."

"I wasn't asking for a recitation of city law. Were you armed?"

"I still have my old weapon. Out of habit I keep it clean and serviceable."

"Did you get a shot off at him?"

"No, I didn't. By the time I thought I could, he was weaving through a crowd of passersby."

"Where did you get on to him?"

"He was at the same concert I was. I hailed a taxi and followed his car. He parked in an outdoor lot. There's a Russian bistro located in that neighborhood. I thought he might have been heading that way, but he changed his direction and started toward the subway. I wonder why he would do that?"

"Because he's a woodchuck," McCann added, "He's holed up in one of the tunnels. That's why we haven't been able to find him. He's probably got a number of safe havens."

"If he's down there, how can we get him?"

"We can't," Santoro inserted, "There are hundreds of places he could be. If we used the entire force we might be able find him, but we're not going to do that. We've got to draw him out into the open."

"How do you propose we do that?" The professor asked.

"If you want to catch the big one, troll with the best bait you've got."

Dirk Spanner was having an unpleasant confrontation with Janus Karper, whose face was crimson red. "What, you didn't get it?" Karper shouted angrily, "What happened?"

"The police were waiting for us. They must have known we were coming. They have most of my men. The 'copter pilot and me are the only ones who got away. My best man was killed by a guard dog.

The place is a fortress. You should have given me more time to. . ."

"It's history; never mind. What will you do now? Time is running out. Do I have to tell you again what will happen if you don't succeed?"

"You're a bastard, Karper, I should have steered clear of you."

"The past, Dirk, recall the past. Do you want that to happen to your family?"

"I'll get it done."

"Good boy, I knew I could count on you. Get out."

"Stick it." Spanner stormed out of the office.

Claudia Morgan tugged on Sergei Trasker's sleeve. "Hey, what's going on with your brother?

Don't you think it's time you told me?"

"Perhaps, but I wonder whether you are ready for what I am about to tell you."

"Try me."

"Mother Nature illustrates how things should be done; she shows by example. I pose two questions. Think about them. Once you satisfactorily answer the two, you will know about Boris."

"Is this about the Fibonacci thing? Alright, Mr. Scientist, I'll play your silly game."

"No, it's not; it's about something else."

"Go on, I'm waiting."

"The first is, what would be the most advantageous state for a species to be in order to ensure its survival?"

"What's the next?"

"What is the one characteristic Bynoe's Gekko, water fleas, and midges have in common?"

"I thought you were going to give me something hard. That sounds easy."

"It is; it's the 'why' that's driving me to distraction. I acknowledge the results, but the question I can't answer is how they came into being. Boris possesses that trait"

"And I thought you were so smart."

"Even smart men yield to Mother Nature."

The pair strolled down the long hall, and then into the courtyard. It was a bright, sunny day, ample reason for anyone to be in a good mood. But Claudia was burdened with Sergei's two questions and he with the reason the phenomenon was occurring in his laboratory.

Yuri Markov was evaluating the black and blue mark on his shoulder. It was the price he paid for evading Jurgens. Turning a corner too tightly, he had not allowed himself ample room to clear the concrete column that obscured him from the line of fire. You're getting too old for this, he mused, maybe it is time to retire to Baku or some other place on the Caspian. Wincing, he applied some liniment to the injured area.

Next time I'll be more careful, he mused. Still, the concert was worth it. Shimsky was excellent.

If the opportunity presented itself, I would go again. But the next time I'd take my pistol. Not doing so was stupid.

The Russian spy turned his thoughts to the matters at hand; now there were two instead of one.

First, he had to dispose of Jurgens. He was the last link to what happened in Potemkin's laboratory. The mission would be more difficult now. Markov chided himself for botching his opportunity that day at Yeshiva. He was sure he would have been successful if only that policeman had not shown up. Now he had been directed to meet with someone he had never seen, his primary contact in the United States.

Casting aside his cloak of secrecy meant the handler thought the situation serious enough to risk exposure. Why did he choose me, Markov pondered, why me? It is because I am the best. It must be very difficult or it's a kamikaze mission, he concluded.

Retirement seemed a distant goal.

Two weeks passed. The guards at the estate relaxed, furrows of anxiety receded from Lev's face, and Sergei and Claudia once again dared to walk about the beautiful grounds. After all the recent challenges the lull was a welcome change. The pair understood the respite might be temporary; the dark forces that coveted Sergei's work had not abandoned their objective. They were just devising other schemes. Regardless, their absence introduced an idyllic intermission and the pair had the good sense to make the most of it.

"Beautiful, it's just beautiful outside," Claudia swooned, "there couldn't be a better day, ever."

She glanced at Sergei. "What's the matter?"

"I've made a decision." The scientist grasped the woman's hand and broke into a slow, loping jog.

"Hey, what's this all about?"

"You'll see."

In a little while the pair arrived at the great room. Sergei pulled an armchair up to the one Claudia settled into and placed both his hands over one of hers. "It's time. After today, you will know everything. I have decided to trust you with the most precious discovery of my life. All I ask is that you guard it well."

Claudia nodded and whispered "I will."

"Most of this happened when I was a 'guest' of the Central Committee in Moscow. Over the years I have built on what I discovered at that time."

Sergei Trasker proceeded to explain how he had constructed a DNA double helix graph on the screen of his computer. "The day before I had been obsessing about the Fibonacci ratio and integrating it with logarithmic values. Just playing around a bit, I manipulated the ratio into a three dimensional form and superimposed it over the DNA. By sliding one figure along the other, I was able to define a series of different sequences based on nothing more than my play. It did not take me long to notice that a pattern was emerging. The values I superimposed were not intended for the Fibonacci ratio; they didn't belong.

What had I come upon? I had to find out. I didn't leave my computer all that day. After supper, I returned and worked throughout the night, reinforcing what I had noticed that afternoon. Yes, there was a correlation; was there any purpose to it? The more I progressed, the more I felt I had stumbled upon something significant."

"In the laboratory, I began to identify and extract those proteins in the order identified by my quixotic manipulation. Again, I was playing, but not really. I tested them, structured experiments to chart new reactions. Little by little, I concocted a gel, the same I used to heal you. Now, I thought, what would this new fluid do?

Since Professor Potemkin's main thrust was stem cell research, I placed a few in the gel. By adjusting temperature and length of time in solution, I found I could alter a cell's differentiation. I could place one cell from my arm into the gel and it would immediately begin reproducing and multiplying at an accelerated rate as long as temperature was held within certain limits and sufficient gel was in solution. I also discovered everything worked better when the solution was alkaline."

"The Fibonacci ratio and my own nonsensical computer play had given me the ability to repair beings for the first time from the inside out."

"And wouldn't you know, I birthed it all, in of all places, Moscow; and, under the close scrutiny and the prying eyes of the Central Committee and Professor Constantine Potemkin. Since then, I have delved further into uncharted territory. Ping, Pang, and Pong, are constructs; living flesh and blood robotic beings, each exactly alike, and each able to be regenerated from a single cell of their own construct. Beyond even that marvelous capability, I can create them from scratch, providing I have my notes and my recipe book."

Claudia stared at Sergei. She could hardly believe what she was hearing, but her own miraculous recovery and the youthful appearance she now enjoyed proved his achievement was fact.

One question remained; Claudia felt now was the time to ask it.

"What's going on with Boris.?"

"Have you found the answers to the questions I posed?"

"I confess; I've been lazy. No, I haven't"

"When you get those answers, we'll talk about Boris. It's my way of preparing you for what I am going to tell you."

Professor Jurgens entered the front door of his home. Nancy, his wife heard the door open.

"Nance?" he called.

"Oh, you're safe," his wife purred as she embraced him.

"Get packed; I want you to go and stay with your mother. I'll call when it's okay for you to come back."

"What's going on?"

"There's a mad dog on the loose, that's all. It will take a while to find and eliminate him."

"Was that why you disappeared?"

"I assumed they would be watching the house. It's me they want, not you. Still, I don't think they're above snatching you to get to me. Get packed, I'll take you to the airport." Jurgens walked over to the window, peered outside and then drew the drapes shut. "No one; come on Nance, move it."

Fifteen minutes later, husband and wife were on their way.

Chief Davis, detectives Santoro and McCann were sitting in his office, strategizing. "It's been quiet. Do you suppose we've scared them off?" Davis asked.

"It's not likely; the stakes are too high. They'll try again; but they'll be more cautious, now that they know we're involved," Santoro replied.

"How much longer are you going to keep the stake out car at the estate entrance? Have you gotten any flak about that yet?" McCann asked.

"I spent an hour with the Mayor yesterday. It seems he's been aware of the situation longer than I have. The Triple I boss, Janus Karper is a sleeper, a Russian agent. He runs the spy show for the Russians here in the northeast corridor. He's pretty slick too, hardly ever uses a throwaway cell phone, never a land line. He never writes notes. He communicates every order by word of mouth"

"How'd they get on to him?" Santoro was intrigued.

"When you talk, your lips move, right?"

"Lip reading; Jesus, we're even into that?"

"Well, it's not just that. The Feds have a deep cover guy working in Triple I. They say he's pretty sharp, one of the best. I'll take that back; the best. Karper always closes the blinds to his windows when he has something to say to one of his minions, but we get the info anyway."

"How?"

Chief Davis smiled. "When you're inside, the blinds seem solid but, from the outside, they're transparent when you shine a certain light on them You can't see the difference from the inside. Let's hope he never figures that out."

"Who's the guy on the inside?" Santoro wondered.

"I don't know, but Claudia knows him, and so does Wagner. If we crack this ring, we'll know soon enough."

"No, we won't. Agents like that are never revealed; keeping their identity secret is a boon."

"How'd you know a thing like that?" Chief Davis asked.

"A little bird told me," Santoro replied.

The Russian agent's ego had been bruised. The ultimate narcissist, he was obsessing about not having extinguished Jurgens. Now he was going to see the big boss, no doubt to receive a chewing out.

And who the hell was he to be giving Markov one? Had he traveled all over the globe doing whatever was necessary to further the cause? He was probably just another overweight, over-indulged, apparatchik type who got a big job because his father kissed the you-know-what of some official.

This was Markov's frame of mind as he waited in one of Union Square's pedestrian subway tunnels. The weather outside was damp and it was cloudy. There was a mild breeze. All these conditions caused the aromas in the city to rise. The breeze carried them along. Eventually, they reached and tortured the nostrils of everyone in the area. The stench was worse below ground, in the subway.

Ever resourceful, Markov positioned himself above the tracks, so that the blast of air caused by approaching trains would blow clear the gathering odors. The solution was far from perfect, but it served.

The Russian turned to the click, click, click of someone's shoes. The approaching woman was very attractive. She looked uncomfortable. Observing the cut of her clothing, the styling of her shoes and her leather briefcase, Markov deduced she didn't belong in the subway. The woman came closer.

"Mr. Ilyich?" She questioned.

"I am Vladimir," Markov answered, "and you?"

"I am Ulyanov." Vladimir Ilyich Ulyanov was Lenin's real name. "Follow me," the woman directed. Markov fell in behind her. He glanced back to see whether they were being followed; all clear, there was no one.

"We are going where?" Markov asked.

"No questions, please," the woman replied.

The pair took the uptown train to 42nd street, and then the shuttle to Grand Central Station. The woman reached into her pocket and withdrew a rail ticket. "Track 21; the train leaves in five minutes. You'd better hurry."

The woman moved away. Markov chased after her. "How will I know who I am meeting?" He asked.

"He will know you." The woman stopped abruptly, turned, and stared at the spy. "Now go!"

Finding track 21, Markov moved along the platform, finally choosing to enter one of the Pullmans. Not recognizing anyone, the only thing he could do was sit down and wait to be contacted.

Five minutes late, the train pulled out of Grand Central, headed for who knew where. It was a local, which meant it would stop at many more stations than the express. Peering out of the window Markov recognized the Hudson River on his left. The train continued north and soon the Mid-Hudson Bridge near the city of Kingston appeared in the distance. At Rhinebeck, many passengers detrained. An equally large number boarded.

Suddenly, the same woman he had met in Union Square, the one who had given him the ticket took a seat next to his, kissed him, and whispered, "Hello, Darling." She glanced toward the rear of the car. A man in a gray suit and matching fedora nodded. The woman did likewise. Markov was relieved; he had not been followed.

"Come, let's go to the bar and get something to drink," the woman tempted. Markov smiled, and replied "Yes, let's." The pair started forward. Approaching, a man, about Markov's size and wearing exactly the same clothes as he, fell in behind. At the appropriate moment, a compartment door flew open and Markov was yanked out of the passageway. His replacement moved up and accompanied the woman to the bar.

"Who are you?" Markov asked.

"I am Dzugashvili; and you?" It was Josef Stalin's last name.

"I am Iosif Vissarionovich," Stalin's patronymic title.

Janus Karper extended his hand. "Welcome, comrade."

"Thank you. Why have you contacted me, and why must we meet in this way? You have never felt it necessary to reveal yourself before, why now?"

"My, but you are direct. Are you always this way? I am meeting you because I want to impress upon you the urgency of the mission you are about to undertake. There can be no failure. The mission must be successful. As you can see, I have put myself at great risk sitting here in this train, talking to you." Karper handed Markov an envelope. "Whatever the cost, you must do this. I have lost many good men. They tried to achieve what you must now do. It is well known that you are the best of the best. I turn to you in desperation."

"I was thinking of retiring, perhaps in Baku."

"If you survive, I will personally buy your air ticket and a house there."

"You don't expect me to, do you?"

"No." Karper raised his cell to his face. "Time to come back now," he commanded.

As before, the switch was made in the hall and Markov, arm in arm with his darling, returned to his seat.

Detraining in Rensselaer, the station across the river from Albany, the pair split up. Markov took the next train back to the city.

Claudia found Sergei in the laboratory. On the way, she stopped in to observe Boris. Still immersed in the gel, his complexion was improving. And now, she had a strong suspicion why. "I've done the research you said I should. Is it true?"

"I'm afraid it is, and, I can't explain how it happened."

"Every animal and insect you gave me had one thing in common. They reproduce in ways other than the normal way. Is that what Boris is all about?"

"Yes, and also the men who were assassinated."

"Why them? Did they have the same problem?"

"Potemkin was afraid they might. That would reveal to the entire scientific community what we had stumbled upon, the possibility of never-ending existence through regeneration; cloning one's self every five decades."

"How is that possible?"

"Cells split and one might say they reproduce; the water flea and the gecko begin their reproductive efforts in response to some sort of trigger. Even though the two processes are different they still possess a similarity in that their function is to perpetuate the species. Seeing that kind of innovation, you ask yourself 'What if I cranked up the dial a little more; what else might be possible?'"

"You're saying, ergo Boris. The others who were murdered, did they have this capability? Were they killed because of that? Who did it?"

"I don't know who, but it was Potemkin who issued the order. He wanted to keep the secret a secret. That's why he came here, to find out how I achieved that." The scientist waved his hand in Boris' direction. "I didn't even know what he had discovered until Boris appeared in the lab. Potemkin came upon the anomaly before I did."

"What's your next move?"

"The professor will soon be leaving. While I don't trust him entirely, he's the only one I can have assist me when Boris' time comes. I have no idea how to keep him here and I'm still not certain I can convince him to stay. His allegiance to the motherland is still the big question. I don't know whether I can turn him away from his obsession for glory and have him become a participant in what I am about to attempt. Even so, I have no other choice but to ask him for his help." The arc of Sergei's eyebrows and the corners of his mouth were all inverted and his eyes had lost their sparkle.

"Call him out, Sergei, appeal to his humanitarian side. I think there's a lot of good in him. He's suffered a lot, seen men die, been afraid and perhaps even been targeted for extermination himself. He can't be all that bad. You have built up a lot of capital with him during your years together. Make a large withdrawal."

The scientist grasped Claudia' hand, raised it to his lips, and tenderly kissed it. "Thank you," he half-whispered.

Markov detrained at Grand Central. His stream of thought was consumed by his meeting with Janus Karper, the man he had met but whose name he still did not know. The agent had met the director of all espionage conducted in the northeast corridor. That alone was a noteworthy event.

The mission, whose plan resided in an envelope inside Markov's coat, was of such gravity that the director exposed himself to impress Markov of its importance. Still, he chose not to reveal his identity or where he might be reached. The agent was deeply engrossed in evaluating why his superior would choose to do so.

As he climbed the steps and came up from the subterranean maze of train platforms, that rumination was the main reason for his lack of attentiveness, not the diversion from the myriad shops and restaurants in the terminal. He stopped to indulge his hunger and purchase a very substantial vegetarian wrap from a nearby Sbarros located in one of the alcoves connected to the grand concourse. He also purchased a large, steaming cup of coffee to quench his thirst. For the moment he forgot who and where he was, concentrating instead on simply enjoying his meal.

For one engaged in the business of espionage, dropping one's guard can be dangerous. Dropping one's guard twice can signal the end of a career.

So steeped in the profession, it was not natural for Markov to behave in this way. Eventually realizing his vulnerability, he resumed his defensive posture. Too late; the pressure against his left side was all too familiar. A voice behind him whispered "Do something stupid. Give me an excuse."

Jurgens had apprehended Markov.

McCann burst into Santoro's office. "Jurgens has Markov; he's bringing him in now."

"Great; where'd he get him?"

"He got him at Grand Central. He didn't want to take any chances, so he called out to a shield who was patrolling the terminal. He called it in and a squad car was dispatched. They're just leaving." McCann was grinning. "Talk about a break, this is it. This is the big one."

Santoro had a different opinion. "I'm not so sure. This guy is a professional; we're not going to get him to talk. He knows we're not going to torture him. He will stay tight-lipped until hell freezes over. Sure, we've got him, but what have we got besides a murderer?"

"At least we'll make things right for Peters and Collins."

Santoro nodded.

"Jurgens said he had a sealed envelope in his pocket; maybe his marching orders?" McCann added.

Santoro became excited. "Sometimes you bring bad news, McCann, and sometimes, good. This time you may have outdone yourself." Sporting a wide grin, McCann sat down and made himself comfortable as the pair awaited Markov's arrival.

Dirk Spanner couldn't sit still. He paced the floor, racking his brain for another way to reenter Sergei Trasker's estate, get what he needed and depart. He had dispatched the Great Dane that killed his comrade. The beast wouldn't be causing him any problem this time. He knew there were guards. What other surprises awaited him? It was just Remsen and him now. The helicopter could get them in alright, but the noise would alert everyone else. What about the rest? The problems seemed insurmountable; he didn't even know where the goods might be, and he damn well knew he wouldn't have all day to find them.

Perhaps upside down might work. Might he use Remsen and the landing of the 'copter as a diversion and enter by another means? After all, he had used the capture of his team that way. Why not employ that strategy again?

He decided to spend some time surveying the estate to determine what vehicles were allowed to come and go; from previous reconnoitering he already had a partial list, so getting the rest would not take that long. Karper and his unrealistic timetable could go to hell. If only he had held his ground and not been goaded into acting by that dolt before he was ready the last time. But that was history. What mattered now was success, by any means.

The doorbell rang. James opened the door and, to his surprise Sergei Trasker, Lev, and Timon stood in the hallway. "Come in, please," James invited, "Professor is in that room over there. Can I get the gentlemen something to drink?" The guests shook their heads.

Professor Potemkin was not a little taken aback to see the three enter the room. As he rose to greet them, Trasker motioned for him to remain seated. Lev and Timon retired to another room.

"Well, what is it? Have you come to tell me what a terrible person I am? Speak up, I haven't all day. I leave for Moscow at the end of the week; empty-handed, as you well know."

"You know about Boris." Potemkin nodded he did. "Can you put aside your ambition to have my notes for a while and help me when his time comes? Or will I have to look elsewhere, to someone else, and have to answer ten thousand questions about why this is happening? You risked everything to help those four men. Would you do any less for me? I am seeking the man who risked his life to save four others. Is he still in residence?"

Potemkin sipped his tea. He remained silent for some time. "I have cancer. They say I have three years, most likely less. That was why I was pressing you. I wanted to leave this world a gift, from me and you. After I am gone, I want someone to say, 'Oh yes, that Potemkin, he was a great scientist. He did so and so.' That is all I ever wanted." The professor stared at Trasker; it was a knowing glance. "Of course I will help you.

If Moscow finds out, they will execute me. What of it; death will have come a little sooner.

The way our legal system works, I shall be dead by the time they find me guilty."

Sergei Trasker, full of emotion, could hardly speak. "Thank you, thank you."

"James! Call the embassy. Tell them they have to extend our visa. We're staying in America."

The valet, who had been eavesdropping, entered the room. "Extend, for how long shall I say?"

"Say, for two months, renewable as needed. That should do it."

Arrangements were made for the professor to move to the estate, but clandestinely. Many of his belongings would remain at Dakota House, in the event anyone questioned his motives and came to search the apartment. Sadly, Potemkin's worlds, both here in the United States and at home in Russia, were replete with distrust.

Espionage is a game of stealth and intelligence. Hiding the identity and purpose of any one of its participants are its two most important elements. Master spies accomplish this with incredible ease. That is because experience and the instinct to survive drive their every decision. One of these was imbedded in Triple I. John Drake's mission was to monitor company activity, ascertain what their objective was, and how it might jeopardize national security. In the seven preceding years he had worked at the firm, simple industrial espionage seemed to be Triple I's objective; American firms stealing industrial secrets from one another. While unseemly, such an activity did not rise to the level that might cause him concern. Until recently, his assignment had been a ho-hum affair.

Now, the Boris Trasker situation, Claudia's sudden involvement with Sergei Trasker, and then Ted Wagner being hospitalized for a gunshot wound changed that. Something significant was occurring and Triple I seemed to be in the thick of it.

The spy already was aware of the following: The thwarted attack on Sergei Trasker's estate was a matter of record. Claudia's condo had been raided. Three assailants were found dead at the scene. She was nowhere to be found. Three other individuals had been murdered; a lawyer, a police detective and a judge. There was a fourth attempt to murder a college professor. The police were unusually tight-lipped.

How much more did they know but were not revealing? It was rumored the entire force was searching for a murderer; for which one? Were the killings connected? Just this morning, the police announced the dragnet had been pulled. Had they captured the assassin, or one of them, or all?

Contacting his superiors, the deep cover agent found out the rest of the story: that Becker Pharmaceutical was involved, that Professor Potemkin was in the United States hoping to reconnect with Sergei Trasker, that scientist Trasker, because of his having discovered something of extraordinary consequence had barricaded himself in his estate located somewhere in Westchester County, that several Russian agents were still at large, but had not as yet, been identified.

Both Claudia Morgan and Ted Wagner were acquainted with this undercover agent, but not his true identity. They had dined together, even vacationed together during an unexpected lull in the mad happenings that characterized working for Triple I. Claudia even thought he might be a good catch, but that was before she met Sergei and became entangled in the web that surrounded him. At one point the undercover agent might have considered teaming up with her. But again, that was history. He was there when she returned from vacation, a beautiful, copper-toned goddess, full of life and goodness. Where was she now?

Agent Drake had to find Claudia Morgan, and soon. How much of that impetus was based on duty and how much on his personal desire to be her protector, one could only guess.

"Heterotia binoe," Claudia Morgan proudly stated, "Bynoe's Gekko. Then, there's the water flea, the order of Daphnia. Last, but not least, there's the Midge, Chironmidae."

"I see you've done your research," Sergei Trasker remarked.

"Oops, I missed one; order of Diptera, that's for the Midge."

"Very good; and, what have you learned."

"I learned something crazy, maybe? All the critters can reproduce without sexual intercourse. Is that what you wanted me to discover?"

"Sit down. I'm about to tell you a story no one has ever heard. Promise me you won't interrupt.

You believe that everyone is either a man or woman." Claudia nodded in agreement. "That's not entirely true. At least three percent of human beings fall into what we call the intersex category, being partially male and female. I'm guessing there are many more, but social stigma keeps these individuals from reporting their true state."

Claudia raised her hand. The scientist waved it down.

"Most of the anomalies are corrected at birth, with the 'extra hardware,' bluntly put, surgically removed or incorporated into existing tissue. Still, there are some individuals who show no external signs of being intersex until later in life. Their gender-anomaly is only discovered when blood work and genetic investigations are performed."

Claudia raised her hand and vigorously waved it. Sergei stopped and looked at her. "What is it?"

"So, what's this all about?"

"As a race, we may be evolving. Tell me, what is the best method of guaranteeing the survival of a species?"

"Sex, I mean, reproduction."

"What if all the females are dead; or, what if all the males are dead?"

"Then, it's kaput, buddy, total kaput."

"Yes, but what if every individual in that species could reproduce without the benefit of having to mate?"

"I get it, the gecko, the Water Flea, the Midge; they can reproduce on their own. That's what you wanted me to discover."

"Yes, that there are already examples in nature of this kind of reproduction, and intersex shows us that we, as a species, might also be well on the way to that end, if only we can dispense with the social stigma associated with the transition."

Claudia stared at Sergei. "Is that what's happening to Boris?"

"Somehow, the gel has called forth a process I cannot explain, or even imagine. It seems the capability for parthenogenesis or a similar process is already hidden within the human genome. Purely by accident, I have set them in motion."

"Let me get this straight. Boris is going to. . ."

"Yes, he is conceiving. In less than two months, it will be time. Since he doesn't have the rest of the apparatus, it will have to be cesarean. That is why I need Professor Potemkin; he has experience in these procedures. When he was young he served as a hospital obstetrician for a time."

"So, these are your secrets; you can repair the body by calling forth any stem cell you need, and now, you can totally reproduce that person providing. . ."

". . . I can anticipate what will happen; which, I can't."

Santoro and McCann sat across the table from Markov in the interrogation room. Chief Davis and several FBI agents watched from the observation room situated behind the one-way glass panel.

"Why did you murder those three men?" Santoro asked, dispensing with the 'softening up' routine. This person was a professional. It would be absurd not to treat him as one.

"I killed them because I was ordered to do so. I do what I am told, and I am successful at what I do. That is why I get the hard jobs."

Santoro glanced at McCann. Perhaps questioning this assassin would be easier than they thought.

Why were you in Grand Central? Was it to meet someone? Who was it?"

"Do you have a glass of water? I'm getting thirsty," Markov asked. McCann turned to the glass pane and nodded. Someone went out to get the water.

"You know we've got you, don't you?" Santoro opined.

"You have nothing. You've seen Boris Trasker kill three people. My name is Yuri Markov. I'm not Boris Trasker. There is nothing you can charge me with. In a month my government will trade me for one of your spies."

"Oh, you think so, do you?" McCann interrupted "How's your shoulder? Trasker may have removed the slug, but I bet you have a scar there. I'll get a doctor to have a look at you." McCann rose and started to leave.

"Wait," Santoro ordered. "What size shoes do you wear?" "Eleven, triple E," Markov replied.

"Take them off," Santoro ordered. The Russian did as he was told. Santoro gave the shoes to McCann and both left the room.

Noticing the questioning look in his partner's eyes, Santoro whispered, "Remember what Claudia Morgan gave us in that envelope? I wonder if there is any of that same gel in the seams in these shoes.

Why don't we examine them and find out?" McCann grinned, then left; there was a spring to his step.

Santoro returned to Markov.

A clerk entered and handed the paper cup filled with water to the Russian, who nodded and smiled at the accommodation. "I'll be leaving tomorrow." Markov stated. "We'll see about that," Santoro replied. "I think I've had enough. If I spend any more time with you, it will ruin my supper. Remember this; killing a cop in this state is a mandatory death sentence."

"I'll be leaving tomorrow."

Two patrolmen escorted Markov out of the room to a holding cell where he would be spending the night.

Santoro entered the observation room. Chief Davis was concerned and angry. "He's a cool one, alright; doesn't seem to care a bit about the death penalty. But we've got him and pay he will. Are you going to question him any more today?"

"Hit men are given a target. They seldom participate in any kind of planning. I doubt whether questioning him further will yield much more. What bothers me is the way he kept insisting he would be leaving tomorrow."

Just then, a policeman threw open the door. "That guy, Markov; he's in the holding cell. I think he's dead."

A physical examination and the observed pallor of the individual indicated he was, indeed, dead.

The scar from McCann's bullet was also observed.

"He probably downed some cyanide. Look at those blue lips," Santoro observed. "Shit, and we had him, too. Get him to the morgue first thing tomorrow morning," the frustrated detective exclaimed.

It was anticlimactic when McCann showed up at Santoro's office the next morning and mentioned that traces of the gel were indeed found on the Russian spy's shoes. It didn't matter now.

Once again Markov had thwarted the police.

At the estate, Professor Potemkin and Sergei Trasker had just concluded a meeting which lasted several hours. Discussing Boris' present condition, they were marveling at the changes that had occurred.

Both emerged from the laboratory confident and determined. They felt they could successfully manage the situation, but the stress it had placed upon them was carved into the deep lines on their foreheads and faces.

Claudia Morgan had been waiting impatiently for Sergei Trasker for hours. When he finally appeared she was happy to see him. What he could not know was the woman he had entrusted with the most precious knowledge he had, had been giving the matter at hand a great deal of thought.

"You haven't had supper, yet." Claudia's statement was one of fact, not a question.

"I *am* hungry," the scientist admitted. Supper was served, and eaten in silence. The scientist appreciated the hiatus; his session with his former colleague had drained him.

Supper over, the pair moved to the great room. Potemkin had retired early. At his age, the present level of activity was too much for him. Sleep restored his strength, and he needed plenty of it.

"Sergei, I have questions, many of them." Claudia began.

"Go ahead and ask."

"Could Adam's birth of Eve have been like what's happening downstairs?"

"You mean as a form of parthenogenesis? I never looked at it that way."

"And Mary; Jesus had no earthly father, that's what everyone says. You said we were evolving toward that end. Could there have been a few that preempted that condition?"

"My grandmother told me that Adam was like God; he was both man and woman. Then God split the one from the other when Adam came to live on the earth. You see, you're not the only one who has had that idea."

"What do you think?"

"When I was twenty, I thought I knew a great deal. These days, I wonder if I know anything at all. It's interesting that the opening pages of Genesis mentions the birth of a woman from a man, and that according to the New Testament the Savior of the world is born of a woman without the benefit of a man.

It's as if the second is meant to counteract the effects of the first. If events like that were to occur today, we might call it parthenogenesis, or one of its many alternatives. I can't say any more, because I don't know any more."

"Do you believe that we might be headed back to the original condition of Adam?"

"Theology infers that we have to become like Adam before sin. How was he before sin, before he birthed Eve?"

"Fantastic."

"Incidentally, about half a dozen years ago, a discredited South Korean scientist unknowingly produced the first human embryos resulting from parthenogenesis. The human genome, Claudia, it's all there, we just have to find out how to uncover its potential."

"What about Boris?"

"Constantine and I are going to concentrate on delivering the infant. We think it might be a cesarean birth, but now that might not be so."

"What do you mean by that?"

"Mother Nature has been preparing the way for some time now, I just wasn't aware of it."

"Why weren't you?"

"You don't look for situations you can't imagine."

"I'm getting into the back of the fuel truck. They make a delivery every other Wednesday. After I get in I'll lay low until nightfall. Around ten, I'll contact you. Are you good to go with that?"

"I don't know; do you think you can carry this off alone?" Remsen asked, "I know we've prepared for this job, but things have changed. You saw what happened to McCarra. Do you want that to happen to you? What about your wife and kids?"

"Are you getting cold feet?"

"One of my buddies is dead. The rest, except for you, are in jail. I don't want to lose anyone else."

"In, or out, tell me now."

"You know I'm in."

"Get the 'copter ready, I'll be in touch."

Spanner agreed with his buddy Remsen that it would be difficult if not impossible to breach the estate house by himself. But there were no other options. He chose to ignore the most obvious choice; quit, and call it a day. He had crafted a plan, one that stood some chance of success.

The last time he was at the Trasker estate he and McCarra had checked out most of the rooms adjoining the hallway except the last two. Those were situated closest to the pillbox, which was probably the underground laboratory. So his first objective would be to get to those two rooms.

What would be his next move? The door leading to the lab would without a doubt be locked, perhaps guarded. He would need to subdue the guard and blast the door open. He needed explosives.

Once inside, he would have to react to whatever or whomever confronted him. He was also aware that he would be searching for something and that he had no idea what that something was. It took a great deal of effort for Spanner to keep brushing aside the recurring thought that what he was attempting was really stupid.

Sergei Trasker took Constantine Potemkin aside and whispered "We have to talk." The professor's response was a smile, one of those 'it's about time' smiles. Claudia Morgan, at Boris Trasker's side, glanced over and noticed the men leaving the room. "Will he be all right with me?" She asked. Sergei indicated he would.

Claudia resumed her conversation with Boris. Her presence seemed to calm him.

"We have a problem," Sergei began. "No, we don't," his colleague answered. "I know what you're going to tell me. It's not a surprise."

"You'll be alone for the next pair of procedures." Sergei Trasker's tone was terse.

"I'll train Lev to assist. I performed many procedures during the war with non-medical assistants.

It's not recommended, but I have done it. I'll just be an observer, unless something requires my attention.

It will be fine." The new challenges energized the old scientist. There was a bit more spring to his step and his voice took on a gusto it had not had before. Even James noticed the change. Sergei Trasker wondered what effect Potemkin's mood reversal might have had on his cancer. He was convinced it would be positive.

Boris Trasker's time was approaching. Completely healthy now, he was visibly annoyed with his protracted immersion in the gel, although Claudia's daily chats did much to assuage his apprehension.

Sergei and Constantine had not yet informed Boris and Claudia of what they had concluded about the approaching phenomenon. In Nature, procreation is sometimes followed by one of the mates passing away. The disturbing contradiction here was that this time, there would be only one host. Would the same protocol follow? Would Boris wither away and die? Sergei Trasker and Constantine Potemkin could not answer that question. They were standing at the edge of a huge body of knowledge without the means to determine any of its parameters.

In the meantime, Potemkin was using every available moment to indoctrinate and train Lev to the medical way of thinking about the human body. He took great pains to identify and explain the uses of surgical instruments, the proper way to give injections, and how to assess the condition of patients who had just emerged from surgery.

Lev did remarkably well. He worked doggedly at absorbing the tidal wave of information thrust upon him because he understood how important it was to be competent in his new capacity.

As if all this was not enough, one evening Sergei Trasker called his faithful servant into the sitting room.

"Here is the address of the law firm that handles all the affairs of the estate. I have made an appointment for you at eleven o'clock tomorrow. Go and see them." Lev glanced at his boss. "I know this seems strange to you, but go; they will explain everything."

The next morning, Lev did as he was instructed. The Lander, Lander, and Lander Attorneys offices were in a building just two blocks from Wall Street. As he entered the elevator, Lev wondered why he had been sent to this place. He thought hard about it, but couldn't see any reason for it.

After a very short wait, the secretary ushered him into the office of Bruce Lander, the eldest of three partners. Mr. Lander offered him a seat.

"Mister Trasker wants you to take over all the affairs of the estate and all his other holdings. You would make him very happy if you agreed to that. If you agree, he will explain everything when you get back. Will you?"

Lev's face turned crimson; the reason for his response subject to speculation.

Bruce Lander smiled. "Sergei said that you were a modest man. I can see that. Please don't be alarmed, you need not be afraid."

"I am not afraid, I am worried. Is Sergei going to die?" The head guard's anxiety showed in the unsteadiness of his voice. "He can't, he can't."

"It's nothing like that. Your boss is going to live forever. Why, he'll probably outlive you."

Those words were just what the scientist's number one guard needed. Relieved, he grinned broadly. "Show me where I sign." The lawyer placed the papers in front of him and Lev signed.

"I'll be sending along some other information. Look it over carefully. You are in charge now.

And, don't forget to stop and see Sergei. I'll call and let him know everything went well." Lev, still shaken from the experience, stopped to relieve himself on the way out. There was a scream and Lev, apologizing incessantly, burst out of the Ladies' room.

The mortuary wagon had only one cadaver in it; Markov. Since there was no rush to get to the morgue, the driver stopped by his usual haunt, Ruth's Little Coffee Shoppe, to get some breakfast. The conversation came around to Yankee pitchers, a subject of some contention. Back and forth went the slings and arrows, without anyone gaining an advantage. Sure, the Yanks had some poor pitchers, but they also had some darn good ones, too. Muttering to himself, the driver started his rig and drove off. The Yankee fan driver never even noticed that Markov's body bag had been cut open until he arrived at the morgue.

Becker Pharmaceutical's Moroka phoned Karper and inquired about 'the goods.' Skilled at providing information and not substance, this time the Triple I CEO faltered. Moroka understood; Karper had failed.

"Do you have someone who can get the goods?" Moroka probed.

"I have my best man on it," the CEO replied confidently.

"Your best man; do you mean only one person is working on this?"

"He is in charge. I'm sure he will get as many people as he needs to make the mission a success."

"How long will it take him?"

Cornered, the flustered Karper blurted out "He'll have it to me Monday, by noon."

"Then we'll have lunch at Eugene's. Let's say 1:30; I will meet you there."

Karper bit his lip; it was too late to retract what he had said. His only alternative now was to squeeze Spanner and get the goods by Monday - before noon.

The fuel truck arrived as scheduled at the Trasker estate. Spanner had managed to insert himself into the compartment containing the valves and nozzles located at the truck's rear. He noticed that in previous deliveries the guards never checked it.

As the truck rolled unchallenged through the gates, the lone intruder was relieved. But now a new problem surfaced. How might he get out of the compartment without being seen? The truck stopped.

Spanner listened as the driver's door slammed shut. The sound of footsteps got louder as he approached the compartment. The latch clicked and the door started to open.

Suddenly, a voice called out. "Helicopter; it's over there."

Spanner reckoned it was one of the guards. The driver moved away from the back of the truck.

Both men moved to the front of the vehicle. It sounded as if the guard was running away, toward the sound of the rotors. Spanner seized the opportunity to make good his escape. He could hear Remsen guiding the helicopter skyward and then its sound fading away in the distance.

Several spreading yews gave Spanner the cover he needed. Composing himself after nearly being discovered, he decided he would wait until the fuel truck departed before entering the building.

That would reduce the likelihood of anyone being present when he finally emerged from the shrubbery.

Within moments, the guard returned and engaged the driver in conversation while the fuel oil was being pumped into the storage tank.

Twenty minutes later it was on its way and the guard gone. Dirk Spanner was free to proceed with the on-the-spot scheme he had devised to enter the house. It was late afternoon, that time of day when important things have already been accomplished. And, with sunset approaching, a quiet and satisfying evening seems near.

Sergei and Claudia were in the lab engaging Boris in small talk. Potemkin, as was his habit during this part of the day, was napping. Even Lev felt confident enough to sneak away for a catnap. The chef was busy preparing the evening meal and the guards on duty manned their posts without the threat of further disruption.

As long as he wasn't discovered, the intruder could move about as he wished. Spanner went to the place he had made his last entry, the French doors. Surveying them closely before attempting to enter, he spotted what might have been several alarm devices attached to the doors and panes. He decided to seek another way in. That was more difficult. Most likely every door and window on the first floor would be locked. It appeared Spanner's plan was doomed to failure. Then he heard the voices. They were coming from above, on the second floor. Someone had opened the doors to the balconied bedrooms and was placing blankets on the railing for an airing.

Soon the doors were shut and the voices faded. Spanner waited, weighing his options. Climbing up to the balcony during the fading daylight would be risky. But if he waited too long, the doors would open once more and the blankets retrieved. The doors would be locked shut for the night.

Spanner decided to risk the daylight climb. His grappling hook caught the railing on the first toss.

Two minutes later he was on the balcony. Entering, he could hear the staff in the next room chatting as they worked. Now, all he needed was make his way undetected down the stairs and then to the far end of the hall. A few moments later he was at the door that might be the entrance to the Trasker laboratory.

He was correct. Fortunately for him Claudia had inadvertently left the door ajar. Spanner couldn't believe his good luck. He had made his way this far without being challenged. He considered it a good omen.

Ping was the first to yap the alarm. Sergei glanced at Claudia. Before either could say a word, Spanner stood in the doorway, pistol drawn.

"Hello. You know what I've come for. Let's not waste any time."

Ping, Pang, and Pong had been sitting. The intruder caused them to glance at their master.

They were awaiting his command. "Rest," he said. The three terriers rolled over on their side and closed their eyes. "You know you have come here at great risk to yourself."

"I lost a good man to that Great Dane of yours. Now, I'm going to get what I came for, even if I have to hurt a few people." The intruder stared at the scientist. There was no mercy in his gaze. "Let's get at it. I don't have all day," he demanded, waving his pistol at the pair.

Sergei Trasker reached into his pocket, retrieved his keys and a small, clear plastic container.

"Claudia, please stand over here, behind me. I need to get at that cabinet." The request seemed odd; she was already out of the way. Still, she complied.

The scientist knelt down as if to unlock the cabinet. He opened the container and texted three fleas to fly, the same prototype 'blahas' he had smashed into the Lucite.

"Come on, come on; let's move it. What's taking so long?" Spanner anxiously demanded.

The scientist rose, faced the intruder and handed him a dossier. Spanner leafed through the pages.

"What the hell is this? It's your income tax return for last year."

"What better place to hide my work. It's all encrypted. If you let me use my cell, I can print out the encryption code for you."

"Go ahead, but it better be fast. I'm losing patience. Maybe I'll kill her first." Spanner took aim at Claudia Morgan. "Will that make you move any faster?"

Sergei Trasker's text command to the fleas was going to be WOUND. Now, he punched in KILL.

Dirk Spanner fell to the floor in a heap.

The scientist commanded the fleas to RETURN. Dripping with cranial fluid, they returned to the container.

Remsen waited and waited for Spanner's call to pick him up. It never came. The pilot went back to his room, packed his bags and took the first bus home. His gut told him the mission was over.

Markov was furious. Why had the boss stuck him with this assignment? After all, he was an assassin, a professional; he wasn't a secret-stealer. The more he thought about it, the mission sounded like a one way ticket to oblivion. Why, because others, competent others, had tried, and failed. They were secret-stealers. If at all possible, they would have succeeded. It was their area of expertise. But they hadn't.

The two areas of endeavor were different; the approach, the surveillance, the entire operation.

Markov was struggling. His strong inclination was to go back to the homeland, but his indoctrination and training demanded he complete the mission, oblivion or not. Most of all he needed time to think it through.

He spent the following days surveying the property, its defenses, escape routes and personnel, much the same way Dirk Spanner had. But there was a difference. The Russian was also using the hiatus to evaluate his options and decide which should be the primary one. He reminisced frequently about his short stint in Baku when he was a young man, and how he had enjoyed the warm waters of the Caspian Sea. He had even encountered a beautiful young woman, one with shining black hair and dark, alluring eyes. The desire to return to those days was getting stronger; the call to duty, weaker.

The assassin had come to the same conclusion as Spanner; the fuel truck was the best way to get into the estate. But things had changed; Lev had also deduced that Spanner gained entry via the truck. If previous inspections of the vehicle had been considered thorough, the new protocol was 'super' thorough.

The 'truck way' into the estate was no longer available.

Despite his attempt to move ahead with his assignment, the Russian's uneasiness persisted. This was because he was recognizing the signs that were shouting 'you are past your prime.' He had had three close calls, the first at Yeshiva, a second after the concert at Carnegie Hall and finally, the third at Grand Central, the place where he was finally apprehended. None of those incidents would ever have occurred when he was young. No one could have put him at such a disadvantage. Yes, he had been that good.

Inexorably, Yuri Markov was coming to grips with his situation.

Who knows I have this assignment, thought the assassin; only the boss. He's short on manpower.

The incident at Claudia Morgan's condo must have wiped out the other team. That must have meant there were three dead. Was there a fourth? Was he also killed at the scene? If they were exterminated, was he, the boss, the only one left?

Markov knew what needed to be done. The plan was simple. He wondered whether that raven- haired beauty in Baku had married.

There are periods when time seems to slow and there are periods when it seems to fly by so swiftly that a person must cling to it with all determination.

Sergei Trasker, Claudia Morgan, and Constantine Potemkin stood at the precipice of the latter.

Spanner's remains had been removed by the authorities. Santoro and McCann were in charge of the investigation and interviewing those involved. Already familiar with the previous assaults and the fact that Dirk Spanner was an armed intruder, there appeared to be no need for any further inquiry. Still, an intruder experiencing an aneurism of the brain while attempting to commit a burglary did seem odd.

Santoro and McCann chose not to delve deeper. Death was due to an aneurism, period.

All that was history. Boris was about to make medical history and give birth. If there was a time when intrusion of any sort would be unwelcome, it would be now. Sergei, Constantine. and Lev had prepared. They had anticipated every possible complication.

The delivery went well. The infant was born in the same manner as Caesar.

The condition of the infant surprised the scientists. Well along in development, the babe was able to get to its feet within hours, in the same manner that offspring of grazing animals are able. Sense of equilibrium, the ability to turn to sound and discern various objects were already functional. Sergei turned to Constantine. Both were dumbfounded. Past experience could not explain what they were witnessing.

Within hours Boris began to wilt; his roseate bloom faded. He had accomplished his mission of producing an offspring and now there was nothing further required. In some inscrutable way, Sergei understood the cycle he was seeing played out. Boris' work was over. Now he was expendable.

Sergei Trasker sensed he might be witnessing the primal paradigm that had been promised from the beginning of time. Had the way been opened for the Adam of Eden to return?

Weary, Sergei disrobed, showered, dressed, and went upstairs. Claudia would be waiting.

"Well? How did it go?"

"I am an uncle," Sergei answered as he slipped onto the sofa. "How could this have happened?

You'll never believe it. You must see the child. It's as if he's already nine months old, perhaps older. It's incredible."

"How can a man be born again? That's what Nicodemus asked Jesus. That question has been asked over and over again? I'm frightened. We've used the gel. Will we be next?"

"What does that have to do with what just happened? My brother just had a baby. I'm too tired to hear all this. Tomorrow, Claudia, we'll talk then." The scientist headed for bed. Drained physically and emotionally, he wondered whether he would be able to manage the stairs.

Claudia remained behind at the computer, striving to make sense of all that had occurred. She was too agitated to consider going to bed. She was also unaware of Boris' condition.

Markov parked his car in Triple I's parking lot, where he could observe the firm's main entrance. Claudia Morgan was the only link to Sergei Trasker that he knew. He had read the dossier Karper handed him on the train. Everything he needed was there; schedules of entering vehicles, location of entrances, the name of the firm that installed the security systems, and a map showing the types of devices installed. Missing was the number of personnel guarding the estate, their routes and timetables.

Markov decided not to follow orders. He had something else in mind. Steadying his high-power binoculars against the steering wheel, he began observing the personnel entering and exiting the building.

Not sure of what he would find, nevertheless he felt there was a good chance he could connect someone at Triple I with the Trasker operation. From experience he knew that agents usually worked alone, but that handlers remained close by for support.

The day dragged on; he was disappointed. Since this was his first day, he decided to stick it out and remain at his post until nine o'clock. By then, most of the executives, those who usually remained after hours, would have gone home. By eight, the Russian was toying with cutting his day short and heading home. Fortunately he decided to wait until nine.

At ten to nine, Janus Karper walked out into the parking lot and headed for his car. Markov grinned. "Hello, my secretive friend," he whispered.

A professional spy is hardly ever observed spying. Depending on the circumstances regarding his cover and identity, he chooses to be seen a great deal, seldom, or not at all. John Drake was a master at making the appropriate choice of when and when not to be seen. His expertise at remaining alive and completing difficult missions were the reasons he was chosen for the Triple I investigation.

Drake had managed to learn a great deal about Triple I. He knew, for example that the chief accountant, Henry Burrows, had a habit of directing one thousand dollars a month to a firm called Random Stationary, a firm he owned through a holding corporation. Marcy Myers, a legal secretary, worked on the floor below in the accounting department. She was Burrows' paramour. They regularly vacationed together at upscale European resorts.

Carl Lancer, one of the firm's lawyers, was a mole for Crater Investments, a large firm holding a chair on the New York Stock Exchange. It was his job to monitor who Triple I's clients were targeting and inform them when an assault on them was imminent.

Janus Karper was another matter. The man was extremely cautious. Drake had shadowed him for months and still could not discover anything onerous. The executive used throw away cells and never even once, initiated a call from his company to anyone other than business associates. That degree of caution indicated to Drake that Karper did, indeed, have something to hide. Installing the chemically treated window blinds helped. Lip reading is not a perfect science, but it gleaned enough information for Drake to conclude that Janus Karper was engaged in espionage and held a high position in the pecking order.

Drake knew he had to bide his time. Eventually, some situation would force Karper to shed his cover. The agent had no way of knowing the very incident he had been waiting for was about to happen.

He had taken up a position near the parking lot to monitor Karper's comings and goings. It did not take him long to notice that another person, Markov, was doing the same, but from a vehicle parked in the last row of the lot. With two people to watch, Drake called for help.

"That's a new one. The Feds want to know if we can spare a person for some stakeout. It's to help one of their deep cover agents. They think the guy in the parking lot is some low level character," Chief Davis informed Santoro and McCann.

"Is it anyone we know; is the person a felon? Who's the deep cover guy?" Santoro asked.

"He can't make the guy. He's got some photos of him and we should be getting them any time now." Davis' secretary burst into the room and handed the chief an envelope. "Thanks," the chief responded, but the woman was already closing the door. He opened the envelope and spilled the photos out on his desk. "Does he look familiar? Can you identify him?"

"It's Markov," Santoro sputtered.

"And I know just the guy for the job," McCann exclaimed.

Santoro turned to Chief Davis. "Can we get Jurgens reinstated to the CIA for just this one assignment? It would be great if he was the one to nab Markov this one more time."

Davis seemed elated at the request. "If they don't activate him, then, goddamn it, I'll find a way to do it."

The estate and its inhabitants were now most vulnerable. Boris' present condition demanded there be no more disturbances. Soon, Professor Potemkin and Lev would be taking care of Sergei and Claudia. The burden of protecting the group in the laboratory and those recuperating fell to the remaining cadre. Lev and Sergei had chosen well. Each of the protectors were dedicated; they respected and loved Sergei and their boss, Lev. Claudia Morgan and Professor Potemkin were also under their protection because they were Sergei's friends. That was enough of a distinction for the guards.

Unknown to all, the recent skirmishes, both at Westchester and Claudia's condo had all but wiped out the contingent charged with obtaining Sergei Trasker's discovery. Markov, Karper and Moroka were all that remained.

Markov was the only one who had recent field experience. The other two, former spies, were now administrators. At this late stage in their careers they were not anxious to reenter the stark world of doing field work.

Moscow had decided that additional agents would not be reassigned from their current activities.

Unspoken yet powerful, there had always been a lingering suspicion at the Central Committee that Constantine Potemkin had overstated the importance of Trasker's breakthrough. Thus, Moscow was waiting, somewhat listlessly, for the message that indicated the mission was a success.

Disaster

Two CIA agents visited Professor Jurgens at home and informed him he was being reinstated just for this one assignment. When he learned it concerned Markov, he had several questions. If circumstances allowed, could he apprehend the Russian? The answer he received was swift and decisive; no, he couldn't. Other operatives were involved and an untimely arrest might jeopardize the entire operation. Who would be his handler? Jurgens was told he would be contacted by the agent in charge, and soon. Other information, such as the handler's identity, were on a need to know basis, and Jurgens was not one of those in the loop.

That night, Jurgens decided to follow a hunch he had. The last time he had encountered the Russian, the man had parked his car. It looked as if he was heading for the subway entrance. might that have been where he was hiding? Telling noone, he elected to stake out the entrance. It would be an all- night vigil. Armed with a bag-full of sandwiches and two thermoses of coffee, he took up his position in the parking lot adjacent the entrance and waited.

Markov emerged at eight the next morning, got into his car and sped off. Already aware of Karper's routine, he knew how much time it would take to get to Triple I and how long he would have to wait until Karper arrived. Jurgens noticed the Russian was carrying a gun case. He would have alerted his handler, but he didn't have his number. Jurgens elected not to follow. Being discovered now would have been catastrophic.

Jurgens cell rang. Drake, without identifying himself, described the layout of the Triple I parking lot and where Markov's car was located. He was not to be apprehended until Drake gave the go-ahead.

Jurgens was to observe his prey from the slope to the east of the lot. That left the slope to the west as the perch for the Triple I operative.

"Our mystery man is arriving at the parking lot. Wait, he's leaving. I am in no position to follow.

What is your location?"

Jurgens stepped on the gas. Perhaps he might get there in time.

"Wait, he's not leaving, just taking another parking space closer to the entrance."

"He's going to shoot; he's got a rifle, stop him," Jurgens shouted over the phone.

"Hey, calm down," Drake said, "He's not going to do anything with all these people around."

"Damn it, I wish you'd listen to me. I'm telling you he's got a rifle."

"And just how would you know that?" Drake asked.

"I saw him this morning coming out of his cave. He was carrying a rifle case."

"You know where he hides out?"

"Not exactly, but I know which subway entrance he uses to come and go."

"We'll talk about the subway thing later. Get up here as fast as you can." That ended the conversation.

After Jurgens arrived on the scene, the two settled in for another long day of surveillance.

About nine that evening and right on time, Janus Karper opened the front door and headed for his car. Suddenly, he fell to the sidewalk.

"He's been shot," Jurgens transmitted over his cell. Markov got out of his car and went over to his target. Lowering his weapon, he shot several more times.

Jurgens saw Drake get out of his car, take out his pistol, and begin firing at the shooter. Don't do that, don't expose yourself, Jurgens whispered to himself. He watched Markov run and take cover among the parked vehicles. Drake jumped into his car and headed for the place he last saw the shooter. No, don't do that. Stop and take cover, damn it, take cover, Jurgens muttered.

Suddenly, Markov stood up, took aim, and fired several times at the approaching vehicle. The car swerved suddenly, and then crashed into several others. Drake opened the door, stumbled out, and fell to the ground in a heap.

Jurgens sat quietly in his vehicle and watched Markov make his getaway. Any movement would have alerted the assassin there might have been another observer. After the car was out of sight, Jurgens raced to Drake's side. There was no need for an ambulance. One of the rounds of explosive ammunition had blown open a cavity where Drake's heart should have been.

Claudia Morgan was standing beside Boris Trasker. "It's the Adam of ancients reclaiming his original place; it's being born again, to a new life. It's being him again, with Eve still inside, as God intended. You simply accelerated the process. Remember the water flea, the midge, and the gecko? They all possess this same power to create. I'm wondering whether this is going to happen to us. Are we going the way Boris is? Sergei, are we going to die too?"

Sergei Trasker remained silent while Claudia Morgan rambled on. Everything she proposed was to say the least, highly speculative. Still, he remembered what his grandmother had told him. Others had been thinking and mulling over this 'born again' idea for some time. He wondered how many others had arrived at an interpretation of those words which differed from the accepted one. Certainly, none had come to the point where they might be thinking about delivering their brother's baby, and certainly no one would be considering having one themselves without being impregnated.

Claudia's ideas seemed on the cusp of sanity, but the present situation did raise questions.

Moment by moment, Sergei Trasker was coming to a different understanding of age-old concepts. He felt sure she had already concluded they would be next.

She sat down next to the scientist. Flipping through several marked sections of various volumes, she recited again and again the concept that one had to be 'born again' to be eligible for heaven, no matter how one might interpret that statement. The further she investigated, the more she found that many more writings alluded to becoming transformed, being 'born again.'

Claudia Morgan's discourse ended. She glanced at Sergei. The scientist had that appearance people get when they are deep in thought – and distressed. "Sergei, Sergei; are you all right?" She tugged at his sleeve.

"Yes, I'm here," the scientist replied finally, "I'm all right. I was thinking."

"I know. You were somewhere near Saturn. I'm glad you returned."

"We're next, you know. I believe you have come to that conclusion all by yourself. Boris' work is over. He is the host of a new Boris; the first to have been born again, if that can be believed. For some time now scientists have said that only certain traits could be transmitted to offspring. Were they mistaken?"

Claudia embraced Sergei. "I don't know, but if you believe even a little of what I've read, you'll begin to understand what's happening to us."

"What's the matter?"

"I'm frightened." Claudia burst into tears.

Sergei embraced her. "Come, let's see how my little new brother is doing."

Claudia wiped the tears away. Arm in arm, they went to visit the child.

Boris' offspring was already remarkable. Sergei noticed several characteristics that mimicked exactly the movements of his brother when a child. That was where the age - for age similarity ended.

Child Boris was eons farther ahead in development. Sergei was uncomfortable in the child's presence. A few times he caught the infant watching him. It reminded him of his brother. The experience was unsettling; had he created a way for his brother to leap into the next generation via his offspring? The scientist decided to test the child's responses. He cupped his hands in the same way he had when he and Boris were young. It was a little game they played just before going to sleep. Papa and Mama were in the kitchen and the boys' game produced no sound. All was well.

Sergei approached the child. To his astonishment child Boris immediately recognized what was being offered and engaged the scientist in the game exactly the same way his brother would have. Absent any hesitation the terrified scientist and the child played the game to its conclusion. This time Sergei won.

He placed his hands at his side. Young Boris followed suit. Sergei leaned forward and gazed into the child's eyes. He saw his brother, intact, but younger in years.

Regardless of the wonder he had witnessed, Sergei still had to prepare both he and Claudia for their journey; experiencing death and then hoping that their issue would be the missile that thrust them intact into a new life. No one could ever have been exposed to a more excruciating challenge.

New Boris had filled him with this hope of cheating death and being able to bridge the gap into the next generation, and the next, ad infinitum. The concept bordered on the insane, but he clung to it.

There were no other options.

Markov observed all the speed limits and traffic signals on the way back to his cave. There was no reason to hurry. Silencing Karper was his last mission. He felt certain that no one would conclude it was he who had dispatched the Triple I executive.

It had been reported previously that the person attempting to kill Professor Jurgens had been wounded. Both Potemkin and Karper knew the identity of the assassin. Neither knew whether he had survived the attempt. After the meeting on the train, Potemkin remained the only one unaware that Markov had survived.

With Grigorev and company having failed so miserably in trying to kidnap Claudia Morgan, Markov rightly concluded that Karper would have been reticent to make that disaster known to his superiors. The Russian agent also rightly deduced that the mission Karper had given him were known only to them.

If this reasoning was correct, Markov was home free. No one knew of his whereabouts. He had not initiated contact. Under such circumstances, he would have been presumed dead. Karper's death most likely would remain unsolved, just another anomaly in police case files. With the last four bullets, the Russian agent had severed himself from his profession as an assassin and spy.

First, the agent went to his main lair, the one at Carnegie. After collecting all the paraphernalia he deemed important and destroying the rest, he returned to his second, the one located in the subway. He packed his bags, burned a number of documents, and then sat down to relax. Since there was no rush, Markov decided he would leave the next morning. He called and made reservations for the next available flight to Baku, via Vienna; first class, of course.

The evening Karper was murdered, Albert Moroka was attending a summit of pharmaceutical executives in Denver, Colorado. The attendees were from all over the globe. Conversations lasted far into the night. It seemed everyone at the affair assumed obtaining Sergei Trasker's discovery was a foregone conclusion. Various firms were bidding for 'a piece of the cake,' even though they had no idea what the content of the discovery might be. Greed was palpable. The Becker executive had called the meeting, certain that before long, he would be in possession of the coveted material. Eventually, the weary group succumbed to their need for rest.

Albert Moroka got up rather late the next morning. Everything having gone so well the previous evening, he felt now would be the perfect time to ring up Janus.

"Hello, this is Albert Moroka. May I please speak to Janus Karper?"

"What's your business with him?" Bob McCann replied.

"Is he there?" The tone of McCann's voice made Moroka cautious.

"I'm Investigator Bob McCann. Mister Karper is dead. This is a police investigation. What is the nature of your business with him?"

Moroka slammed down the phone. In half an hour he was on the way to Stapleton International Airport. The remaining executives appeared for breakfast, only to find the person in charge of the meeting was nowhere to be found.

Baku. . . Markov could feel the hot breeze caressing his face. Glancing around his lair one last time, he grasped both pieces of luggage, walked along the narrow tunnel walkway and headed up the stairs leading to street level. It was early, the city still had not switched from the cool of the evening air to the sultry heat of the day. Pulling together the collar of his light coat, the Russian agent began walking toward his car.

"Don't move," a voice behind him whispered.

Markov put down his bags. He glanced up at the sky, now getting lighter with each passing moment. "I was on my way to my haunt on the Caspian Sea. There's a hotel there I frequent. Would you like to come? I have enough money for both of us. You can even bring your family."

"And what about Peters, and Silverman and Collins, can they come too?" Jurgens replied.

"You are a good man, faithful to your comrades. I admire that." Markov reached inside his coat, drew out his pistol and spun around. This time the former CIA agent was ready. As the pair of bullets tore through the Russian agent's body, he whispered to himself 'proshchai Baku,' goodbye, Baku.

After making sure the agent was dead, Jurgens holstered his weapon. He placed a call. "Hello, Detective Santoro; I got him. Yes, he's dead. Send someone to pick him up, will you? I've got to call my wife and tell her she can come home."

Claudia Morgan sat in the great room peering through the large window at the pool where two Merganser ducks were splashing water over themselves. A shadow of a smile wisped across her face as she surreptitiously participated in the mini-maelstrom she was observing. The little fowls were at their comical best, cavorting, diving, surfacing, flapping, making waves and just enjoying the moment. Claudia wished she could have been like them. Boris' death had certainly been difficult enough, but it had also opened the door to a possibility Claudia had never considered; certain death, and soon. Whatever the reasoning, whatever the premise, hope or promise of life beyond the shroud of death, it still lacked verification. The reality of it all shook the young woman to her core.

Who was Boris' child? Was he, indeed, the reincarnation of the host? How could anyone really know the answer to that question? The more Claudia thought about it, the more it upset her. Logic and the power of deductive reasoning had run its course.

"A penny for your thoughts." It was Sergei. He had been observing Claudia for a while. "You seem pleased with what's out there. May I look, too?"

"It's two silly ducks having the time of their lives. I wish I were with them."

"You mean they don't know that they're going to have to die soon, is that it?"

"It seems you read minds, too."

"The same thoughts crossed mine as did yours. You're not alone in this, you know."

"I think it's time for the truth, don't you. I couldn't bear going to my grave without telling you how much I love you. I think I've always loved you, even before we met. I have always loved your kind of person. I didn't believe one actually existed."

"Claudia, I, I. . ." Sergei hesitated. "It's hard for me to trust anyone. All those years when there wasn't anyone, I withered up inside. God, I do love you, I do, but I can't trust you - not yet."

"We don't have much time. I have no choice but to trust you with my life, my baby and my new self. Doesn't that stand for something?"

"I didn't do this to myself - it's them, they did it! Every night I curse them for it, because now I have met you - and I can't respond. I'm still afraid." Sergei left Claudia to her splashing Mergansers.

Moroka was back in his office at Becker. If Karper was dead, did that mean 'his man,' the one who was directing the theft, was also dead? Was there anyone else involved in the operation? Who else knew? Certainly, he didn't. Perhaps Potemkin did, but where was he? Was he hiding, or had he gone over to the other side? I must find Potemkin, the executive mused, he will know all about this.

The Becker executive spent most of the morning calling everyone he thought might help him find Potemkin. It was his only option. Such dire consequences would not reflect well on this giant in the field of espionage. Moscow of late had begun to sour on operations in the United States. This, because of the repeated mission failures and subsequent rounding up of their agents. Russian spies were beginning to appear more and more inept while their American counterparts more and more skilled.

Desperation, at times, causes one to ignore common sense, and this was the precipice that Moroka was approaching. Instead of waiting for answers from individuals he had spent the morning calling, the executive felt it necessary to act, do something, anything, immediately.

Aniushka, 'little'Anna, sat just beyond the door to his office. She was the one who met Markov at Union Square and had given him the train ticket. Her boss had no idea she knew Karper, or that she was one of his operatives. Her position as Moroka's executive secretary provided the Triple I CEO with 'disaster insurance.'

Karper had also taken her as a lover. While in his case it was a stratagem, in hers it was a pure and sincere case of love. Not stupid, Anna realized the relationship might not have been all she wished, but she accepted its limitations. There was always the hope that at some point in the future, the bond between them might strengthen.

Moroka pressed the intercom button. "Anna, please come." The door opened and the woman entered.

"I need you to do some investigative work for me."

"Of course, sir, what do you want?"

"Janus Karper was murdered last night as he left his office. We were in the midst of a very important negotiation. I must find out who the other principles are." Were he not so embedded in his own thoughts, Moroka would have noticed that Anna started to swoon, but managed to regain her composure.

"Of course, you understand this investigation is to be covert." He glanced at Anna. "Are you all right?

You seem a bit pale. Should I get you a glass of water or something?"

"No, no, it's just that murder, oh, my god, how terrible." Anna began to sob. He guided her to a chair.

"I'll get the nurse. Perhaps she can give you something to calm you." The executive hurried out of the room.

Anna was well aware of the 'negotiations' between her lover and Moroka. Janus had related every detail of the mission to obtain Sergei Trasker's discovery and the pressure her employer had placed on him to deliver the goods. Anna had worked long enough with her boss to know that he had two personas; the first, a considerate and efficient administrator and, the second, a ruthless savage when he felt circumstances dictated the necessity for such a posture.

She concluded it was Moroka who had ordered Karper's murder.

"Please sit," Sergei Trasker suggested to Lev. The scientist explained to his long-time friend and head guard the reasons for him shifting all assets and responsibility to another person. Not insensitive, Lev had already begun to suspect that a significant change might be coming. He never expected it would be what was now coming from the lips of his employer.

The scientist went into great detail, explaining the reason for the abbreviated medical training, the shift of assets, and what he expected would occur after the three blessed events were over. The most important point the scientist made over and over again was that no one except Lev, Potemkin, Boris, Claudia, and Sergei should know what was happening.

As far as everyone else was concerned, and this included the cadre of guards, everything was progressing normally. Sergei, Claudia, and Boris were travelling abroad, and Potemkin had gone back to Russia. The Potemkin timetable rested on his being able to survive the ordeal at the estate, delivering several babies, and then being able to return to the motherland before the cancer took his life. Sergei provided Lev with the names of several obstetricians in the event the cancer incapacitated Potemkin before he could perform the deliveries.

"You are my best friend. I know this is a great burden. But I have no one else whom I trust as much as I do you."

"I will not fail you. Don't worry; everything will be fine." Lev had many questions. Some he would not have dared to ask before this. But now, he rained them down on the scientist, and he, Sergei, unabashedly provided the answers.

What Sergei Trasker did not mention to his friend was the forming of a deepening conviction that he, Sergei Trasker, might indeed be experiencing being 'born again.'

Moroka called executive secretary Anna Kremenko into his office.

"I have contacted a number of my associates. Here is a list of people and the phone numbers Janus Karper is known to have contacted. Find them and see whether they had anything to do with the operation I entrusted him with. With or without him, this endeavor must be successful."

Annuishka stared at her boss. He believed she was showing resolve. It was smoldering rage. "I shall give this my full attention, sir. I will see to it, and perhaps get you more than you expect."

"That's my Anniushka," He whined. More than you expect, he mused, what a woman.

Anna had been a part of Janus Karper's life long enough to be familiar with his habits and haunts, even though he had been very careful about discussing them with her. Being devious was part of the corporate world and Anna was very skilled at it. Ascending to her present position was not an accident.

One by one, the secretary called each telephone number. Many of the people were unavailable, had moved on, or were unwilling to converse with a person they had never met. One, however, did pique her interest. She decided to see him. 'Josef' condescended to meet her at a given time at a restaurant in Greenwich Village. Once called Humpty Dumpty's, now called Karavas Place.

Josef was sitting alone at a table outside on the sidewalk. As he saw Anna approaching, he arose and acknowledged her. "Please, sit down."

"How is it that you know me? I have never met you."

"There is much back room talk about the big boss trying to complete a mission about to fail. He's been calling everyone, from the highest to the lowest. He must be very worried, not so?"

"You're not very respectful," Anna said as she glared at the man.

"He's a pig, they're all pigs. They send us out on these stupid assignments and expect success every time. They have no idea the danger they're exposing us to."

"How do you know me?"

"Someone from the embassy informed me I might be getting a call. They even forwarded your picture, and so on and so on. Now, would a smart boss telegraph anyone who was meeting their representative by posting that person's name and picture and. . ."

". . .so on and so on. I admit that was very stupid."

"Maybe he wants you killed, or arrested. Did you ever think of that?"

"No, I didn't." Anna was truly surprised.

"Perhaps he found out that you and Janus were lovers." The woman stared at Josef. "You are a good agent, Anna. There are few secrets in our community. Everyone knows what everyone else is doing.

It's like having an insurance policy. In our business one never knows when someone will decide to collect."

"Moroka sent me to investigate who might have ordered Janus' death."

"He did, of course. He has no tolerance for failure. And that's why he sent you out. He probably wants you out of the way, too."

"You think someone is out there waiting for me?"

"Yes, I do; maybe it's me." Anna stiffened. She slipped her hand into her purse. "Put that away. I was just making a very bad joke. What do you say we collaborate and kill Moroka? I hate the bastard.

Once, he gave the order to have me killed. I talked him out of it after I dispatched the assassin. He's no good, you know, the worst of the worst. Well, what do you say? He killed your lover didn't he?"

Anna stared into Josef's eyes. Was this a trap? Was this her boss' doing? She studied the man sitting across the table from her. He had already shown his brashness. Now she had to decide how sincere he was. Josef must have read her mind. He placed his hands on his open shirt and unbuttoned it.

"Here is your Albert Moroka. This shows just how much he values human life." The bullet wound had not quite healed. More important than the evidence Josef presented was the passion Anna saw in his eyes. He wanted him dead.

"How shall we do it?"

"I would like the pleasure. Is that all right?"

"Do it so that I can watch." Anna hesitated; was it a trap, one set by her boss? Suddenly, she was suspicious. All of this had been too easy. She drew back.

"What's the matter? Don't you want him dead?"

"Before we go any further, I must give this some thought. I need some time. I'll call you in a few days. Will that be all right?"

"Going to tell Albert about our conversation?" Josef's eyes were now slits; his lips were drawn."

"You have no idea how much I hate that man, do you?" Anna patted Josef's arm. "Two days, I will call then."

James turned the light on, got up from bed and headed for the door. Someone was rapping on it, lightly, but urgently. It was Potemkin.

"Come in," James invited. The light shining on the old scientist's face provided the reason for his visit. "Are you out of morphine? You appear to be in pain. I have some in my bag." The valet guided the scientist over to a chair. Potemkin collapsed into it. Retrieving the pills, James returned with two of them and some water. Potemkin wolfed them down and sighed.

"Ah, now I shall be able to sleep. Thank you, good friend."

"Is it getting worse? Are you able to handle the pain?"

"The pills are supposed to give me relief for four hours. They last only three."

"I'll get Sergei," a concerned James replied.

"No, no, don't. If he sees how sick I am, he'll have me sent to a hospital or somewhere else for treatment. He needs me, James, and I must help him. He has no one else. I know you understand what I am saying."

The valet nodded.

The professor fell silent. He appeared very tired, most likely from a protracted period of enduring pain without relief.

"I want to go home, back to Russia. I've had enough of this travelling. I want to see my family, I miss them," James said.

"It will be just a little while longer, and then we both can go," the professor answered. "I, too, have had enough of this life; research, academia, and all that. I think I'd like to get a good Italian rattan chair and just sit in the warm sun. That would be good. I'll leave the rest of the work to Sergei and others like him who are building their careers and hoping to astound the world with their next great discovery.

Do you think that's an admission I'm getting ready to die, James?"

"You've realized it's time to dismount, Constantine. You always were a bit arrogant, you always thought you rode better than the others. I believe the cancer has caused you to put your life back into balance. In that way your malady has been a blessing."

"Constantine, you haven't called me that for years."

"I did, when we were friends. I never called you that when I was your valet. Just now I was speaking to you as a friend."

"Forgive me, James. We were friends." Potemkin reached out and grasped James' hand.

"We are friends." Potemkin winced. "Tomorrow, go out and get some more morphine. I'll contact the embassy and have someone write several prescriptions. Don't fill them all at the same pharmacy."

"I could be arrested for that."

"You are the best sneak in the world," Potemkin answered, "You won't get caught. The professor sighed. "The drug is starting to take effect. I feel better already."

"Let me help you to your room," James suggested.

"What, a healthy, slightly cancer-ridden man like me? No, thank you. Besides, I don't want anyone to think I won't be able to do what I came here for." Potemkin winked.

James shook his head. "You are still intolerable, Constantine."

Potemkin slept well. James did not.

"He's in the wagon again. This time he won't be doing any Houdini act," Santoro mentioned to Jurgens.

"I'm the only one left," Jurgens observed, "Collins, Peters, and Silverman, they're all gone. I can't believe it. The Russians tried to kill us once, but that Russian doctor saved us, gave us our lives back. Why did they decide to change that? Was it sour grapes?"

Santoro glanced at McCann. "Probably that was it," McCann said. "No doubt about it, sure, that must have been it," Santoro chimed in.

"Well, it's all over. I've called my wife and she'll be coming home this evening. I've got to get to the airport and pick her up." He bid both detectives goodbye and left.

"Was that bullshit you were giving him, or what?" Santoro barked at McCann, "You don't have the slightest idea why those Russians came after them."

"You're right. Thanks for backing me up. Well, now he has answers. He can put the whole caper to bed."

"What was I going to do, leave you out there to dry? I'll even admit you might have been right.

He did need closure. You gave it to him, even though it was an out and out lie."

"And, what's going on with this Karper murder? What's that all about?" McCann, ever the bloodhound, was on the trail again.

"Ask that guy on the way to the morgue, he knows. The answer to that question is going to get buried in potter's field. We can't know everything."

"Who knows what evil lurks in the hearts of men, the Shadow knows." McCann laughed.

"Cut that out."

Sergei Trasker opened the door where 'little' Boris was being kept. It had been several months since his birth and the child was already behaving precociously. As Sergei approached, the child turned to the sound of his footsteps and their gazes met. "Boris?" The scientist called out and thought he saw a faint glimmer of familiarity in the child's eyes. There was no verbal response, but the scientist felt sure he was not mistaken. It was Boris. Nodding to the babysitter and asking whether all was well, he made a hasty exit.

What have I done, Sergei Trasker asked himself. Claudia's time is coming, and then mine. What have I done? On the way down the stairs, Sergei met his colleague.

"Disturbing, isn't it, seeing someone of the next generation who is the same person as the one who lived in the last. It's not cloning or parthenogenesis or the host of others forms of regeneration we are familiar with. This is the essence of copying, truly being born again," Potemkin offered.

"How can you say that? You don't even believe in God."

"The look of surprise on your face when you came down the stairs, that's how. You saw Boris, didn't you? Say it, say it. I saw it, too. After this experience, I just might convert."

"I can't deny it," muttered the scientist. "What are we going to do, Constantine?"

"We are going to follow the path that has been provided for us, that's what we're going to do.

Claudia thinks she'll be ready soon, perhaps within the week. Stay with her as much as you can, she seems anxious. I would be too, under the circumstances. I'll go and check on little Boris. He's been doing extraordinarily well so far. He's developing so rapidly I'll probably be playing chess with him by next Christmas - and losing." Potemkin's levity was lost on Trasker.

The scientist found Claudia sitting in a chaise on the patio, soaking in the brilliant sunlight. She smiled at him as he approached. It was wistful, uncertain, not one of gladness or joy. Sergei kissed Claudia on the cheek.

"I'm going to be a mother, and of myself. How's that for a show-stopper?" Claudia embraced Sergei, but this time fiercely, longingly. She needed reassurance, someone who would tell her everything was going to be all right.

The scientist realized her need and told her what she needed to know. Without one reinforcing speck of scientific insight that what he theorized would come to pass, he whispered "It's all going to be alright. I'm staking my life, yours, and young Boris' on it. You and I are going to live for a very long time."

"Thanks," Claudia replied and released Sergei from her embrace. "I know you don't really have any answers, but I find reassurance in what you envision, not in your words, but of what I see in young Boris. He seems familiar, as if he was the adult Boris I knew, yet in a child's body. Boris the young is Boris the old, a generation advanced. I'm betting everything on that."

Silence reigned at the supper table. Neither Sergei nor Claudia seemed disposed to small talk, or any, for that matter. An occasional glance was the best that could be had. Without addressing it, both were aware that her time was nearing.

Then Lev and two others entered. They had wheeled in a huge three-tiered white cake. Bride and groom dolls positioned in a bed of sugared roses adorned its top. Claudia was the first to spot it. She rose, raced over Sergei and kissed him passionately. Lev et al grinned.

"If I can't marry you in this life, perhaps there will be time in the next," Sergei blubbered. "I love you, Claudia."

"What's the reason for the cake?"

"I thought we might have our honeymoon before our wedding. I've given my life much thought.

My captors will not steal you away from me because of what they've done. I won't let them. . . I trust you Claudia, with my life."

"Shall I cut?" Lev inquired.

"Please." Sergei embraced Claudia. "We'll begin the night with the cake. Dessert will come later."

Cake-eating went briskly; some might say at breakneck speed. Afterward, Sergei led Claudia up the stairs to the bedroom. Throwing the door open, He carried her across the threshold.

Sergei's trembling fingers could not unbutton Claudia's blouse. Gently, she guided them. His face turned crimson when he saw her breasts and reached out to touch them. He was panting. As if to memorialize the event, he closed his eyes. Who knew what terrible memories he was replacing with this lovely moment? His behavior was sophomoric almost infantile, for this was, indeed, his first time. Even with the availability of the 'girlfriend' the Russians had provided, he resisted, not willing to trust anyone, even her.

Sergei Trasker was a virgin.

The love-waltz continued, but it was unlike any other, for this event included an exorcism, a rite of passage, and an entry into the promised land of being loved and loving in return. Moment by moment, Claudia Morgan was erasing Sergei's fear and apprehension, the two ogres that had been his companions for so many years. Not an easy task, still, it needed to be done.

When time and event allow, there appears that eternally joyful face of consummated love that all lovers exhibit. Claudia's face radiated with that light, and deep, deep within himself, Sergei understood and participated in her elation. After a time, the brief lovemaking ceased; after all, a child was on the way.

Exhausted and deliriously happy, Sergei lay on his back looking at the ceiling. Claudia rolled over and placed her head on his chest.

"Whatever follows, at least now you know that I love you," he whispered.

"I've always known," she replied, "even during that moment at the police station. I just had to make you aware that I knew."

"There were too many ghosts. I couldn't respond; I wanted to, but was afraid."

"That's all behind us. Now we must face what comes next. I'm not so sure I can manage, but I'll do my best."

"I'm sorry, Claudia, I didn't realize. . ."

Claudia placed her finger on the scientist's lips. "Please be quiet, love, and let me enjoy the moment. I've just been seduced by the man I love. Let's leave the rest for the future."

Sergei kissed Claudia on the forehead. Both enjoyed the customary lovers' respite.

"Well, what have you found?" Josef seemed irritated. Anna had promised to contact him in 'two days,' but today marked one week since they had met. Glaring at her from the other end of the table, he awaited her response.

"Everything you told me was true. It took some time and a little begging, but I found out what I needed to know about you."

"That's nice. I'm not a liar. Neither are you. I checked up on you, too. It's a requirement, let's say, of the profession. They say you are competent. I'm not surprised. And you don't feel bound by what you promise. If something takes more time, you take it."

"Yes, I do, even if it irritates those around me, correct?"

Josef smiled. "Yes, that is correct." He lowered his voice. "Now, what are we going to do?"

"Remove the problem. The only question that remains is by what method?"

"I prefer explosives. There is no chance of survival or retaliation."

"Will you do it?"

"I would prefer it that way."

"Do you need money?"

"Keep your money. What I need from you is a time and a place. Once I set the device, he will need to be the one on the scene, and at the proper time."

"I can arrange that."

The remainder of the meeting concentrated on a review of the executive's comings and goings.

Claudia's time had come. Sergei was by her side. Potemkin and Lev were standing by.

"See you soon-I hope." Claudia managed a smile. Sergei went upstairs to wait. He could barely manage the stress.

Little Boris came into the living room from somewhere else, no doubt many steps ahead of one of his many part-time 'governesses.' The child paused for a moment and looked at Sergei. It was one of those long, penetrating gazes, the kind an officer might give while inspecting his troops.

It's Boris, I know it, Sergei told himself. It's him, it's him. The child, having completed his inspection, ran off. A huffing, puffing Timon entered, looking for him. Sergei pointed the way. The guard resumed his chase.

Seeing the child was encouraging. Everything that was happening was new, illogical, and unprecedented. All he could cling to was his understanding, which was infinitesimal, and his hope which, of necessity, needed to be infinite.

Less than an hour later, Potemkin rapped on the open door. An apprehensive Trasker turned to greet him. Potemkin was grinning. Nothing more needed to be said. The scientist arose, approached the professor, and embraced him.

"It's a beautiful baby girl. And if I say so, she's even more beautiful than her mother."

"How is she?"

"She's fine. Go and be with her. You don't have much time."

He went to be with Claudia. Potemkin was right. Time indeed, was of the essence.

It had been a long day. Moroka's unprecedented departure from the Denver meeting left his associates no choice but to contact him at Becker Pharmaceutical. Most were confused. Some were angry. The rest were unwilling to accept his excuse that he had experienced a cardiac episode. They attributed his sudden departure as a maneuver to deal them out of the profits that would be generated from the new discovery.

It was almost midnight when the exhausted executive decided to leave his office. He buzzed and Anna came in. "You look tired, sir. Isn't it time to go home and get some rest?" she asked. "Hans and Charles are asleep, dozing on the couches. Shall I wake them?"

"Now that's something, both my bodyguards asleep. No, I will. You go home, I'll close up. It's been a very frustrating day, as you might have guessed. My associates are not patient men. You should have heard the names some of them called me."

"I can only imagine."

"Go on, Anna, I'll see you tomorrow."

Moroka began the protocol of leaving his office. He locked the center drawer in his desk, went over and made sure the wall safe was closed and its dial spun off the last number. He flipped his reminder pad to the next day, then turned off the desk lamp. At the entrance he switched off the light, closed the door and entered the reception room.

"Time to go, boys," Moroka ordered.

Hans and Charles awoke. Realizing they had fallen asleep on the job, they rocketed off the couches and were upright in an instant, "It's all right," Moroka said, "but it better not happen again." The Grand Canyon could not have accommodated the silence that followed.

Soon, the three were in the elevator heading down to the parking garage. Protocol dictated that Hans drive while Moroka sat in the rear. Charles would be driving a second following vehicle, the one carrying the weapons, just in case.

As the three entered the garage, Moroka had a sudden need. "Where's a rest room?" he asked.

"I'll show you," Charles offered.

"Hans, get the car started, I'll be with you in a minute."

"Yes sir."

Charles guided his boss to the next level where there was a rest room.

The explosion knocked the two men to the ground. "Hans," Charles yelled, and ran down the stairs to where Moroka's car was. When he opened the door to the garage, a wall of flame burst through and burned his face. Charles thrust his shoulder against the door and shut it. The flame had seared his eyelashes off and blinded him. His boss, following, found him a few moments later in a heap, in the corner of the stairwell.

Retrieving Charles' cell phone, the executive called for help.

Anna, sitting in her car on the street, smiled. She started her car and sped off.

"Where is it," Santoro asked the fire chief.

"It's on the first level, in the rear. All the big shots park there. There's one dead, a body guard. He was the one who started the car. The second one was near enough to get badly burned. His eyelids are singed. That leads me to believe his eyes might have been damaged, but the doctors at the hospital will have the final say on that."

"Whose car was it?" Bob McCann asked.

"Albert Moroka; he's the chief exec for Becker Pharmaceutical. He's the only one who came away unharmed. He had to take a piss at the last moment. That's why he wasn't in the car."

McCann stared at Santoro. "Is this ever going to stop?"

"What's up? Is there something I should know?" The fire chief asked.

"Not really," Santoro answered, "there have been some attempts at industrial spying going on lately, and we think people at Becker might be involved. We don't have any names yet."

"Do you think someone has it in for the exec?" the chief asked.

"It sure looks like it," Santoro replied. "Where is he?"

"He's over there, getting checked out by the ambulance guys. He's the one in the $1,000 suit," the chief replied sarcastically.

Santoro and McCann walked over. Moroka appeared dazed - and frightened. He knew only too well what the car bomb meant. He had failed or angered someone; who, he did not know. But this he did know; if they did not succeed this time, they would try again, until he was finally extinguished. It was a frightening realization. He had become someone's target.

"I'm Detective Santoro and this is Detective McCann. We'd like to ask you some questions.

Do you feel well enough to answer them?"

"Go ahead, I'm all right." Moroka answered as he stared at the pavement near his feet.

"Do you have any idea who is responsible for this?" Santoro asked.

No. I don't. I have enemies and competitors but they wouldn't resort to this. There are better ways of getting back at me than blowing me up."

The corners of Santoro's lips turned up a tad. "Sir, have you hired anyone to steal the Trasker discovery?" Santoro glanced at McCann; he nodded.

Moroka shuddered as if a bolt of lightning had hit him. "N-no, I never heard of any Sergei Trasker."

"Really? I didn't say Sergei. Have you ever done any business with a firm Called Triple I?"

"We use them from time to time, yes."

"You do know Janus Karper is dead, don't you?"

"Yes, I do."

"Do you think the same person who murdered him could be after you?"

"I don't know, I don't know." Moroka cupped both his hands over his face.

Santoro retreated; the executive's panic was palpable. "That's all for now. We'll be contacting you if we need any more information."

The attendants helped the man into the ambulance. "We're taking him to the hospital. He may be going into shock," one of the ambulance personnel said.

Anna Kremenko began her usual regimen. She got up at the regular time, sure that Moroka wouldn't be at the office. Providing the police could find all the pieces, what was left of him would be laying on a slab in the morgue. Anna maintained her schedule, not wishing to draw any attention to her as a possible conspirator. She understood how the police worked.

The trip to the office seemed less hectic. Her knowledge of Moroka's demise had reduced her anxiety. Bypassing several parked police cars while humming a little tune to herself she entered the Becker elevator and pressed the appropriate button. When the doors finally opened, she found the office in a state of confusion. Several uniformed policemen were moving from person to person questioning them.

As Anna headed toward Moroka's office she was intercepted by Santoro and McCann.

"Are you Anna Kremenko?" Santoro questioned.

"Yes, I am."

"We'd like to talk to you. Please, in here." The three entered her boss's office.

"What's happening, where's Mr. Moroka?" The secretary inquired.

"We'll ask the questions," McCann replied.

"Is he all right? Was he wounded? Is he in the hospital? Where is he? I want to see him."

"Please calm down. Right now, he's probably at home, well protected by some new bodyguards."

"What of Hans and Charles, were they injured?"

"The Hans guy is dead, and Charles experienced some burns while trying to save his buddy."

McCann added, "Your boss got away without a scratch."

Anna sank into a chair and feigned swooning.

Several of her answers made Santoro suspicious. Wounded, injured; how would she know?

Little Claudia was three weeks old. Sergei Trasker sought out Potemkin. As he approached, their gazes met.

"It's time," the scientist proclaimed.

"I'll call Lev. Are you able to get to the laboratory? Can you manage?"

"Yes, I can. Let's get this over with," Sergei exclaimed.

A half hour later, Constantine Potemkin and Lev were busy operating on Sergei. Not quite conscious, the patient's thoughts turned to the first cesarean operation; the method used to deliver Rome's royal next of kin. He wondered whether that was all the event had been. As he sought to delve deeper, he was brought back to full consciousness and found that he was not prepared for the event that had just taken place. It was both a magnificent and horrendous moment, being the bow that fired an arrow of life into the next generation while relinquishing its place in the present one. He likened himself to that already familiar Chinook salmon that deposits roe in the headwaters of the Columbia River, and then patiently awaits its own demise.

Simultaneously, Sergei Trasker understood everything and nothing. It did not bother him. His successor was beautiful; words could not describe the emotions that coursed through him upon seeing his offspring.

"You know what will be happening now," Potemkin said.

"Yes, I know. Can I see him once more?" Lev brought the child. "Good luck, young Sergei, may your journey be better than mine."

"You didn't do that bad," Lev replied.

The waterfall events had passed. In a short while, only the children would remain.

"You failed, now I will have to do it," an angry Anna Kremenko shouted at her fellow assassin.

"We will try again," Josef fired back.

"Do you think he will give you another chance? Do you think he's some fool? By now he's gone into hiding. He won't trust anyone now, not even me. The fox is aware he is being hunted. There is no way to know where he will go or what he will do. He might even suspect you're the one who is trying to kill him. Did you ever think of that?"

"No."

"Next time, use a speed detonating device. Set it for say, 50 miles an hour. That way you'll be sure to get him."

"That's a good idea. I'll do that."

"It's settled then."

"Yes."

"Walk me down to my car. It's dark outside."

"You're afraid?" Josef laughed.

"Come on," Anna enticed.

The pair walked down the steps from Josef's second story flat and into the street. He opened the car door for Anna and she got in.

"So, when shall I see you again?"

"Never," Anna replied as she shot Josef three times in the chest and sped off.

Lev had barely placed the newborn Sergei in the bassinet when Potemkin's maneuvering began.

"Where does Sergei keep his files?" The professor asked. Lev did not respond.

"Where are they," Potemkin persisted. Seeing the glint of suspicion in the guard's glance, he sought to reassure him. "We're together in this, are we not?"

Lev pointed to Ping, Pang, and Pong. "There, that's where Sergei keeps his notes; in them."

"He keeps them in the dogs? How is that possible?"

"They are robots, made of flesh and blood. It was one of his achievements."

"That is remarkable. How does one access their information?"

"Ping, sit," commanded Lev. The dog sat. "Ping, access records," he ordered. The dog barked.

"He wants the password," Lev explained.

"What is it?" Potemkin asked.

"It's Genghis Khan's name when he was a youth, Temujin." Lev faced the dog and ordered,

"Ping; Temujin!" A mini-disk drive appeared. "Place a blank disk in the slot and Ping will fill it with data," Lev instructed. "Give Pang and Pong the same instruction, and you will have everything you need.

I have to go upstairs. I have three babies and two parents to attend to."

Potemkin called James down to the laboratory. Together, they retrieved the information everyone had sacrificed so much to acquire.

Now I shall be famous, Potemkin thought to himself.

Lev informed his master of what Potemkin had asked for and received. Sergei, in no condition to retrieve the disks, told Lev what he had allowed was fine. The scientist knew that it would be some time before Potemkin and his minions might be able to break the encryption he had fashioned. In addition, there was a wipe clean command that would automatically run if certain key strokes were engaged.

Chances were very good that his notes would never be deciphered.

In the interim, Sergei had to prepare Claudia for her passing. Then he had to prepare for his own.

Much needed to be done and time was short. One of the last things that Sergei did was to allow Timon to be brought into the inner circle of those who knew what was really happening. Now Lev would have an ally, someone he could rely on.

Albert Moroka had commandeered a private jet for his flight to Moscow. It was not to be a direct flight. There would be several stopovers. Anyone trying to find him by conducting a surveillance of all commercial flights would be frustrated. He would be long gone before anyone realized how he had managed to leave the country. But the Becker executive had erred. He paid by credit card and used a cell phone to make the reservation.

He was waiting in the lounge of the company that was to fly him the first leg of his long trip.

Another half hour and I'll be on my way, he mused, and all this will be a memory. Suddenly, a hand pressed lightly on his shoulder. The executive's heart sank. The slight rush of air and the tiny prick he felt in the back of his neck meant he would not be seeing his homeland again. A familiar voice cooed "This is for Janus." Anna Kremenko moved forward and stood before her boss.

"Anna, I didn't. . ." was all Moroka was able to say as his chin came to rest on his chest.

"Here, let me help you, sir." Anna cranked the chair to the reclining position, pulled the executive's head back so that it rested on the headrest. "There you are, sir; pleasant dreams."

One passenger seated across the aisle quipped to his partner "Now that's what I call service."

Unexpected

Potemkin wasted no time in leaving the estate. Two months after little Sergei's birth, he was packed and ready to leave. Lev didn't approve; he felt the professor should have stayed longer. What if there were complications? He stated his case, but Potemkin dismissed all of his concerns as trivial.

"James, call the embassy. Tell them my work is done here and I shall be leaving on the first available flight. I shall be at the embassy in an hour and will need a direct line to Moscow. Tell them it is of the highest priority."

"What about your things at the condominium?"

"You stay behind and see to it that everything is left in order. After that, get the next fight home.

Go and spend some time with your family. I'll call after I get settled. Until then, you are officially on paid vacation."

James grinned, stepped forward and embraced his old comrade. "Have a safe journey."

"I am marching into history, James. I have waited a long time for this. You know, I don't even mind dying after I receive the acclaim this will bring me. It's too bad Sergei couldn't have shared it with me. It was his discovery, you know."

James lowered his eyes. "Yes, it was. I hope you give him the proper credit."

"Boris is gone. He and Claudia will soon be gone; bringing his name up will only confuse the issue."

"It's your decision, Constantine. I think you would have decided differently if you were younger."

James left the room before the professor could reply. His meaning was clear.

Sergei Trasker made no sound. He was approaching the last moments of his life. Lev entered the room. What he saw saddened him. The energetic and brilliant scientist he had served for so many years was in decline and there would be no recovery.

"Can I get you anything?" Lev could hardly utter the words. Sergei shook his head. "You are sad; why?" The guard questioned.

"Potemkin, it's him, it's what he's going to do that makes me sad. He's going to give my work to his superiors and they will use it not for good, but for their advantage. What have I done?" The dying man burst into tears.

"It's my fault. I shouldn't have told him how to get the data," Lev answered.

"No, it's not. It's our quest for fame that lies at the bottom of it all. And it will never change."

The scientist raised his hand and beckoned Lev to come closer. "And who could have a better friend than you." As the two men's fingers intertwined, Sergei Trasker left this world.

Timon and Lev had the graves dug on the pretense that some plantings had been ordered and were to be placed in an area of the garden the two had selected. And that indeed, was true. But first, three interments had to occur. Lev chose an evening when there was a crescent moon. It would provide some light, but not too much. There was little talk. Both men were dealing with having to bury three of the best friends they had ever known. The one redeeming and almost insane reality was that the three children of their friends were being readied as the generation to come.

The task accomplished, Lev reminded Timon that the plantings would be coming tomorrow.

"In the afternoon, I hope."

"Yes, late in the afternoon," Lev replied.

"I'm going to get drunk," Timon announced.

"I've already started," replied Lev.

The two went back to the house to drink to the memory of the dear departed.

Anna Kremenko was the only one left now. Everyone else involved with trying to steal the Trasker discovery were gone. She phoned the embassy and requested leave to return to Russia. The several cells she had been associated with were out of service or terminated.

Her request was granted.

During her conversation with the embassy official, he mentioned that someone else would also be returning to Russia with the much-touted Trasker discovery and that a state reception was being planned at his arrival at Sheremetevo International Airport.

Anna burst into tears. That should have been Janus, she told herself.

Now the work would really begin for Lev and Timon. They would have to maintain the estate, keep up the strength of the cadre of guards, select new ones when required, and oversee a host of other activities to carry forward the entire operation in the defensive mode it currently exhibited. Most important though, would be the selection of educational institutions for their three charges, and controlling the children's interaction with others. No one outside the estate could be allowed to understand enough about Boris, Sergei, or Claudia's existence to be able to comprehend their true status.

The two, both in their late thirties, understood the gravity of their commitment. They would be close to retirement before their three charges would be able to resume control of the estate.

Aeroflot 31 lowered its flaps and began its descent. Touchdown at Sheremetevo Airport was ten minutes away. All those aboard could feel the slowing descent of the sleek jet. An occasional slight shudder meant the air spoilers were being manipulated.

Professor Constantine Potemkin was riding the crest of a wave. I shall be famous, he mused.

The data stuffed in the briefcase jammed between his back and the fabric of the seat would insure that.

How shall I broach the subject? Shall I tell the Central committee that I have the power which will allow them to live forever, or, esteemed comrades, I can give you all eternal life, but in return, I expect this or that. The professor thought the last alternative was too crass. His musings turned to his departed comrade Sergei; transformed comrade might be more accurate.

True, he, Professor Constantine Potemkin, had gone back on his word. He had promised Sergei the regenerative solution and the procedure would never reach Moscow. So, he lied. Why would Sergei care? He had the ability to produce the liquid over and over again, insuring that he, Boris and Claudia would live who knew how long? Potemkin considered getting the treatment himself. He would round up several friends and they would form a pact. They would help him, and he would do the same for them.

Russia's overseers wouldn't be the only ones who might be living forever.

He had enjoyed the last leg of his journey, his flight from Paris. The Russian jet Aeroflot 31 was modern and comfortable. His seatmate was a charming Russian woman; young, well-dressed, attractive and very articulate. He couldn't quite place her dialect. That annoyed him.

As the jet entered its final approach on Moscow's airport, the woman arose, reached into the overhead compartment and retrieved a leather briefcase. Considering its size, it seemed heavy. She managed. Placing it on the floor in the space under the seat in front, she turned and smiled reassuringly at the professor.

"That seems such a heavy case for such a small woman. When we deplane, please let me carry it for you," the professor offered.

"There will be no need. Besides, it's only some candy for you apparatchiks," the woman replied.

Potemkin saw the hate flash across her countenance. 'Candy for you Russians;' the professor had heard that phrase before; it was in one of the notes Chechen terrorists left behind after an attack.

Alarmed, Potemkin stared at the woman. "You are Chechen."

"Yes, I am. And you are one of those pigs who will be dying today; Proschai." She reached under the seat and turned the handle of the briefcase. Aeroflot 31 disintegrated.

Anna Kremenko was over the Atlantic in Air France 667 when the airliner's TV announced the crash of Aeroflot 31. The tragedy closed forever the Russian attempt to rob Sergei Trasker of his discovery.

Knowing a great deal about the effort and the players, Anna spent the remainder of the flight reflecting on the unnecessary loss of life in attempting to gain access to the Trasker discovery.

Was his work that essential, she mused, really? What did he do, discover a way to live forever?

Janus Karper's death reoriented Anna Kremenko's way of perceiving the world. Quite unexpectedly he had opened the door to better things for his former lover.

Convinced that incompetence and ineptness were the reasons for his demise, Anna became a driven person. No longer did she sit quietly in meetings and allow the malaise of non-participation to continue. She began demanding that superiors become more aware of what their agents were doing and to engage them more frequently.

It wasn't long before her supervisors started to marginalize her. Anna found herself not invited to more and more meetings. At considerable personal risk she attended them anyway. She continued to reiterate her concerns about the slipshod techniques which many superiors chose to run their operations.

To many it appeared her career was drawing to an end; expulsion appeared imminent. Anyone even remotely connected to the woman had better be careful.

Then, it happened.

Two highly touted espionage cells were discovered by the parent country where they had their operations. Three more failed terribly in achieving their objectives. Aware of this, Anna brazenly took her concerns to her supervisors' superiors.

This time, they listened - intently. Anna was promoted, once, then again, and again. Eventually, she became head of operations in the Americas.

The sophomoric behavior drew to a close. Supervisors began to periodically monitor what their agents were doing, charting their progress frequently. Anna demanded, and received, highly detailed reports weekly, and sooner if the operation had priority.

Still, one unknown remained. What *was* the nature of Sergei Trasker's discovery? So many had perished trying to obtain it. Not knowing gnawed at her.

And so it was, that two and a half decades after she had returned to Russia, Anna Kremenko returned to the United States. Whatever reason she gave her superiors for the trip, her real purpose was to find the answer to the one question that had plagued her for all those years.

"This is private property," the guard informed the driver, "You cannot enter."

"I have come a very long way, from Russia. A person I loved very much died trying to obtain the secrets that are hidden somewhere in this place. I just want to know, was his life lost in vain."

Something about Anna Kremenko's pleading had an effect on the guard. He called the main house. Lev answered the phone. "Is she alone? Check the trunk and see if it's empty. After that, send her up."

When Anna, escorted by the usual terrain vehicle and armed riders, pulled up to the main house, Lev was waiting for her. Timon stood in the doorway, his AK-47 resting in the crook of his arm.

Anna and Lev proceeded to the great room with Timon trailing a few steps behind. Lev offered her a seat and then sat down next to her. His silence intimated she was to be the one to speak first.

"A man I loved very much died many years ago. He was assassinated. He was involved in trying to get Sergei Trasker's discovery for the Russian government. I don't care about that now. He is dead, and so are many who tried the same thing. I can't change what has happened. The question that I keep asking myself is this; was the expenditure of all those lives worth it?"

Someone outside shouted "Kick it to Boris, to Boris, Claudia." Anna got up and went to the partly open French door. She noticed three young adults on the lawn playing soccer.

"My, but they are a handsome trio. Who are they?" Anna asked.

"They are the Trasker's offspring. They are my responsibility until they come of age; in two years."

"They seem old enough right now. May I meet them?"

"I'm not so sure that would be possible." For reasons unknown, Lev relented. "I'll call them in. They may need a few minutes to freshen up."

"Of course. I understand." Anna seated herself once more and waited.

Soon, Boris, Claudia, and Sergei burst into the room, full of the energy that only young adults can foster. "Hello, and you are?" Sergei bubbled, as he extended his hand.

"I am Anna Kremenko. I used to be Albert Moroka's executive secretary. I worked at Becker Pharmaceutical." Anna noticed the flash in Sergei's eyes.

"I wouldn't know anything about Becker. I'm sure my father would. He's passed on, you know."

"Then you are his double. I have pictures. Here, see for yourself." Kremenko reached into her pocketbook and supplied Sergei with numerous pictures of himself, Claudia, and Boris. Surveillance in the past included photography.

"Yes, I do look like my father. Everyone tells me that." Sergei replied. "Why are you here?"

"Many men perished attempting to get your father's discovery. They failed. Still, I have yet to hear of it in any of the scientific journals or anywhere. Is his discovery still a secret?"

"I have no more knowledge of it now than when he was alive. I'm afraid whatever he discovered will remain with him."

"Thank you for clearing that up, Sergei." Anna turned her attention to the other two young adults.

"And you are called Claudia and you Boris, is that not so?"

"Why, yes, Claudia answered.

"Well, that's enough for me," Anna answered, "I'll be going. I still haven't found the answer to my question. I suppose I never will." Anna dropped her notebook.

Sergei reached down and picked it up. "Life does not always provide us with answers. There are times when we must rely on faith." He handed it back to Anna.

"Yes, faith, I think I understand," Anna replied. "What do you think of the design, Claudia? I had the notebook made especially for me. It's all aluminum. The pages are treated with some kind of plastic so that they're easy to erase - even ink. Isn't that clever?"

Claudia examined it. Curiosity getting the better of him, Boris asked to see it.

"That's very clever," he commented.

"You wouldn't be trying to kill us, would you," Sergei asked, "If you were, Lev, here, would provide you with your own reward."

Anna heard the snap of a bolt being drawn back and released. She laughed. "The days of ricin and such things are over. These days, we behave professionally. If I wanted you dead I would have used cyanide. Besides, I have no reason to harm any of you." She glanced at her watch.

"I have just enough time to return to my room, pack, and catch my plane; goodbye." Anna left.

"She knows," Sergei announced.

"How could she," Claudia replied, "She has no proof."

"My, but you are naïve. She has our fingerprints," Boris added.

Claudia placed her cupped hands over her lips.

Once more over the Atlantic and headed home, Anna Kremenko gazed out of her window and surveyed the vast ocean below her. Her thoughts were many; she had fallen in love and had her lover ripped out of her life. She had served the motherland in the United States for ten years. That came to nothing. Her stint in the foreign land had been a disaster. Her only success was exacting revenge on Albert Moroka.

As the trio feared, she had indeed verified the fingerprints to be those of Boris, Sergei, and Claudia. Armed with that, and additional information gleaned from conversations with Janus Karper, Anna was able to deduce the profound discovery Sergei Trasker had made.

Janus, my love, she mused, if you only knew the prize you were seeking, how elated you would have been. We could have had a life together, you and I, forever. But now, that will never be.

The sun was setting. Soon it would be dark. At this moment the distant horizon posed a special meaning for Anna Kremenko. She had encountered three souls who had been given the opportunity to journey beyond it. She raised her glass in a toast. "To Sergei, Boris, and Claudia; safe journey."

The End